CUPID'S KISS

Miss Delafield's gaze dropped to her lap. Her fingers trifled with the knot of ribbons at her waist. She spoke softly. "I have a theory, Lord Burton. While I have never experienced the physical expression of love between a man and a woman, I am convinced that when one does, one would also become acquainted with raw emotion. My dilemma is obvious. To fulfill my quest, I will need a . . . willing participant in the endeavor." Her violet gaze lifted. "Could you? Would you? Lord Burton, be my mentor?"

His lordship felt as if he had taken a direct hit to the breadbasket. While he prided himself on being worldly-wise, the implications of what Miss Delafield had just suggested floored him.

"You want me to . . . you want me and you to . . ."

In spite of being a country girl, Gowland's knowledge of the physical side of love, coming as it did from romantic novels, was surprisingly sparse. She hung her head, her cheeks flushed with shame. "I am so sorry, Lord Burton. I should not have asked such an intimate favor, but never having been kissed—"

Startled, Lord Burton leaned forward and firmly cupped his beloved's chin obliging it upward until their eyes were level and locked. Then he lowered his head, and his lips, as if of their own volition, bestowed a trail of small kisses. . . .

BOOK YOUR PLACE ON OUR WEBSITE AND MAKE THE READING CONNECTION!

We've created a customized website just for our very special readers, where you can get the inside scoop on everything that's going on with Zebra, Pinnacle and Kensington books.

When you come online, you'll have the exciting opportunity to:

- View covers of upcoming books

- Read sample chapters

- Learn about our future publishing schedule (listed by publication month *and author*)

- Find out when your favorite authors will be visiting a city near you

- Search for and order backlist books from our online catalog

- Check out author bios and background information

- Send e-mail to your favorite authors

- Meet the Kensington staff online

- Join us in weekly chats with authors, readers and other guests

- Get writing guidelines

- AND MUCH MORE!

**Visit our website at
http://www.zebrabooks.com**

MY DARLING VALENTINE

KATHLEEN BECK
CAROLA DUNN
ALICE HOLDEN

Zebra Books
Kensington Publishing Corp.

http://www.zebrabooks.com

ZEBRA BOOKS are published by

Kensington Publishing Corp.
850 Third Avenue
New York, NY 10022

First Printing: February, 1999
10 9 8 7 6 5 4 3 2 1

Printed in the United States of America

CONTENTS

MISS DELAFIELD DISPOSES

by

Kathleen Beck

Dedicated to the memory of
my beloved husband Bernard B. Beck.
Soldier—Officer—Gentleman

ONE

"Do not raise your brow at me in that condescending fashion, Lord Burton," Lady Rettinger admonished. "I tell you, the Bellefleur nose is cursed."

Obligingly, Lord Burton Dance lowered his offending brow. "Forgive me, Lady R, but I fail to see where a 'curse' is involved."

"Then you have not been paying proper attention," Lady Rettinger replied tartly. "I shall have to start at the beginning."

Lord Burton suppressed a groan. He was a tall, young man with the superb physique of a natural athlete. His features were regular, his hair a thick rich brown, and his eyes a deep emerald green. Couple his physical attributes with a sizable fortune, and he was indisputably the most sought-after prize of the past Seasons. Yet, when in the company of Lady Rettinger, he felt restrained, as if by the curbing tug of leading strings

It was boredom that had driven him to answer her summons to her drawing room on this blustery afternoon in early January, and a misplaced sense of duty that kept him there.

As a gentleman, Lord Burton felt he owed Lady R a certain amount of his time and attention. Not only was she older than God, but, as the fates would have it, she was his closest neighbor in the grandeur that was Grosvenor Square.

From Lady Rettinger's loftier perspective, the affiliation was reciprocal. She, too, felt Lord Burton owed her his time and attention, and in return, she magnanimously granted him the right to oblige her.

Lady R was not a handsome woman, possessing as she did the thrust-forward stance and weathered mien of a ship's figurehead—one that had been too long at sea. Yet, all things considered, hers was a commanding presence.

Settling her considerable bulk, corseted to the nines, against the sofa cushions, she began, "The Bellefleur nose can be traced back to the Norman Conquest when a certain Frenchman, Bellefleur by name, infiltrated England and subsequently married into one of its finest families. Down through the ages, the females in the line born with the Bellefleur nose have been cursed with contrariness. They disregard duty and will marry only for love!"

If Lady Rettinger was expecting a horrified reaction to this apocalyptic tidbit, she was disappointed. His lordship merely stifled a yawn. "I do not think a honker, however sinister, holds much sway in such matters. Young ladies often marry for love."

"I beg to differ with you, Lord Burton. Love has nothing to do with marriage. I despised both my husbands, but I did my duty. That is what marriage is about. Duty!"

Lord Burton stole a surreptitious glance at the clock on the marble mantelpiece. "But cannot true love be intertwined with duty?"

"Tiens! You think like a man! What takes place in the bedchamber is just so much foolishness for a woman. If I had a daughter, I would tell her what my sainted mama told me on my wedding day: 'Lie back and think of England.' With Horsley, my second husband, I thought of Wales. Never enough time for more."

Unaware that this surprising bit of information had set his lordship back on his elegant haunches, Lady Rettinger continued, "The Bellefleur nose has been known to skip several generations, then hit in deadly succession. My goddaughter, Grace, was so affected. She had an offer from a duke. Instead, she threw herself away on a scholar"—Lady R's lip curled with disdain—"and all because of love."

A contemplative silence filled the room. True love would be nice to have, Lord Burton reflected. Too bad the pursuit of it was so bloody boring.

His lordship, having enjoyed his quota of *chère amie*, was now seeking a wife. Not because he wanted a wife per se, but because he wanted children.

After several Seasons of plumbing the marriage mart, however, his lordship found himself thoroughly bored with the offerings. He had had it up to his gunnels with maladroit maidens and matchmaking matriarchs. Boring parties, boring conversation—

Lady R's sigh, sounding like an overworked bellows, waylaid his lordship's bout of self-pity.

"As you know, Lord Burton, I have no children of my own."

Small wonder, thought his lordship.

"I loved my goddaughter, Grace, as if she were my own. She died when Gowland was but a year old." Lady R's voice trembled dramatically. "Gowland has the Bellefleur nose. I fear she will follow in her mother's footsteps."

Again a bellows-like sigh. "I feel a commitment to Grace to save her misguided daughter from herself. I see where my duty lies. In spite of my tenuous connections to the family, I shall make the journey to Chigger Hall."

Wondering briefly if Lady R had finally gone around the bend, Lord Burton tactfully inquired, "You fear, then, that Miss Delafield plans to marry a *scholar?*"

"For heaven's sake, Lord Burton, you have read the letter. How can you remain so thick to the situation?"

"The sentiments expressed in the letter seem quite innocuous to me," his lordship returned tartly. "Miss Gowland Delafield writes to invite you, her grandmama's bosom bow, to attend a Valentine's Day Ball to be held at Chigger Hall to celebrate her twenty-first birthday. She adds, quite sweetly, I think, that if you are free to come in January she would be most happy to have you, and any guests that you wish to bring with you, for an extended stay."

"Your brains are obviously still rattled by the excesses of the Little Season," harrumphed Lady Rettinger. "You have overlooked the most important indications of the impending peril. Note how Gowland hints at a special announcement to be made at the ball, and how often the name of her drawing master, Cosmos Wombwell, is mentioned. I tell you, Lord Burton, drawing masters named 'Cosmos' are up to no good."

Fearing the answer, yet feeling compelled to ask the question, Lord Burton inquired, "And what is it exactly that you wish *me* to do?"

"That will be apparent. On Valentine's Day, Gowland celebrates her twenty-first birthday. On that date, she becomes an heiress in her own right and may marry whomever she wishes. *I* do not wish her to marry a fortune-hunting drawing master."

Lady R's commanding manner continued. "I will require your presence at Chigger Hall. Since Mr. Delafield obviously has been neglecting his duties as a father, Gowland will need the guidance of an older man to dissuade her from this madness."

"Older man?" his lordship sputtered. "If you are referring to me, Lady R, I will have you know that I am but two-and-thirty—"

"Do not be so overly concerned with advancing age," Lady Rettinger scolded. "It is not becoming. I, myself, am five-and-sixty, but you do not hear me lamenting."

Lord Burton glowered at her. The old griffin had whittled ten years or more off her age. He would bet a monkey on it. He drew himself up. "I cannot—would not—presume to counsel a young girl, especially one I have never met."

"Nonsense," Lady R reassured him. "You are more than

qualified. While it is true you have been unsuccessful in finding a wife, you have been around the track once or twice, and in doing so have picked up valuable knowledge of the female mind. Of course, if you do err, I shall be there to correct you."

Fuming at the off-handed affront, his lordship glared at his nemesis. "Really, Lady R," he chided, "you go too far."

"Tut, tut, Lord Burton, that was not meant as censure. I fully believe it is perfectionism, not inability, that keeps you from settling."

His lordship clenched his jaw. "Thank you, Lady R, for that astute insight into my character."

Sarcasm was lost on Lady Rettinger. With a regal nod she accepted his lordship's gratitude. "I pride myself on my perception of people's character, and I am happy to say, I have never been wrong. I intend to leave for Chigger Hall within the week. When can you join me there?"

The nerve of the old harridan! "I am afraid a journey at this time is out of the question, Lady R. I have pressing matters that need my attention."

"Nonsense. What do you have to do? Nothing stirs in the City at this time of year. You have no wife or child, no country home of your own to racket off to. Admit it, Lord Burton. You are bored. Teetering on the brink of a serious ennui. Join me at Chiggers. A touch of bracing country air might be just the thing to snap you out of these unbecoming sulks of yours."

Infuriated by Lady R's heavy-handed insistence, Lord Burton shot to his feet. "My joining you at Chigger Hall is out of the question, Lady R. If you will excuse me?" He bowed stiffly and strode from the room.

Lady Rettinger watched him leave. Had she been a shade too demanding? Nonsense! Her notable perception was matched only by her exquisite tact. She would try another approach. It was imperative that Lord Burton join her at Chigger Hall.

TWO

Miss Gowland Delafield, the cause of Lady Rettinger's concern, was an intelligent young woman, yet something of an intellectual paradox. Raised in a protective, scholastic milieu by a doting but detached father, she had a wide knowledge of abstruse subjects while retaining a childlike innocence concerning more practical matters.

Since the Delafields were the first family in consequence in the rather large village in which they lived, Gowland had grown accustomed to lavish praise, even for the most mundane of her accomplishments. Thus, when Cosmos Wombwell became her drawing master and pronounced her an artistic genius-in-the-making, she had believed him without question. Never having been exploited or lied to, she thought no one capable of exploitation or deceit.

At Wombwell's urging, Gowland had had one of the best bedchambers converted into a luxurious studio. The chamber possessed a lushly quiet atmosphere and a good northern light, elements which Wombwell had decreed essential for an artist of her potential.

Wombwell was a tall, extremely thin young man with jet black hair, a milk white complexion and dark, piercing eyes. He habitually wore voluminous white linen shirts open at the throat and trouser suits of black velvet. He had lived and studied in Italy which entitled him—he felt—to indulge in morose moods and petulant outbursts.

"Position, please, Miss Delafield."

Obediently, Gowland stepped up to the easel. She was a striking young woman with an unusual flair for fashion. For her drawing lessons she wore an enormous turban of fine blue wool set at a rakish, off-side angle on her close-cropped golden curls, and a long, loose coatdress that boasted panels of bright embroidery from its elevated waist to its hemline.

"Now, Miss Delafield, we will begin! Extend your arm. Move it from the shoulder, elbow stiff, wrist relaxed, fingers holding the pencil as though it were a brush."

A moment of silence, then Wombwell thundered, "Ovals, Miss Delafield! Small ovals starting in the center of the paper, growing progressively larger until, as if of their own volition, they career off the confines of the sheet and fly into space."

With intense concentration, the stiff-armed Gowland ovaled her way around and around, the pencil careening and flying according to Wombwell's instructions.

She stepped back, studying her drawing much as da Vinci might have studied the first brush strokes of the Mona Lisa.

Wombwell approached. His eyes narrowed. He, too, studied the drawing. He took a deep breath and slowly exhaled it. "Yes!" he whispered. "Yes!"

He whirled around and faced his pupil. "And what think *you*, Miss Delafield?"

Gowland hesitated, but only momentarily. Her previous drawing master had never solicited her opinion of her own work, although he had often given his, with lowering effect.

Of course, she rationalized, her previous drawing master had not studied on the Continent, as had Wombwell, and so, had not recognized her immense raw talent.

She sighed to signify that she was less than satisfied. "I feel there is a definite improvement. Only last week, my ovals had a decided tendency to list to the left. Now they are rigidly upright." She glanced at Wombwell to gauge his reaction. "Are they perhaps a shade *too* upright?"

Wombwell bowed his head as if deeply moved. "You are too modest, Miss Delafield. Your ovals are *magnifico*. Through diligent exercise, you have perfected the one technical fault that had kept you from progressing to the elevated heights your innate talent can command. Portraiture will be your avenue of expression. I can sense it."

Across the room, Gowland's companion, Miss Camilla Clarke, rose to her feet and applauded. "Bravo, Gowland. Well done!"

Gowland blushed modestly. "You are both too kind. To show my gratitude, my first portraits will be likenesses of the two of you."

Wombwell blanched at the offer. Fortunately, his complexion was so pale that Gowland failed to notice. She brushed the pencil dust from her fingers and sighed. "I must go. I have promised Lady Rettinger to sit with her and await Lord Burton's imminent arrival. She will wonder what has become of me."

Wombwell did not comment. He appeared lost in Gowland's composition. Slipping an arm around Gowland's waist, Miss Clarke walked with her to the door.

"Gowland, my dear, I would be remiss in my duty if I did not confide to you my fears. I grow concerned for your health. You are attempting to do too much. You have the Valentine's Day Ball to plan for and must also attend to Lady Rettinger's entertainment. She claims so much of your time. And now, to add to your duties as hostess, she invites Lord Burton Dance to the Hall. Does she not understand that your *Art* suffers when challenged by the selfish demands of others?"

Gowland was quick to come to Lady Rettinger's defense. "It is true Lady Rettinger does not possess an artistic sensibility, but she was a doting godmother to my mama, and as such, I owe her my regard. She is also very kind to others. Lord Burton has been Lady Rettinger's friend and neighbor for many years. She tells me he has been blue-deviled of late, and if it were not for her bracing company, he would surely fall into a decline. I have promised to do all that I can to see to his well-being while he is with us."

"But your lessons—"

"Do not fear, Camilla, I shall miss but few lesson days. And, after the ball, I shall be free to devote all my time and my fortune to the establishment of the Wombwell School for the Arts." She smiled dreamily. "Imagine! I shall be Wombwell's devoted patroness as well as his most ardent student."

Miss Clarke looked at her sharply. "You have not told anyone of your plans to endow a school for Wombwell, have you, Gowland, dear?"

"I hinted at a special announcement to be made at the ball in a letter to Lady Rettinger, but my intentions remain a secret between us three."

"Please do not say another word to anyone, especially Lady Rettinger. You know how Wombwell feels when any undue adulation comes his way."

"I do know. And yet, if the dear man had not offered to forgo his own dreams of artistic immortality in order to teach other gifted artists like myself, none of this would be possible. He is all that is noble."

"You are so good-hearted, Gowland."

"Nonsense. It is you who are good-hearted, Camilla. You are the best of companions, and without you I would not have made the acquaintance of Wombwell. He is my inspiration. Until later, then."

After Gowland had gone from the room, Miss Clarke carefully locked the door behind her. As she did so, her expression changed. Her forehead tensed in annoyance, and her eyes hardened. She stalked over to where Wombwell stood staring at Gowland's ovals.

"I do not like this, Cosmos."

Wombwell sighed. "Nor do I. Miss Delafield's drawings are enough to make a dog sick."

"I was not referring to her drawings."

"What then?"

"Lady Rettinger. She does not like you."

"*I* do not like *her.*"

"She brings Lord Burton Dance to the Hall."

"So?"

"Ask yourself, why would Lord Burton Dance come from London to Kent in February to attend a country ball? Surely a gentleman of his stature must have his own country estate in which to wile away the winter. I greatly fear that Lady Rettinger plots a match between this Lord Burton and Gowland."

"You worry too much, Camilla."

"And you worry too little," Camilla snapped back. "Our future depends on Gowland remaining single and in control of her inheritance until you can get your hands on it."

"Do not talk nonsense. Miss Delafield is not seeking a husband. She is in love with her *great* talent. It is all she thinks about." He looked slyly at Camilla. "And do not forget, the silly chit is half in love with *me.*"

Miss Clarke frowned. "And *you* do not forget that there are boundaries, Wombwell."

"I do not forget."

"What are we to do about Dance?"

Wombwell yawned. "If he comes smelling of April and May, I am sure you will think of something to put him off. Until then, leave our budding little artist entirely to me."

"That I shall never do," Miss Clarke declared fiercely.

Wombwell smiled. His sloe-eyed gaze left Gowland's drawing and slowly traversed Miss Clarke's slender figure. With her ash-blond hair, large gray eyes and shy demeanor, Camilla seemed a prim and proper lady. He knew better. He slipped his hand beneath the bodice of her gown. "Make sure the door is locked," he whispered, "and I will show you what a bona fide artist is capable of producing."

THREE

In spite of the long journey in weather cold enough to freeze the accouterments off a brass monkey, Lord Burton Dance felt in fine fettle. Lady R's unflattering insinuations had ceased to plague him. Old? Sulky? Perfectionist? He was none of these!

Bored? Quite possibly.

He grinned ruefully. What else could explain the fact that at this very moment, his traveling carriage bearing him and his shivering, scarf-muffled valet was lurching down the ice-rutted drive that led to Chigger Hall?

His lordship had held firm against Lady R's entreaties that he join her at Chigger Hall, and she had left for Kent in a pique to do her *Duty* alone. A cryptic note from her a scant week ago, however, had caused him to reconsider:

Lord Burton, come at once. Wombwell runs tame in the household, and Gowland is besotted with him. Mr. Delafield is a Bedlamite. I fear the worst. Desperately need your assistance. Lady Rettinger.

The wording of the note had snared Lord Burton's interest as Lady R's high-handed insistence had not. What could be a more bracing stimulant to boredom than a lecherous drawing master, a Bedlamite, and a young lady sporting a honker with a mind of its own? To say nothing of

Lady R's heavy-handed pursuit of *Duty* to stir up the mix. Observing such a rare menagerie was certainly preferable to spending February in the City.

Ignoring his valet's groan of protest, his lordship lowered the window glass and leaned out, his eyes narrowing against the sudden blast of cold air and the brilliant winter sunshine. Chigger Hall was coming into sight. It was an imposing pile of rosy brick, not an ancient pile to be sure, but a large, modern country house with a pampered, well-kept look to it. It had almost an . . . enchanting air about it. The capricious thought amused his lordship. Usually, he was not given to flights of fancy.

As the carriage rattled closer, he whistled softly. The three-storied Hall boasted twenty windows, at least, across its front, not counting six dormer windows on the attic floor. With the window tax being what it was, Mr. Delafield must be quite plump in the pocket.

His lordship's eyes were next drawn to the eight tall chimneys soaring up from the Hall's roofline, each one painting cheery plumes of smoke against the sky. Another good sign. His host-to-be was not one to stint on coal.

Lord Burton turned from the window and addressed his valet. "Have heart, Peabody, warmth is ahead—"

Abruptly, his lordship turned his gaze back to the Hall. Were his eyes playing tricks on him? Was there someone sitting on a third floor window ledge?

Dear God, there was! It was a man, an older gentleman, white hair shining silver in the sun, long legs complacently crossed at the ankles and swinging back and forth. Was it the loose-screwed Mr. Delafield?

Lord Burton's blood ran cold at the sight. Although he was a superb sportsman, equally handy with his fists or his guns, and a crack whip, his lordship had one fear: heights. Just observing the ledge sitter was enough to make his mouth go dry and his throat tighten.

The ledge sitter lifted one arm in salute. He appeared to

be waving a welcome to the carriage! His lordship's arm involuntarily lifted to return the wave, but he caught himself in time.

Indignation replaced his panic. Why was the old gentleman not being properly supervised? Whatever the reason, the household must be warned of the impending disaster at once. He leaned out the window and shouted up to his coachman, "Faster, John, faster!"

The horses responded to the crack of the whip. The carriage thundered up the remaining drive to the front entrance, its braking wheels spewing up an impressive shower of ice shards.

Leaving the stunned Peabody to his own devices, his lordship leapt from the carriage and ran through the ice-crusted snow to the corner of the Hall. Waving his hands frantically, he called up, "You there. Go back inside. You will surely fall if you do not."

With renewed vigor, the old gentleman waved back. Damn! Was he perhaps preparing for flight?

His heart pounding like a blacksmith's hammer, his lordship quickly retraced his steps. Taking the broad stone stairs two at a time, he beat his fist upon the oaken entrance doors.

His frantic drubbing was answered by a staid butler. His lordship pushed past the startled servant and pelted into the entrance hall. "I am Lord Burton Dance," he shouted over his shoulder as he raced toward the staircase. "There is someone sitting on a third-story window ledge on the east side of the house. He is in great peril. We must go to him at once—"

An Oriental rug proved to be his lordship's undoing. The toe of his boot caught on one dog-eared corner. He tripped and landed heavily upon the marble floor.

The impact knocked the wind out of him. Dazed, he lay spread-eagle, dimly aware of the soft hastening scuffle of kid slippers, the pleasant scent of lavender, then the comforting rustle of a woman's skirts directly in front of him.

Winching his chin a notch off the floor, his lordship focused in on a wide panel of bright embroidery that had materialized before him. He forced his gaze upward, following the vertical panel until it met with a sweetly projecting bosom.

"Please, madam," he gasped, "there is a lunatic about to fall from a window ledge—someone must go to his assistance."

A sound of amusement came from on high. "Have no fear for the lunatic, Lord Burton. He is my papa, and he often sits on the window ledge to clear his thinking. Streech, our butler, has gone to assist him, an act of service that, I am sure, will annoy Papa greatly. I am Miss Delafield."

Thoroughly deflated, his lordship lowered his chin to the floor. "Delighted to meet you, Miss Delafield," he mumbled. "Forgive me for not rising."

Miss Delafield crouched down beside him. "If you are not too sorely injured, Lord Burton," she suggested, "perhaps you should attempt to rise?"

It seemed like a sane proposal, the only one voiced so far. Lord Burton carefully eased himself up on his elbows. Miss Delafield, her head tilted to one side, peered into his eyes.

Vis-à-vis with the Bellefleur nose at last, his lordship stared in astonishment. He gasped, too stunned to speak or move. Dear God, why had not Lady R warned him?

The Bellefleur nose was not a honker of renown, but a work of art, a thing of exquisite beauty. Delicate and refined, yet somehow *tweakable,* curving from its bridge like a fine scimitar, the shell-like nostrils slightly flaring—

"Lord Burton? Are you quite all right?"

"Beg pardon?"

"Your eyes. They are crossing most alarmingly."

* * *

"Foxed and floored! Lord Burton, you are a disgrace!"

Lord Burton glared at Lady R. After his unfortunate entrance, Miss Delafield had insisted that he be escorted up to his bedchamber for a rest. His rest had been short-lived. He had no sooner changed from his traveling clothes when Lady R appeared.

She continued her reproach. "And after I went to such great lengths to describe you to Gowland as an older gentleman of wisdom and decorum, one worthy of her trust and respect. How could you?"

The two were in the small but comfortable sitting room adjoining his lordship's bedchamber—the door to the hallway properly left ajar to preserve Lady R's virtue, such as it was.

His lordship occupied a wing chair before the roaring fire, his one hand clutching a wineglass as if it were the Holy Grail, while Lady R sat primly perched on a matching chair. In her gray satin gown and turban, his lordship thought, she resembled a dyspeptic gargoyle.

"As I have told you countless times now, Lady R, I was not foxed"—Lord Burton took a needed sip of his host's excellent Madeira—"but I intend to be, before I have the pleasure of meeting another member of this *interesting* household."

Lady R glared back. "Not foxed, heh? When I came from the drawing room, Peabody was helping you up the stairs."

Defiantly Lord Burton took another sip of wine. "My unsteadiness was caused by the nasty header I took over that dashed loose rug, to say nothing of the earlier shock I sustained when I saw my host sitting on a window ledge three stories above ground like some deranged simian."

"You cannot say I did not warn you about the peculiarities of the household."

Lady R had warned him of some peculiarities, his lordship thought acidly, but she had not warned him of the most important. Why? he wondered.

He gave her a keen-eyed glance. "Tell me, Lady R, why did you not mention the exquisite beauty that is the Bellefleur nose?"

Lady R looked at him askance. "You are daft, Lord Burton. There is nothing of beauty about the Bellefleur nose. Gowland is a beauty *in spite* of the nose, as was her mother, Grace."

Lord Burton was taken aback. Had his fall rattled his brain box? Had he only imagined the serene significance of Miss Delafield's sniffer?

Lady R was regarding him in a singular fashion. "Surely you noticed Gowland's exceptionally fine eyes and the perfection of her complexion?"

Lord Burton had not, but he was not about to acquaint Lady R of this failing. "Of course I did," he lied testily. "Perhaps I found the Bellefleur nose more *passable* than it actually is, because I was expecting a proboscis of heftier proportions."

"You must practice temperance, Lord Burton. Do not let wine cloud your intentions. You are here to save Gowland from Wombwell."

Lord Burton frowned. "Ahh, yes. So tell me, how does the situation stand?"

"It is most odd. While Wombwell dumps the butter boat on Gowland and praises her prodigious talent—a recent phenomenon as far as I know—no one in the household is permitted to see her work."

"Hmmm. Could it be that Wombwell is leading Miss Delafield on about her artistic abilities in order to make an advantageous marriage?"

Lady R sighed. "I fear so. Gowland is infatuated with him and allows him privileges usually not granted to a mere drawing master. He occupies one of the best bedchambers and takes his meals *en famille*. I have never seen the likes of it. She behaves like a mooncalf in his company, and when he is absent, her conversations are riddled with references to him. It is enough to drive one mad."

Upon hearing this, Lord Burton experienced an odd feeling of resentment. He asked sharply, "Does Wombwell return Miss Delafield's sentiments?"

"I am sure that he does, though all is decorous on the surface. Wombwell, aside from spouting Italian phrases and sulking about, does nothing to give offense. He and Gowland are never alone, not even during her interminable drawing lessons. Miss Clarke is always in attendance."

"Miss Clarke?"

"Gowland's companion, a genteel young woman who hails from a financially destitute family. Miss Clarke is a good influence on Gowland. With my keen perception of character, I saw that at once." Lady R sighed again. "If only Gowland were more like Miss Clarke."

Lord Burton's tone was oddly defensive. "From my first impression, albeit I was flat on my face at the time, Miss Delafield seemed to be all that is proper and gracious."

"On the surface, perhaps, but she was raised in a loose fashion. Given free rein to books she should not be reading, encouraged to say and do as she wished.

"I do not blame Gowland, per se," Lady R continued in her infamous, holier-than-thou tone. "She is cursed with a robust vitality that life as an unmarried country gentlewoman fails to challenge. At a time in her life when she should be thinking of marriage and children, she suffers a lack of malleable young men. There are few gentlemen of her station in the vicinity, and those there are she dismisses as bores. I place the blame for her faults on the Bellefleur nose, *and* Mr. Delafield."

Lady R harrumphed mightily. "Because of Mr. Delafield, Gowland has not had a Season. He does not care for the City and will not hear of turning her over to a relative to bring out. In truth, he is very attached to his only child and is loath for her to leave him."

"I can understand Mr. Delafield's sentiments," Lord Burton mused. "Miss Delafield would indeed be a delight to dandle upon one's knee."

Glimpsing Lady R's elevated eyebrows, his lordship stammered, "Ahh, yes, where were we? The ledge sitter, is he much with the company?"

"At mealtimes only. The rest of the day he is in his book room, doing whatever it is a scholar does in a book room."

"Does he approve of Wombwell?"

"He is sycophantically approving of the man. He will be more hindrance than help in our effort."

Lady R rose reluctantly. "I must dress for dinner. It is up to you, Lord Burton, to make Gowland see the error of her ways. You must treat her with avuncular kindness, win her trust until she confides all to you. Then, give her the guidance of your years."

Suppressing an urge to tell her ladyship to go to the devil, Lord Burton tossed back the remains of his Madeira and poured himself another glass.

FOUR

Lord Burton's inborn skepticism, coupled with a half bottle of the excellent Madeira, had convinced him that Lady R had the right of it. His perception of the Bellefleur nose *had* been faulty. No nose on earth could be so breathtakingly beautiful as to have caused his eyes to cross.

And so, supremely confident, brushed, buffed and polished to a high degree, his lordship took up a candle and left his bedchamber to make his way down to dinner.

Charged by Lady R with the winning of Miss Delafield's confidence, his lordship had dressed to convey "trustworthiness." While his single-breasted evening coat of navy wool with navy breeches and white jacquard waistcoat might be considered a shade too somber, Mr. Weston's superb tailoring and his lordship's own broad shoulders and excellent legs elevated the outfit to a degree of quiet elegance rarely seen in the country. A fine linen neckcloth, tied in the Oriental and garnished with a discreet diamond stickpin rendered Lord Burton a perfect pattern card for a well-dressed gentleman.

He traversed the long, dimly lit hallway without mishap and turned to descend the main staircase. He was met by Streech holding aloft a blazing candelabra. "Your lordship," he huffed, "the others await you in the drawing room. I shall escort you."

As Lord Burton followed the butler down the stairway,

he was struck by the elegant ambiance of the Hall. The candlelight emphasized the delicate rococo ornamentation adorning the pastel-tinted walls and ceilings of the stairwell. His lordship felt right at home. The Delafields belonged to the untitled aristocracy. A family that could trace its lineage back to the Norman Conquest was certainly deserving of the attention of a duke's younger son.

Two matching pedestal cupboards, an Adam hallmark, flanked the tall doors leading to the drawing room. They were crowned with tall vases of delicately scented flowers.

Two footmen, also matching, opened the doors, and his lordship stepped over the threshold. The scene that met his eye could have been painted by Reynolds. Miss Delafield sat playing the pianoforte. She wore shimmering gold silk, her close-cropped curls replicating the color and texture of her gown to near perfection.

A tall young man in black stood behind her turning the pages of the music, while Mr. Delafield and another young woman listened in rapt attention from a spot in front of the fireplace.

Lady R, stationed by a window, was the one discordant element in the scene. Dressed in rusty brown, she looked for all the world like a potted shrub in dire need of watering. In ringing tones, the butler announced his lordship.

Miss Delafield stopped playing at once, rose gracefully and swept toward him. "Welcome, Lord Burton."

As he bowed, she dipped into a curtsy. They finished their respective courtesies together, ending up face-to-face.

His lordship stared in amazement. Miss Delafield *was* a beauty. Why had not he noticed it before? Her large, wide-set eyes were the color of violets, her mouth generous and sweetly curving, her luminous complexion warmed with undertints of softest peach.

And her nose? The Bellefleur nose? His gaze shifted to that portion of her countenance. Long moments passed.

"Your lordship?"

"Beg pardon?"

"Your eyes . . ."

"Have they crossed again?"

"I fear so."

"It must be caused by a chill I caught on the journey."

"Of course. Lady Rettinger has told me that you have been down-pin of late. Do come and meet the others."

"I would enjoy that."

Neither moved. His lordship had the sudden odd sensation that he and Miss Delafield were alone under a glass dome and not an earthly sound or sigh could breach their quietude.

Lady R's battering ram of a voice, however, succeeded with ease. "Lord Burton!" Almost guiltily, Miss Delafield eddied to one side as her ladyship marched upon the pair.

Like an irate vicar eyeing a fledgling curate for signs of dissipation, she nailed his lordship with a trenchant eye. "I do hope you are *well,* your lordship."

His lordship correctly translated *well* as meaning *sober.* Glaring at Lady R, he sketched an insouciant bow. "Charmed, as always, Lady R."

As if cued, Mr. Delafield stepped smartly forward. He was tall and dapper with silver-gray hair and bright blue eyes. There seemed nothing of the Bedlamite in his host's mien, his lordship thought. Perhaps like poor King George's, Mr. Delafield's mental ailments ebbed and flowed.

"Welcome to Chigger Hall, Lord Burton. Delighted to see you again. We met this afternoon while I was taking the air on the window ledge."

"Of course. Your servant, sir."

Miss Clarke was introduced next. She was a mouse of a woman with features tending toward plainness, except for her eyes. They were large and gray and glittering.

That left only the gentleman in black to be made known to his lordship. Miss Delafield did the honors. With an arresting lilt and obvious devotion in her voice, she chimed, "Lord Burton, may I present . . . Wombwell."

Tossing an errant dark lock back from his forehead, the drawing master sauntered forward. At four-and-twenty, Wombwell had the face of a sin-riddled seraphim: large, heavy-lidded eyes, full sulky lips, and skin so white it looked blue.

He wore black velvet trousers, overly long and wide-legged, called cassocks, and a loose-fitting black velvet jacket that resembled a workman's smock. His shirt was fine white linen and his Napoleon necktie a bright violet-colored silk.

For some reason that Lord Burton could not quite fathom, the hairs on the back of his neck bristled as Wombwell approached.

His lordship bowed. "Mr. Wombwell."

Clicking his heels in the continental style, the sound somewhat spoiled by the folds of cloth overhanging his heels, Wombwell returned the bow. "*Wombwell,* only, if you please, Lord Burton. I am an *Artiste. I* need no title to enhance my standing."

Dampening an almost overwhelming urge to beat the bejesus out of the drawing master, Lord Burton good-naturedly shrugged his broad shoulders. "As Shakespeare so eloquently put it, 'What's in a name?' "

He turned to his hostess, taking care not to look directly at her nose. "*Your* given name intrigues me, Miss Delafield. Is 'Gowland' a family name?"

Miss Delafield had been looking adoringly at Wombwell. Reluctantly, it seemed, she shifted her gaze to his lordship. "No, Lord Burton. I was named after a lotion, *Gowland's Lotion.* My mama had a morbid fear of freckles, you see."

"Ahhh . . ." said the thoroughly baffled Lord Burton.

On that comment, the group proceeded in to dinner.

* * *

During the long walk to the dining room through the chilly corridors of Chigger Hall, Lord Burton was not sure if his feet touched the floor or not. He knew he was in love, bewitched by a nose that was appended to the face of a girl named after a freckle lotion. How had this happened?

Gowland was equally aware of Lord Burton, but for a different reason entirely. Since their first encounter when she had come upon him sprawled upon the entrance floor, she had wanted to secure his image on paper.

With a series of quick, oblique glances, she studied him. He was quite tall, as tall as Wombwell, but with more . . . substance across the chest, and quite handsome—even when his eyes were crossed. He was also much younger and *much* more handsome than Lady Rettinger's comments had led her to expect.

She imagined herself, hand and eye working as one, capturing the contours of his lordship's broad shoulders, his lean hips, his long, strongly muscled legs—

"Gowland, my dear," Miss Clarke's voice rang out, "you have led us past the dining room."

Leaves had been removed from the long refectory table to create a cozy setting for six. The ambiance of the room itself was most pleasant. Heat from two crackling fireplaces fevered the air, and an array of silver sconces holding several candles apiece gave light and substance to the scene.

Gowland presided over the head of the table with Lord Burton on her right and Wombwell on her left. As his lordship unfurled his napkin, Mr. Delafield addressed him from the opposite end of the table. "Do you have an interest in art, Lord Burton? Wombwell, fine fellow that he is, tells me my daughter is a combination of the best of Lawrence and Haydon rolled into one."

Placing her napkin on her lap, Gowland gave a soft, self-deprecating laugh. "Wombwell said I have the *potential* to become an artist of renown, Papa. It will take much study and forbearance on my part."

His lordship sipped his wine. Across an ornate epergne, his green eyes were level with Wombwell's. "I *pride* myself on my artistic discernment, Mr. Delafield. Mr. John Soane and his wife are close friends of mine, and I am often invited to comment on their latest acquisitions."

Lord Burton's response, directed to Mr. Delafield though meant for Wombwell, said much for his lordship's expertise. Soane was an architect of great note—he had designed the Bank of England—but it was his personal collection of books, arts and antiquities that made him famous.

After taking another sip of wine, Lord Burton placed his glass to the side of his plate; then, never taking his eyes off Wombwell, he added, "As something of a connoisseur of art, I look forward with pleasure to a showing of Miss Delafield's paintings."

Wombwell dropped his gaze and commenced toying with his dinner knife. Camilla had been right, he thought. It was obvious that his lordship had to be kept from Miss Delafield's pitiful scratchings at all costs.

With as much nonchalance as he could muster, the drawing master shrugged. "Miss Delafield is by no means ready to exhibit. Talent as great as hers must be carefully nurtured until it is ready to withstand the light of undisciplined—however well-meaning—curiosity."

"We speak of a portfolio, Wombwell, not a full-blown exhibit," observed Lady R tartly. "Surely, after six months of study, something should be forthcoming."

Miss Clarke leaned forward and spoke quickly. "You did say recently, did you not, Wombwell, that Miss Delafield should have a portfolio of her work ready for display soon after the ball?"

"Quite so," he said. He favored Gowland with a dazzling smile. "After the ball we shall plan a little showing of your best work. The choices will be difficult to make."

Dinner commenced. As the dishes were served and savored, the talk revolved around general topics. During the first course, which consisted of soup and fish, several meat and game dishes, and various sauces and vegetables, the talk was of the weather and the latest fashions.

During the second course, lighter than the first, the conversation concentrated on neighborhood happenings, then branched out to include Byron's recent journeyings around the Continent.

At last, the cloth was removed and the apples and walnuts passed around. As the candles burned down, a circumspect silence descended over the group. Six sets of thoughts went off in six different directions.

Miss Clarke gnawed nervously on her lower lip. Lord Burton's obvious attraction to Gowland had turned her blood to ice. Damn Lady Rettinger! Lord Burton was young, handsome, wealthy *and* an art connoisseur. Did Wombwell realize the potential dangers associated with his lordship's presence?

Wombwell, however, with his usual arrogance, had already dismissed his lordship and any potential problems connected to his arrival. It would not be difficult to keep Miss Delafield's work safely under wraps, he had decided. By his orders, the door to the studio was kept locked, and no spectators were permitted during the lessons. By the time his lordship learned that his hostess had the talent of a donkey, Wombwell and Camilla would be in sunny Italy spending Miss Delafield's inheritance.

He signaled the footman to refill his wineglass, idly wondering if Camilla could get away and join him for a *tête à tête* in the studio later this evening.

With painstaking precision, Mr. Delafield dissected a walnut shell and carefully extracted the meaty kernels. He knew the Bellefleur nose to be a powerful proboscis. It could sniff out—often over great distances—the most suitable mate for its possessor. Once sniffed, both sniffer and

sniffee were powerless to stop the attraction. Had Lord
Burton been picked by the Bellefleur nose? he mused. His
lordship looked promising. All the signs were there.

Lady Rettinger's thoughts were more self-congratula-
tory. How wise she had been to enlist Lord Burton's aid
in freeing Gowland from the wiles of that wretched drawing master. Veritably his lordship's involvement would be
twice-blessed. In assisting her to assist Gowland, he would
be forced to focus on something other than his own lonely
and misguided life. He was fortunate indeed, she preened,
to have the benefit of her keen perceptions.

She glanced across the table to where Miss Clarke sat
staring into space. The poor dear looked drawn this evening. She was so ladylike and so diligent in her duties.
Gowland had found the perfect companion.

Miss Delafield nibbled on a section of peeled apple. The
thought of rendering a portrait of Lord Burton was becoming more inviting with each passing minute. Because
of Wombwell's restrictions, she could not ask his lordship
to sit for her, but, she reasoned, if she could memorize his
face and form, she could paint him from memory at a
later date. She would make two paintings, she decided.
One for herself and one to send to him as a gift. A memento of his stay at Chigger Hall.

Having accepted his lightning-strike love for Miss Delafield as "Divine Intervention" at work, Lord Burton was
determined to win her. He saw Wombwell as his only ob-
stacle.

Covertly, he studied the drawing master across the table.
Was he a fortune hunter as Lady R implied? A despicable
cad who would do anything to make an advantageous marriage, to include leading on a green girl about her artistic
talents?

His lordship focused in on the problems confronting
him. First off, he would have to find a way to examine a
sampling of Miss Delafield's work. If Wombwell was fabri-

cating her talents, Mr. Delafield must be informed immediately. While Lord Burton longed to give the drawing master a doubler or two, and would if he got the chance, it was Mr. Delafield's prerogative as master of Chigger Hall to send the blackguard packing.

There was one other problem to be dealt with, one that Lord Burton was loath to think about. But think about it he must. In exposing Wombwell, Miss Delafield's lack of artistic talent—if such proved to be the case—would also be revealed.

His lordship stiffened his upper lip. He had to be firm in his commitment, whatever the consequences. Surely, it was better to have his new-found love endure a week or two of disappointment—a disappointment he would do his best to ameliorate—as opposed to her spending a lifetime married to a cad.

He already had a plan. The ball was a scant two weeks away. Caution was called for, but swiftness was required. Time was of the essence.

FIVE

After the gentlemen had finished their port, they joined the ladies in the drawing room. From the depths of his favorite chair, Mr. Delafield requested that Gowland play the pianoforte for the enjoyment of the company.

She acquiesced, but only if Miss Clarke would consent to sing. Wombwell then offered to turn the music for the ladies, which left Lord Burton free to settle next to Lady R on the settee and tell her *sotto voce* of his plan for later in the evening.

"It will not work, Lord Burton," Lady R pronounced the moment he had finished.

His lordship gave her a testy smile. "I am assured it will work, Lady R. It is quite simple, really. After the household is abed, I will steal into the studio and examine the fruits of Miss Delafield's artistic labors." He gave a slight shrug. "While I realize it is not the conduct of a gentleman to slink about after dark in the home of one's host, I feel the breach of etiquette is more than justified in this situation."

Lady R merely sighed, the kind of female sigh that signifies all men are fools. "Your plan will not work, Lord Burton, because the studio is kept locked, and Wombwell keeps the key. *I*, however, have a plan that *will* work."

Ignoring his lordship's muttered oath, Lady R cautioned, "Keep your voice down and listen carefully. Your bedchamber is situated on the east corner of the Hall. The studio occupies the west corner. Simply climb out your window, walk along the ledge and enter the studio by one of its several windows.

His lordship choked over his saucer of tea. "You expect me to balance along a ledge three stories above ground in pitch darkness like some demented circus performer?"

"If you are careful, and I trust you will be, and do not drink to excess, there will be little danger."

"*Little danger*? I have no head for heights. What if I should fall? What if my hostess should come upon my broken body lying lifeless upon her drive?"

"Tut, tut, Lord Burton. Do not let the possibility of a fall cause undue concern to your male vanity. Gowland is aware that you have been blue-deviled of late; she will think you jumped."

His lordship's strangled cry of rage was neatly tempered by Miss Clarke's courageous if inadequate attempt to hit high C.

Damn Lady R! Taking a labored breath, Lord Burton opened the window of his bedchamber and crawled out on the ledge. Gingerly, he straightened up, his back to the wall, his hands pressed against the cold stones of Chigger Hall. A chill blast of wind iced his beaded brow. Bile rose in his throat.

Not daring to look down, he forced himself to stare up at the stars. With seemingly sinister intent, the stars stared back. The night had a thousand eyes, glittering eyes behind a domino's mask.

Unbeknownst to his lordship, another pair of eyes watched him from above. On a window ledge one floor up, Mr. Delafield sat taking a bit of air. He took note of his lordship's unexpected appearance with the sharp interest of a bird stalking a worm.

Ignorant of Mr. Delafield's regard, his lordship forced

himself to lift his left foot and move it an inch toward his objective. With the left firmly settled, he moved the right.

Inch by inch, he edged along the ledge until he was within thirty feet his goal. Pausing before a window to take a shuddering breath, he leaned back, relaxing a bit, a wooden window frame pressing companionably between his shoulder blades. He had made it this far. Surely God would not permit a mishap at this stage of the—

The thought was never completed. The window behind him suddenly opened, and his lordship fell backward onto a cushioned window seat. He continued his fall, somersaulting heels over head and coming to rest facedown upon a soft carpet.

Candlelight encircled him. "Lord Burton?"

A froth of white, lace-bedecked flounces swirled before his lordship's eyes; the scent of lavender wafted on the air.

With a scrambled sense of *déjà vu,* he lifted his chin. "Miss Delafield?" He got quickly to his feet, settled his coattails and bowed. "Forgive this unfortunate intrusion. I felt unwell and thought a walk might relax me."

"On the ledge?"

"It seemed a splendid idea at the time. Again, forgive me. I shall leave at once and return to my bedchamber."

"If you feel unwell, Lord Burton, perhaps you should rest before you resume your walk."

"Here? Certainly not! It would be the height of impropriety for me to remain in your bedchamber."

Miss Delafield calmly considered the wisdom of his words. "Then you had best leave by the door and walk down the hallway to your chamber," she suggested. "Much less risk of injury if you were to faint."

His lordship looked shocked. "Use the door? And place your reputation in jeopardy should I be seen? That would be a worse impropriety."

Miss Delafield nodded. "You are right, Lord Burton. It

would be best if you returned to your chamber by way of the ledge."

A trifle dashed by Miss Delafield's willingness to allow him to risk his life, his lordship grasped the sides of the open window and prepared to heave himself out.

As he did so, his heart began a rapid tattoo against his rib cage; his palms grew moist. He willed his body forward, but it would not move. He was frozen with fear.

After a long moment, Gowland suggested, "Surely the height of impropriety has been reached for this evening, Lord Burton. I doubt if a short rest on your part would either add to it or detract from it."

Gratefully, Lord Burton nodded. "You are right, Miss Delafield. Thank you." He loosened his grip, turned and slumped down on the window seat. His pulse was pounding like a runaway horse. Miss Delafield shut the window behind him. He leaned his head back against the frigid pane and closed his eyes.

Gowland settled beside his lordship, placing the iron candle holder in its drip tray on the cushion between them. What a fortuitous happening! she thought. Lord Burton's *malaise* had provided the perfect opportunity for her to study his resting face and form. Shifting slightly, she tucked her bare feet under her wrapper and began her artist's appraisal. Where should she begin? she wondered. His lordship's strong aquiline nose, his solid square jaw, the tantalizing cleft in his chin?

Lord Burton's face and form might be resting, but his mind was racing with the speed of a harried hare. While he had not made it to the studio, his tumbling into Miss Delafield's bedchamber was not without merit. Surely his impeccable behavior in such an unexpected and intimate situation would go far in winning her trust.

Leaning closer to her subject, Gowland tilted her head to one side and squinted. How very interesting, she mused. Lord Burton's face was composed of a series of planes and angles, quite unlike Wombwell's. Wombwell's visage gave one the impression of roundness. Rounded cheeks, rounded mouth, a rounded pad of plumpness under his chin—

As if aware of her scrutiny, Lord Burton opened his eyes. His breath caught in his throat. Miss Delafield was just a heartbeat away and regarding him with a look of astral fascination upon her face. It was almost as if she were attempting to *absorb* his image.

He smiled to himself. He was quite accustomed to being the object of feminine focus and desire. The noted Dance charm had once more proved irresistible. Moving an infinitesimal bit closer to his beloved, he whispered, "Would it be impolite of me, Miss Delafield, to ask what you are thinking?"

She did not hesitate for a moment. "I was thinking of Wombwell."

Wombwell! Lord Burton felt as if he had been dashed in the face with a bucket of cold water. Sorely reduced in attitude, he attempted to gather his scattered wits about him.

He realized he had just been given a perfect opportunity to learn more about his rival; it would be foolhardy of him not to take advantage of the opening.

Forcing a smile, he mused, "Ahhh, yes, Wombwell. Such an engaging young fellow. His background interests me. He is obviously a gentleman's son, yet he labors as a drawing master."

Gowland nodded sadly. "Wombwell is a gentleman's son. Unfortunately, his papa shot himself to death over his gambling debts. Wombwell's mama, in a pique over her loss, ran off with her groom—she was a bruising rider by all accounts—leaving Wombwell to face penury alone."

"Poor chap," said his lordship, not meaning a word of it.

Gowland nodded. "It is a great loss for humanity, Lord Burton, when an artiste of Wombwell's talents is hampered by concern over the mundane aspects of daily living." A small, secret smile curved her lips. "Of course, that unfortunate set of circumstances could change in the very near future."

Of course, Lord Burton thought bitterly, Wombwell's circumstances would change for the better when Miss Delafield announced their forthcoming marriage at the Valentine's Day Ball.

The look of happiness on Miss Delafield's face—inspired by the likes of Wombwell, of all people—was more than his lordship could bear. His wounded, near-to-death male ego gave him the impetus to move. He got to his feet and bowed stiffly. "Thank you for your hospitality, Miss Delafield. I am fully recovered now and will be on my way."

Gowland rose and picked up the candlestick, her expression clearly mirroring her disappointment. She had explored Lord Burton's face, but not his form. She knew she would not rest until she had his full proportions firmly in hand.

With jealousy burning like a fever in his brain, his lordship opened the window and hauled himself out. For a long moment, he sat crouched upon the ledge.

Fear once more gripped him in its icy fist. He vowed that if he made it to the safety of his chamber tonight, he would never again as much as open a window above the ground floor.

"Lord Burton."

He pivoted. Gowland was sitting on the window seat, holding the candle aloft. The candle's flickering light shone upon her hair turning her crisp curls to molten gold. Her lips parted in hesitation. Suddenly, his lordship could imagine his fingers entangled in those curls his mouth upon those soft lips.

"Lord Burton."

"Uhh, yes, Miss Delafield?"

Though her color heightened in the candlelight, she smiled artlessly. "If you are out for a stroll on the ledge another evening soon and feel unwell, you have only to tap upon my window."

Renewed hope surged through his lordship's broad

chest. Miss Delafield was concerned for his well-being! Without a thought for his safety, he straightened up and bowed. "You are most kind."

Then, under his angel's watchful eye, he proceeded to stroll jauntily along the ledge toward his own window. He took little notice of the chill wind tugging at his coattails; Miss Delafield's smile had given him the courage of a lion.

When he arrived at his destination, he tossed a nonchalant wave over his shoulder, opened the window and stepped through. As he closed the casements behind him, deferred fear caused his legs to give way, and he almost fell to the floor. His heart pounding with an exhilarating mix of terror and love, his lordship made his wobbly way to the bed and collapsed upon the coverlet.

In spite of his trepidation, he knew he would walk the ledge tomorrow night, and any other night if need be. He would do anything for his beloved. Fear could be conquered; Miss Delafield would be won.

Mr. Delafield had watched his lordship's painful, inch-by-inch progress on the ledge as he would have observed the frantic antics of an overturned beetle, wanting to help but wary of interfering in the natural order of things.

Even his lordship's ungraceful header into Gowland's bedchamber did not overly trouble him. He did not fear for his daughter's virtue, nor did he fear for Lord Burton's well-being. The Bellefleur nose provided equal protection for both its unwitting predator *and* unwary prey.

Mr. Delafield smiled as he witnessed Gowland's lingering farewell and his lordship's ecstatic return along the same ledge he had so fearfully traversed only minutes before. The Bellefleur nose was working its strange magic once again. The natural order of things was proceeding very nicely.

SIX

"I tell you, Cosmos, there *is* an attraction between Gowland and Lord Burton."

Stifling a yawn, Wombwell pulled the drapes aside to admit the coveted north light. It fatigued him to watch Camilla feverishly pace the studio, and he wished she would settle. Where did she get the energy? Her lovemaking had been tireless until well into the morning hours.

Noting Wombwell's indifference to her warning, Camilla cursed the day she had met him and fallen in love with him. What a foolish girl she had been. It had not taken long, however, for the scales of romantic love to fall from her eyes. She had soon realized that Wombwell, though an accomplished lover, was an arrogant bore and lazy as sin. Her mouth hardened. If it were not for her initiative, they would have starved months ago. As it was, getting their hands on Gowland's fortune was their only hope for a future without endless servitude.

She wheeled on Wombwell, her tone terse. "It is still more than a week to the ball, Cosmos. You must keep Gowland from Lord Burton's company as much as possible. Increase her lesson hours, do anything, but keep them apart!"

* * *

"You know I never sleep late, Peabody," Lord Burton grumbled. "Why did you not waken me?"

Peabody brushed a minute speck of dust from the shoulder of his lordship's green worsted jacket. "I tried, sir. You not only wished me to perdition, but suggested several interesting things I could do whilst there."

"Did I? Well, that explains it, then.

"And what of the rest of the household?"

"Mr. Delafield is in his book room, Miss Delafield is in her studio, and Lady Rettinger is, and has been for some time, in the breakfast room. I would assume, sir, that she is waiting for you."

His lordship uttered a colorful oath. On their way to their respective chambers last night, he and Lady R had agreed to meet in the breakfast room at ten o'clock to discuss whatever was found in the studio. It was now half past the hour.

"Damn it, man. Why did you not tell me that Lady R awaits me?"

"It was only an assumption on my part, sir, although Lady Rettinger has inquired repeatedly as to your where-abouts—"

"Enough of your palaver, Peabody. You know the old dragon breathes fire if kept waiting. You have put me in the way of a serious scorching."

As Lord Burton strode from the room closing the door most forcefully behind him, Peabody breathed a sigh of relief. It was not like his lordship to find fault with a fat goose, yet since their arrival at Chigger Hall, he had done just that.

The valet shrugged. What else could one expect in an establishment like Chigger Hall? Its master was a queer card who sat half the day on a window ledge, and the young mistress, as daft as her pater, encouraged a top-lofty pencil merchant to have full run of the house. It was not the way things were done in a proper, well-managed household.

Peabody could hardly wait to return to Grosvenor Square and the sanity of the City.

Cursing his long-suffering valet under his breath, his lordship hurried down the main staircase. As he went, he concocted a Banbury tale to tell Lady R, one that she was sure to believe. He was not about to cough up to the old harridan why he had failed to reach the studio, *or* that he had spent a part of the evening in the intimacy of Miss Delafield's bedchamber.

As he entered the breakfast room, he found Lady R ruthlessly slathering butter on a piece of defenseless toast. She did not deign to glance up. "Good *afternoon,* Lord Burton. I trust you slept well."

"Good *morning,* Lady R. I slept quite well, thank you. And you?"

"Fitfully, at best. The food served at the Hall is too rich; it gives me stoppage of the stomach."

It was more than his lordship wanted to know about Lady R's inner workings. He grimaced and went to the sideboard. Regarding a platter of kidneys as better left untouched, he helped himself to an ample portion of ham and eggs and toast. He took his plate to the table and pulled out the chair opposite Lady R.

She deigned to pour a cup of coffee for him. As he added cream, she glanced suspiciously around the empty room, paying special attention to the corners.

"It is safe for us to talk," she informed him with a sagacious nod. "Tell me what your search of the studio unearthed."

"I did not go," his lordship stated baldly. "I drank brandy while waiting for the household to get itself to bed and wound up too disguised to risk walking the ledge."

Lady R's knife clattered to her plate. "Shame, Lord Burton, shame. I cannot preach temperance enough. Both my husbands drank to excess."

Not surprising, thought his lordship.

"I am sorry to disappoint you, Lady R," he said, "but I assure you that I will search the studio tonight. Not an excess drop of cold tea will pass my lips until I have a sampling of Miss Delafield's artistic work in my pocket."

"Remember those words, Lord Burton. Gowland's future happiness depends on you."

"I am *extatique*, Miss Delafield. You have the *anime* of a true artiste!"

Gowland stepped back from her easel, her shoulders drooping with weariness. Wombwell had been a hard taskmaster today, insisting as he had on both morning and afternoon lessons.

Still, she thought, her last five portraits of Miss Clarke did show a definite improvement. The corklike heads of the first attempts had been replaced with perfect ovals, and this final rendition was the best by far.

"May I see the results?" Miss Clarke queried.

"Please do, Camilla," Gowland responded. "You have been such a patient and uncomplaining model."

Miss Clarke rose stiffly. "Nonsense, my dear, it has been but five hours, and I consider it both a pleasure *and* an honor to sit for you."

"Has your neck spasm quite subsided?"

"Quite."

Miss Clarke smiled weakly, steeling herself as she approached the easel. "Now, to see the final portrait—Oh, dear God." Gowland had painted her with a perfectly oval head, a helmet of matted hair and eyes like a dying fish.Miss Clarke's look of wide-eyed shock signaled yet another spasm in the making. Wombwell quickly intervened. "I had the same initial reaction, Miss Clarke. The mastery of Miss Delafield's work, the confidence of her brush strokes, quite takes one's breath away, does it not?"

"Indeed," Miss Clarke murmured. To say nothing of one's appetite, she thought.

Gowland received her colleagues' compliments with good, if weary, grace. She was not herself today. She had not been able to sleep after Lord Burton's impromptu visit, but had indulged instead in a seemingly ceaseless cycle of self-reproach. Why had she allowed her attention to linger overlong on his face, thus missing the opportunity to explore his splendid form?

"Gowland dear, are you all right? You look a trifle pale."

"A little fatigued is all," Gowland replied.

Recalling her earlier promise, she took Camilla's hand in hers. "Since you take such pleasure in your portrait, Camilla, I would like to present it to you as a gift."

Miss Clarke blenched. "Thank you, dear Gowland, but, however tempting the offer, I must decline. I am certain Wombwell will agree with me; this painting *belongs* in your portfolio."

With a series of weighty nods, Wombwell concurred. "You are very astute, Miss Clarke. I predict that this painting will be the crown jewel of Miss Delafield's offerings."

Lacing his long fingers together, the drawing master made the leap from sycophant to shameless gourmand in one easy bound. "Now, we have earned a rest," he proclaimed. "We shall stop our labors and assuage our *fame*. Supper on trays in the studio. Then, another session, no?"

Surprisingly, Camilla stepped forward. "No indeed," she forbade firmly. "I will not allow it. Gowland, you must rest for what remains of the afternoon and have your supper served on a tray in your chamber."

"I do not think that is necessary, Camilla—"

"I insist! We cannot have you come down sick for the ball."

Meekly, Gowland allowed Camilla to lead her to the

door. In truth, she was relieved to be finished for the day. She was tired, and the thought of another lesson added to her lassitude.

A long rest was what she needed. Then, if Lord Burton should tap upon her window tonight, she would be refreshed enough to concentrate her attention on his superb muscular configuration.

The moment the door to the studio closed behind Gowland, Wombwell turned on Camilla. "And what was that all about?" he demanded. "Did you not tell me earlier that I was to extend Miss Delafield's lessons?"

"I did, but I worried that if we pushed too hard, she would balk." Camilla gazed fixedly at her portrait without seeing it at all—a pleasant state of unawareness. Her gray eyes narrowed in thought. "Did you not sense that Gowland's enthusiasm was less than zealous today? If she grows bored with Art, might she not question the soundness of endowing the Wombwell School for the Arts?"

Wombwell did not like to think of unpleasant things. "Nonsense!" he said petulantly. "She is tired, is all. She said so herself."

"But," Camilla persisted, "what if she were not tired, but preoccupied—with thoughts of Lord Burton?"

"You worry too much, Camilla," Wombwell scoffed. "Lord Burton and Miss Delafield have not had a moment alone together since he arrived. Courtship takes time; seduction requires privacy. They have had neither time nor privacy."

SEVEN

"Damn," Lord Burton muttered. A brief sleet storm earlier in the day had frosted the ledge with intermittent patchworks of ice. He would have to watch his every step. He shivered as a blast of wind, colder than a doxy's heart, sliced through his wool frock coat. In spite of the peril to life and limb, he cautiously inched along.

His approach to the studio went past Miss Delafield's window. He had not seen or spoken to his beloved since their encounter in her bedchamber last evening. Was she avoiding him? Had their unexpected enmeshment been too great a shock for her tender sensibilities? Was she, by her seclusion today, signaling her distaste for his deportment? And yet, he mused—his expectations refusing to die—she *had* invited him to come back.

The unanswerable quizzes put his lordship all at sea. Assuming he did not fall to his death, he had hoped to find the courage to tap upon Miss Delafield's window on his return trip. Not to enter her bedchamber, of course, but merely to pay his respects. Now, until they met in more conventional circumstances, and he could offer a proper apology for his unseemly intrusion last evening, that was out of the question.

Miss Delafield's drapes were drawn, he saw. No candle flickered within. With a sigh that was a melding of regret

and relief, his lordship continued his crablike progress until his objective was within sight.

The studio boasted four windows, two on the front of
the house and two on the side. He exercised a tight, cautious turnabout until he faced the first casement. The studio's drapes were closed. Making a fist, he pounded lightly
on the window expecting it to pop open. It did not budge.
It was locked tight.

Still optimistic, his lordship shuffled his way to the second window. It too was locked. Frustrated, he rested his
forehead for a moment against a freezing pane. He would
have to continue on around the building and have a try
at the two remaining windows. He glanced down and to
his right. The coating of ice looked thicker at the corner
projection. Still, there was no other way. Rigid with both
fear and determination, he doggedly pursued his course.

It was past midnight. Gowland was wide awake and unable to go back to sleep. A series of strange dreams had
roused her, dreams in which his lordship had played a
commanding part. She could not recall all the details, but
she knew the fantasies had been remarkably pleasant—if
unsettling.

Sighing deeply, she dressed in a warm wrapper and
curled up in a chair before the still smoldering fire. The
dreams had disturbed her greatly. Was she losing her
senses? Was the odd restlessness that had affected her in
the past threatening to return?

Last year, at the approach of her twentieth birthday,
Gowland had begun to experience vague longings, a yearning for something more than she possessed . . . something
she could not name.

Wombwell's arrival at Chigger Hall six months ago had
been an epiphany of sorts. With his recognition of her
rare "talent" and constant praise of her efforts, Gowland

had been granted a goal. She had concentrated on her Art, often to the exclusion of other pleasures, and had felt happy and fulfilled.

Now, however, the same vague longing, the same nameless restlessness, had returned. The recurrence, she felt, was in some way connected with Lord Burton's arrival at Chigger Hall.

Since Gowland's lively mind had been given free rein by her doting father, she now set about to find a reason for the curious association between her feelings and the advent of his lordship into her life.

It came to her suddenly. Of course! She must be addled not to have realized it at once. All the great artists had had a special model to whom they were drawn, a symbiotic bonding of two souls, each seeking in his own way to assuage his individual aesthetic needs. Could Lord Burton be the model meant for her? Would her greatest work be a likeness of him?

It must be so. Never before had she experienced such a sharp yearning to commit someone's likeness to paper. As she savored the thought, she heard a shuffling noise outside, on the ledge? Lord Burton?

She rose, tugging her wrapper tightly to her and tiptoed to the window seat. She knelt on one knee and cautiously drew aside the drape. She was in time to see his lordship's tall figure inch past the window. He looked stiff as starched linen. Obviously, his restorative walk had not yet relaxed him.

Going quickly to her bedside stand, Gowland retrieved her night candle and lighted it from the still smoldering coals in the grate.

Now! She straightened up and took a deep breath, her eyes partly narrowed in concentration. Would Lord Burton walk the ledge completely around the house or only as far as the corner, then retrace his steps? If it were the latter, she must conceive of a reason to invite him into her chamber. She wanted, nay, as an Artiste, she was *driven* to commit the contours of his body to memory. By the look of his progress on the ledge she had ample time to think of something. Meanwhile, she should put herself to rights.

She went to her dressing table, placed the candle close to the looking glass and surveyed her reflection. Her cheeks had a natural glow—she had no need for Almond Bloom; her hair, however, was tousled from sleep. Or lack of it.

A light suddenly went off in her mind. Of course! She would pretend to suffer from insomnia and beg his lordship to read to her until she felt drowsy. Certainly, he would not refuse her request.

Smiling at her mirrored image, Gowland picked up her silver-backed hairbrush and began to brush through her curls with short, rhythmic strokes.

"Christ on a crutch!" Lord Burton's distinctive oath floated off on the crisp night air. If he had Lady R here this instant, he would throttle her. All four of the studio's windows were locked, tight as a tick.

Now what? What bright idea would the old griffin come up with when he told her? He cursed again. Perhaps she would suggest suspending him on a rope and lowering him down the chimney? He would not put it past her.

Gritting his teeth, he began to move his feet by small degrees back toward the corner of the building.

In order to expose Wombwell as a liar and a fortune hunter, he had to get his hands on a sample of Miss Delafield's work. But how?

With his feet slipping and sliding beneath him, Lord Burton edged around the corner to the front of the Hall. It was then he saw a pool of candlelight spilling from Miss Delafield's open window.

Moments later, her head appeared, her curls shining like spirals of spun gold. Espying him, she lifted the candle and called out softly, "Lord Burton, if you are finished with your evening exercise, would you join me? I need your expertise in a matter of great personal concern."

At his beloved's summons, his lordship's heart leapt forward. His feet quickly followed. Moments later, he was hauling himself through Miss Delafield's window.

" 'Shall I compare thee to a summer's day?
" 'Thou art more lovely and more temperate;' "

Lord Burton looked up from the sonnet he was reading. "The moment you feel the least bit drowsy, Miss Delafield, you must tell me. My presence in your bedchamber, even though medicinal in motive, is most unseemly."

From the wing chair opposite his, Miss Delafield nodded dreamily. "I love the sonnets of Shakespeare, Lord Burton. I implore you to go on reading. It will not be too much longer. I must confess your voice has a most soporific effect on me."

Taking that as a compliment, his lordship gave Gowland a concerned look. "Do you often suffer from insomnia, Miss Delafield?"

Gowland, who usually slept like a sloth, sighed tragically. "Quite often, Lord Burton."

His lordship nodded sympathetically, then reached for the glass of water that stood on a table beside his chair. Although the fire was banked, the room seemed obsessively warm. His neckcloth felt like a noose. Clearing his throat, he continued:

" 'Rough winds do shake the darling buds of May,
" 'And summer's lease hath all too short a date:' "

When Lord Burton's eyes were safely fastened upon the page, Gowland took up where she had left off. At his lordship's right shoulder.

Using her eyes as though they were the point of a pencil, she slowly traced the sleeve and coattail of his jacket, down one side of his doeskin trousers, around his polished boot, up his muscular calf to the taut tendons of his thigh, to—

Oh, drat! His lordship held the book in his lap in such a way that his exact middle portion was hidden from view. Which meant she would have to paint him that way. But, she reasoned, perhaps it was for the best. The correct linking of limbs to torso was not one of her strong points. Once again, she began to track with her eyes, this time measuring the dimensions of the book. Halfway around its perimeter, she lost her place and had to begin again. She stifled a series of small yawns. Lord Burton's voice was so deep and resonant, like distant church bells. It *was* having a soporific effect on her.

The book's proportions proved far less fascinating than his lordship's. Gowland's yawns grew in number and intensity. In spite of all her good intentions, her eyelids began to flutter.

Minutes later, Lord Burton shut the book with a soft snap and placed it on the table beside his chair. He rose and tiptoed to Miss Delafield's side. She was fast asleep.

Smiling down at her, he leaned over, gathered her up in his arms and carried her to her bed. The four-poster, a fragrant nest of lavender-scented linens, still held the imprint of her body.

Tenderly, he put her down and covered her to her chin with quilts. She burrowed deeper beneath the covers, the Bellefleur nose almost disappearing from sight. Dear little nose, his lordship thought staring down at it. Dear maligned little nose. How he ached to deposit a trail of tiny kisses along its beguiling arc.

Reining in his wayward thoughts, his lordship retraced his steps to the hearth. He snuffed out the candle, went to the window and opened it. Without a hint of hesitation he stepped out onto the ice-crusted ledge and into the cold, dark night.

* * *

From his perch on the floor above, Mr. Delafield had watched his lordship's dangerous trip along the ledge and his unsuccessful attempts to gain access to the studio.

He was much impressed. Lord Burton not only possessed the courage of a lion—not many men would attempt such a perilous feat in evening slippers—he was also clever and resourceful. All told, he was an excellent young fellow.

As a father, Mr. Delafield still was not worried about his daughter's virtue. Yet, he knew from experience that the Bellefleur nose was a powerful aphrodisiac. The time was fast approaching when, as a father, he would have to test his lordship's intentions.

Gowland woke at dawn's first light, castigating herself for having fallen to sleep in the exact middle of his lordship. In her mind, she began immediately to retrace the outline of his tall, supple body, the configuration of his strong torso and lean hip.

She nodded sagely. Yes, his impressive lineament was firmly entrenched in her memory. Sitting up in bed, she hugged her knees to her chest. It was a shame that she had not made it around his lordship's entire perimeter. But surely, she reasoned, one side was much like the other. She could reverse her mental image, and *voilà*, she would have Lord Burton in his entirety. Except, of course, for the middle portion which would be covered with a book.

Filled with a sudden, overwhelming need to create, Gowland swung her legs out of bed and groped for her slippers with her toes. She kept a block of sketch paper and pencils in her nightstand. She would begin work on her masterpiece immediately.

EIGHT

Lord Burton awakened out of sorts and riddled with self-reproach. As delightful as last night's interlude with Miss Delafield had been, he had not accomplished what he had set out to do. Time was growing short. Somehow he had to find a way into the studio.

He took a last gulp of coffee, allowed Peabody to adjust his neckcloth, then stalked out of his bedchamber. He was not looking forward to his imminent meeting with Lady R in the breakfast room. He dreaded having to inform her of yet another failure. That acerbic tongue of hers could etch glass.

That Lord Burton had had reason to dread her ladyship's company was immediately demonstrated. Crashing a piece of toast between teeth that resembled a cockeyed row of country grave stones, Lady R gifted him with an overlying look. "You found all the windows locked, you say?" She chewed thoughtfully. "I think the solution would have been obvious to you, Lord Burton, but let me enlighten you. Tonight when you walk the ledge and reach your destination, you must break a pane of glass, reach in and undo the window latch. I am surprised you did not think of it yourself."

Lord Burton glared at Lady R, taking his ire out on the piece of beefsteak he had just popped into his mouth. After a bout of furious mastication, he replied tartly, "Forgive the lapse, Lady R. While I do not have the benefit of your expertise in such matters, I do believe that the punishment for the deed you so loftily assign to me is *transportation,* is it not?"

Lady R sighed. "You are testy this morning, Lord Burton, but, at least, your blue-devils have left you for the nonce. Of course, you have me to thank for that—"

"Good morning to you all."

"Mr. Delafield!" Lady R cried out. "You startled me. You do not often appear in the breakfast room."

"How very observant you are, Lady Rettinger. This morning, as on most mornings, I had my coffee and toast in my chamber. Upon finishing my repast, however, I decided to spend a few moments in more charming company than my own."

He beamed at his lordship, who was getting to his feet. "Pray do not get up, Lord Burton. I shall take the chair next to yours, if I may?"

As Mr. Delafield settled himself, he directed a quizzing look at them both. "I trust I am not disturbing a private conversation between two old friends?"

"Not at all," Lady R hastily assured him. "His lordship and I were discussing his frequent bouts of *ennui.*"

"Indeed?" said Mr. Delafield. He reached over and helped himself to Lady Rettinger's last piece of toast. Munching contentedly on a bit of crust, he turned his innocent blue eyes on Lord Burton and examined him intently.

"Perhaps more exercise would be the thing," he suggested. "I find a short walk late in the evening hours to be most bracing."

His lordship, who had not blushed since he started shaving, blushed now. Was it possible that Mr. Delafield had witnessed him stealing into his daughter's bedchamber, or had his host's chance remark just happened to hit amazingly close to home?

"Ahh," Mr. Delafield said. "I see the very thought of an evening walk has already sharpened your color. You must make it a regular part of your nightly routine."

He accepted a cup of coffee offered by Lady Rettinger and, after a series of sips, settled his cup down in its saucer. "I feel I should apologize to you both," he said. "Gowland is so preoccupied with her art lessons, and I with my books, that we are neglecting you, our esteemed guests."

Before his lordship could politely protest, Mr. Delafield continued, "We have a billiard room, Lord Burton, and a well-stocked library that might help to fill your days. Our stable also boasts several excellent riding horses, a few gentle enough for ladies. Do you ride, Lady Rettinger?"

"I have not ridden in years, Mr. Delafield. In my youth, however, I was known for my formidable seat."

"I am sure you still are," Mr. Delafield assured her gravely.

Lord Burton glanced quickly at his host. Was there a suggestion of a twinkle in those guileless blue eyes? Interesting, his lordship thought. Bedlamites generally were not noted for their humor.

The gentle twit, if that was what it had been, had sailed serenely over Lady R's turbaned head. Patting her mouth with her napkin, she intoned, "I thank you, Mr. Delafield, for your concern over my possible boredom, but I can assure you, I am never bored." She sent his lordship an arch look. "*I* do not permit myself the selfish convenience of ennui, as do some. This morning, in Gowland's stead, I shall pay visits upon the destitute of the village. After the cook prepares the baskets, and the stable boy lays hot bricks on the floor of the coach, my maid and I shall venture forth into the cold to give comfort to the undeserving poor."

"Do you not mean the *deserving* poor?" his lordship suggested dryly.

The milk of human kindness had long since curdled in Lady R's aristocratic veins. "Do not talk nonsense, Lord

Burton," she observed flatly. "If the poor were deserving, they would not be poor. Am I not right, Mr. Delafield?"

Mr. Delafield nodded thoughtfully. "Yours is an interesting supposition, Lady Rettinger." He adjusted his spectacles, leaned forward and regarded Lady R with scholarly intent. "If I were not so immersed in my study of ancient religions, I would wish to concentrate on the wonder of your mental processes."

Lady R blushed unbecomingly. "Horsley, my second husband, also thought my mind ripe for scientific study, and said so on many occasions."

"An astute fellow, your Horsley," Mr. Delafield approved. He got to his feet and bowed. "Now, I shall bid you both a good day."

As Lord Burton rose respectfully, Mr. Delafield paused. He looked his lordship up and down, head to toe, as though measuring him for a new suit of clothes. "Lord Burton, perhaps you would join me in my book room after you have finished your breakfast?"

His lordship greeted the invitation with a trio of emotions: surprise, pleasure, and guilty apprehension. "It would be a pleasure, sir," he responded, praying that this would prove to be so.

Mr. Delafield nodded complacently. "Excellent, excellent! I think it is time that I introduce you to my wife."

Ostensibly unmindful of his lordship and Lady R's startled gasps, Mr. Delafield left the room, humming softly to himself.

Gowland's attempts at capturing Lord Burton's image on paper had not gone well. She had filled ten sheets with sketches, but had failed to secure the essence of his lordship's manly qualities.

At first she blamed a faulty memory for the deficit, but after much soul-searching, she had decided the fault came from *within.* Wombwell often spoke of imbuing one's work with passion, raw *émotion,* he called it. Gowland had no "raw" emotions that she was aware of. All of hers were decidedly well done.

The deficiency worried her. If she were to be a great artiste, if she were to capture his lordship's likeness in a painting which could prove to be her *pièce de résistance,* she must gain this needed knowledge. But how and from whom?

It must be someone in whose presence she felt comfortable and with whom she could speak freely. Lord Burton came immediately to mind. Gowland's heart pulsed with a new and curious beat. She would do it. Tonight, she would request his lordship's tutelage in the matter.

Wombwell interrupted her reverie. "You seem preoccupied this morning, Miss Delafield."

Gowland winced. She had not remembered Wombwell's voice as being so high-pitched before.

He left his easel—he had been putting the finishing touches to a snowy landscape, one of his own paintings—and went to Gowland's side.

Frowning, he surveyed her work. "Your depictions of the model do not have the same . . . unique qualities as yesterday's endeavors. I wonder why?"

Tossing back the lock of dark hair he had patiently trained to dangle over his forehead, he turned to Miss Clarke. "We will take a rest now. Perhaps you would be so kind to serve Miss Delafield a cup of tea?"

"Of course."

Miss Clarke, whose pose today had been "nymph holding a waterjug," gratefully lowered the heavy jug and moved stiffly to do as she was bid.

Wombwell took himself to a side window. Clasping his hands behind his back, he stared moodily out upon the snow-encrusted grounds.

Miss Clarke correctly read Wombwell's temperamental

stance. He wanted *her* to find out what, if anything, was troubling their *little Artiste.*

She poured two cups of tea and offered one to Gowland.

Gowland sighed. "Thank you, Camilla." She took a sip and sighed again. "I fear my inferior work this morning has disappointed Wombwell."

"Nonsense, my dear. Wombwell, as a distinguished artist himself, is aware that all great artists have their bouts of regression. As long as your determination remains firm, and you remember your artistic aspirations, you will reach and surpass your goals."

Gowland said nothing. She was remembering Lord Burton's green gaze and his broad white smile. He was, after all, her artistic aspiration at the moment.

"Your determination *does* remain firm, does it not, Gowland dear?" Camilla probed delicately.

As Lord Burton's image refused to fade from her mind, Gowland glanced incredulously at her companion. "Not remain firm?" she cried out. "I assure you, Camilla, I have never felt so determined to transcend all obstacles in the pursuit of my dreams. I am literally bursting with a longing to create."

So loud and clear and fervent was Gowland's response that Wombwell turned from the window and shouted, "*Magnifico!* Spoken like the great artiste that you, Miss Delafield, are destined to become."

NINE

Lady R and Lord Burton stood in the entrance hall awaiting the arrival of the carriage that would take her ladyship on her not-so-charitable rounds. While his lordship had recovered from the initial shock of Mr. Delafield's disturbing pronouncement, questions remained.

As usual, Lady R was talking—maligning, actually—both his lordship and her host.

"Do not blame me for your present dilemma, Lord Burton. I told you Mr. Delafield was short a sheet from the very first."

Lord Burton glowered at her. "Releasing yourself from blame, my lady, does not answer my query. Exactly how am I to react when our host introduces me to his hallucination of our late hostess?"

Lady R tugged on a pair of French kid gloves and adjusted the ties of her bonnet. "You must open yourself to the new experience and act accordingly. Your reluctance to do so is another indication that you are showing your years. As is Mr. Delafield. Dear Grace has been dead for almost two decades, and still, he cannot accept the fact that she is gone. The man is an odd volume to be sure."

At her ladyship's words, his lordship experienced a sudden anger, a strong sense of resentment, that a learned man of Mr. Delafield's gentle goodness should be so described.

He rushed to his host's defense. "An odd volume, perhaps," he said heatedly, "but Mr. Delafield's enduring love for his wife is certainly an attribute to be admired."

Lady R gave his lordship a keen-eyed look. "I have never seen you so emotionally fired. I think it is past time you were married. Do not fret the matter. I shall attend to it. After my visits to the poor, I have been invited to take tea with the squire and his wife. Sir John suffers from the gout, and his wife has a pronounced squint. Their unmarried daughter, Elizabeth, who is your age, or perhaps a bit older, is looking for a husband. I shall put in a good word for you."

Defeated, his lordship helped Lady R don her fur-lined cloak. He felt sorry for the undeserving poor who would have to endure her ladyship's concepts of comfort: lofty attitudes and lukewarm soup.

Mr. Delafield's book room was situated at one end of the attic floor, set off a suitable distance from the servants' quarters. Lord Burton hesitated before knocking. He felt nervy, the way he had felt as a lad when called to his father's study for a likely whipping.

Finally, he summoned the courage to rap. The door was opened by an ancient manservant who ushered him into a large, pleasant chamber. It was a "man's" room, solid comfort and no frills, with a fitted Wilton carpet upon the floor and built-in bookcases lining the paneled walls. There was a pleasant smell to the air, of leather bindings, strong coffee, and books yellowed with the years.

At the far end of the room, a rosewood writing table was centered before two draped windows. To one side, Mr. Delafield stood behind a book stand engrossed in leafing through a large, dusty tome.

He looked up. "Ahhh, Lord Burton. Do come in."

Nodding pleasantly to his manservant, he said, "That will be all, Manfred. Please leave us."

As the servant shuffled out, Lord Burton made the long walk between a row of leather-topped library tables to where his host awaited him.

"Good morning yet again, sir," he said in a too-hearty tone.

"Good morning, Lord Burton. Thank you for coming."

"My pleasure, sir." His lordship cleared his throat. "The book you are perusing looks to be most interesting."

"I find it so. It is a study of ancient religious rituals, those that pertain to the more corporeal sentience of antediluvian man. Did you know, your lordship, that in certain primitive persuasions the physical expression of love between a man and a woman was regarded as an integral part of their religion?" There was a small pause. "I have come to the clear conclusion that its followers were exceedingly devout."

Again, his lordship could have sworn his host's eyes twinkled with mirth. But the expression was so fleeting as to be hardly perceptible.

A non sequitur immediately followed. "Do take a look at the view from up here, Lord Burton," Mr. Delafield directed, leading him to the window. "On such a beautiful clear morning, it is without equal. I find a pleasant vista to be very refreshing to the mind. In fact, it is upon this very window ledge that I like to sit and ponder life's perplexities."

Lord Burton did as he was bid. He stared out, his eyes following the long, curving drive as it wended its way through the snow-covered grounds and disappeared from view into a stand of tall trees. His gaze shifted to the formal gardens. Its stone inhabitants, impervious to the cold, sat serenely upon their pedestals, their shoulders swathed in tippets of sun-dappled snow. In the far distance were endless acres of rolling hills dotted here and there with clusters of cottage rooftops.

"Chiggers is a profitable estate, your lordship; the bulk of its income is derived from its surrounding farms. I do not believe in squeezing the land for profit; instead, I embrace it as a living thing. My estate manager feels as I do, or I would not employ him. While we live most comfortably at the Hall, I am proud to say that our tenant farmers share in our abundance. You will not find better-kept cottages and better-fed tenants anywhere in Kent."

"I salute you, sir," Lord Burton said sincerely. "Too often it is an estate's tenants who suffer from the excesses of their masters."

Mr. Delafield chuckled dryly. "Of course, the country does not provide the complex pleasures of the City, but for some, that is considered a blessing."

Lord Burton did not respond. The shards of sunlight sparkling off the blue-shadowed snow were mesmerizing. The whole of the scene seemed to dance enticingly before his eyes. The City and its dubious pleasures were far from his mind.

"Do you have a country estate, Lord Burton?"

"No sir, I do not, but standing here looking out on Chiggers makes me long for one. When I marry and start my family, I will, of course, purchase a country home. Still, I doubt if I will find one with the quality and charm of Chiggers."

Mr. Delafield sighed deeply. "Yes, there is something about Chiggers that gets under one's skin. It is my fondest wish that when Gowland marries, she and her husband will make their home here." He turned to Lord Burton. "Did you know that I had the Hall built for my wife as a wedding present? Together we planned the placement and size of every room. She loved our home above all other places."

"You must miss her very much." The moment the words were spoken, his lordship wished them back. Had his thoughtless remark caused pain to his host? A quick glance showed Mr. Delafield was smiling at him.

"Do not fret over your words, Lord Burton. I assure you,

my wife is still very much with me. If you like, I will introduce you to her."

"Yes," his lordship said, holding his breath, "I would like that above all things."

"Then, you have only to turn and look to the end of the room. She is there."

Slowly his lordship turned. In a small cove to the left of the door hung a life-sized portrait of Mrs. Delafield. His lordship's exhalation was one of relief and lovestruck awe. It could have been Gowland who stood before him, steadfast for all time. The same glorious golden curls, the same smooth, peach-tinted complexion—

"Let us move a bit closer, my lord," Mr. Delafield suggested.

His lordship needed little coaxing. He advanced upon the painting as though approaching an icon. The artist had done a masterly job in the posing of his subject to make the most of her grace and beauty. Her body was turned to face the artist, but her face was in profile. The Bellefleur nose was at its haughty best.

"You have heard of the legend of the Bellefleur nose, Lord Burton?"

His lordship raised his brows in amusement. "That its possessor will only marry for love? Yes, I have heard the myth. Pure foolishness, I would say."

Mr. Delafield's shoulders lifted in a slight shrug. "There is more to the myth. It has been said that the Bellefleur nose has the power to seek out the most suitable mate for its possessor. Distance is no barrier, and once the choice is made, the match is as good as made."

He chuckled. "Pure foolishness, as you say. Equally foolish is the fact that there are some who find the Bellefleur nose without allure."

Lord Burton looked appalled. "Impossible! Whoever finds fault with the Bellefleur nose can only be deemed a barbarian. Never have I seen a nose possessed of so much charm and fascination. See how it curves from its bridge with stern intention, yet ends in a tip that surely must be the epitome of feminine insouciance. It is so . . . so . . ."

"Tweakable?" Mr. Delafield suggested.

Lord Burton turned to him. "Exactly, sir. I could not have said it better myself."

After his meeting with Mr. Delafield, Lord Burton was more perplexed than ever. Was his host a Bedlamite, a sophist, or a wise man? The entire morning had had a dreamlike aura to it. His lordship was not certain what had passed between him and Mr. Delafield, but he knew that something had.

If truth be told, Mr. Delafield was a very wise man. Having lived intimately with the Bellefleur nose for many years, he was well acquainted with its subtle powers. The nose knew what it was about. Lord Burton and Gowland were as well as wed. One had only to wait.

Dinner that evening was a charade, a facade of civility that masked the true thoughts of the occupants of Chigger Hall.

Lady R was feeling very pleased with herself and less than pleased with Lord Burton. During a solitary stroll in the conservatory earlier in the day, she had purposely side-stepped into the potting room to find a rock suitable for window smashing. When she had presented it to his lordship with complete instructions as to its use, he had been most ungracious.

Miss Clarke felt more at ease this evening than she had since Lord Burton's arrival at the Hall. Gowland's passionate avowals had convinced her that she and Wombwell had nothing to fear. Not only did Gowland's commitment to her artistic calling remain firm, but her dedication, it seemed, had soared to new heights.

Camilla glanced to the head of the table where Gowland sat hanging on Wombwell's every word. The *little Artiste's* eyes were bright and her cheeks actually glowing with renewed devotion. So much for Lady Rettinger's matchmaking, Camilla thought scathingly.

So lulled was she, that her practical nature took a holiday. She began to imagine herself in sunny Italy. Blue skies, red wine and Wombwell.

Wombwell's mind was also at ease, but then, he never overly worried about anything. He did, however, have one delicate issue that was niggling at him. When he got his hands on Miss Delafield's money, did he really want to take Camilla with him to Italy? Her ability in the bedchamber was without fault, and his life, since he had taken up with her, had never run so smoothly. Still, the Italian beauties had such ripe charms and torrid temperaments. As he weighed the pros and cons of carting coals to Newcastle, he noticed a dreamy expression wash over Camilla's face. He smiled to himself. Her passionate nature was aroused. He would suggest they meet tonight in the studio.

Lord Burton, meanwhile, was experiencing a myriad of emotions. He was apprehensive about his forced entrance into the studio later this evening, in spite of Lady R's detailed instructions on how to use a rock.

What if, presuming a successful entry, he found that Miss Delafield was indeed an artist of great promise? If that were so, it would prove Wombwell neither a cad nor a liar. Miss Delafield would announce her engagement to her drawing master at the Valentine's Day Ball, and he, Lord Burton, who loved her beyond all thought, would be powerless to intervene.

He allowed his eyes to stray to his beloved. She was talking animatedly to Wombwell. Her eyes were bright, her cheeks flushed. With what emotion? Lord Burton thought jealously. Watching her so obviously captivated by another man, he felt as if his heart would break.

Gowland was very much aware of his lordship. So much so that she barely heard Wombwell as he pontificated on the abilities, his own especially, of gifted artists.

Her mind was in a whirl. Did she have the fortitude to solicit Lord Burton's tutelage in her quest for raw emotion? Would he think her bold? So agitated did she become that she dared not look at his lordship or speak to him directly.

Meanwhile, Mr. Delafield, though seemingly engrossed in the dissecting of a ripe pear, was observing each and every one of his dinner guests in turn. His daughter's agitated state and marked avoidance of social contact with Lord Burton told him all he needed to know. The time was ripe. If his lordship was unsuccessful in gaining entrance to the studio tonight on his own, he, as Gowland's father, must stand ready to help.

TEN

Gowland sat at her *écriture* with pen in hand. Her bed-chamber was in darkness save for the smoldering fire and the flickering light from a single candle.

Pensively, she stared into its flame, composing in her mind the words that would form what could be the most important missive of her life.

After a few moments of cogitation she put pen to paper. Her thoughts already formed, the actual execution of the note went quickly. In no time at all, three rows of neat inscriptions paced across the page.

She read what she had written, carefully sanded the missive and sealed it. Imprinting her initials in the still warm wax, she took a deep breath and hurried to the door. It was imperative that she slip the note beneath Lord Burton's portal before the rest of the company began their nightly trek up the stairs to seek their slumber. It would not do to be seen outside his lordship's bedchamber.

Opening the door a crack, she peeked out. All was quiet. Without benefit of candlelight, she stepped out into the dark hallway and groped her way along the wall. Pausing at his lordship's chamber, she bent over and quickly pushed the note beneath the door.

It was done.

* * *

Shielding his night candle with his cupped hand, Lord Burton strode down the drafty hallway to his chamber. He was heartsick. During dinner, aside from the gracious enactment of her duties as hostess, Miss Delafield had barely acknowledged his presence. Instead, she had breathlessly hung on Wombwell's every pompous pronouncement.

Although his lordship had not thought it possible, the evening had then proceeded to progress from bad to worse. After the gentlemen had rejoined the ladies in the drawing room, Miss Delafield pleaded the headache and, refusing Miss Clarke's solicitous offers of assistance, exited the room as if pursued by wolves.

With her leaving, so left the heart of the gathering. Cards had been halfheartedly suggested by one of the remaining company and collectively rejected by the others. After a dish of tea and some dull conversation, the host of Chigger Hall and his guests had disbanded to the solitude of their own chambers.

As Lord Burton opened the door to his, he sighed heavily. The irony of his present situation weighed heavily on his heart. It was painfully apparent that Miss Delafield, the only woman he would ever love, did not love him in return. And, forthwith—if his suspicions proved correct—he would be the instrument that would wound his beloved to the quick. Because of him, Miss Delafield would come to loathe the man she presently loved and planned to marry. Would she also loathe the messenger who had brought the bad news?

Whatever had he done in his life, his lordship lamented, to deserve this double-edged sword? Once inside his chamber, he turned to close the door behind him. It was then he noticed a square of white paper directly beneath his boot.

Puzzled, he retrieved it and held it up to the candlelight. The incised initials "G.G.D." stared up at him from a blob of red sealing wax. It was a note from Gowland!

Breaching the seal with a quick flick of his thumb, his

lordship set down the candle, unfolded the single sheet and read what was written:

> *Dear Lord Burton, Forgive this intrusion, but I find myself plagued with an issue of the utmost import. If not resolved, I fear my future happiness and fulfillment will suffer. There is no one I can talk to who has the experience to understand and ease my plight, save yourself. If you would come to my chamber by your customary path, I shall be waiting.*

It was signed,

> *Most gratefully, Gowland Grace Delafield.*

Lord Burton had but one thought. His beloved needed him! Without a wasted moment, he went to the window, opened the casements and stepped out onto the ledge.

Heedless of his own safety, he traversed the narrow projection between their chambers as if it were an innocuous garden path. Gaining his destination, he rapped softly upon Miss Delafield's window.

She opened it immediately. Anxiety shadowed the hollows of her finely molded face. "Lord Burton, you have come."

He stepped over the sill and across the window seat. Resisting the urge to take her into his arms, he ducked down and peered into her face. "What is it, Miss Delafield? What plagues you?"

She paled under his questioning. "I am plagued, Lord Burton, with a lack of . . . something."

"Something?" His lordship straightened up, a baffled expression on his face. "Could you be a little more specific, Miss Delafield?"

She turned from him, her silken skirts rustling like a lover's sigh. She still wore the blue gown she had worn at dinner, he noted. Her long, graceful neck and delicate back, so artlessly displayed by the low-cut bodice, gave her a vulnerable look, like a fledgling fresh from its nest.

She went to the hearth, indicating with a vague gesture the chair his lordship had occupied last evening.

"Please make yourself comfortable, Lord Burton, and I shall do my best to be more definitive."

When he was seated, Gowland placed a large tapestry pillow at his feet and sank gracefully upon it. For a long moment, she studied her slender hands. "How can I convey to you what it is that I covet?" she whispered.

His lordship's lips moved in the smallest of fond smiles. She was like a child, he thought, a beautiful child, about to ask for a special treat. What innocent desire could she have?

"Do you trust me, Miss Delafield?" he asked softly.

She lifted her face. The light from the fire silvered her violet eyes to dusty lavender. "I do trust you, Lord Burton. We have not known each other long, but I feel as if we have been friends forever."

"Then certainly, you can tell me what is troubling you," he coaxed.

She drew a deep breath and sat up straighter. Her voice was suddenly firm. "I wish to experience raw emotion, Lord Burton. Without it, I cannot be the great artist I aspire to be."

His lordship's eyes goggled. As he struggled to seek a suitable reply, a terrible suspicion seized him. His green gaze suddenly glinted with anger. "Is it Wombwell who suggested your pursuit of raw emotion," he demanded, "and has he offered to *help* you gain your goal?"

Miss Delafield looked at his lordship askance, as if he had somehow offended her. The Bellefleur nose lifted to its haughtiest height. "Wombwell often talks of an artist's need for raw emotion, but he knows nothing of my current search for it."

At her words, Lord Burton's sensibility was effectively split asunder. While his male ego was flattered that Miss Delafield would seek *his* counsel above Wombwell's in such an intimate matter, there were *some* subjects that were not discussed between a man and a young, naive maiden.

He resolved to test the waters with a neutral query. "Ahh, tell me, Miss Delafield, how do you intend to seek such . . . knowledge?"

Miss Delafield's gaze dropped to her lap. Her fingers trifled with the knot of ribbons at her waist. She spoke softly. "I have a theory, Lord Burton. While I have never experienced the physical expression of love between a man and a woman, I am convinced that when one does, one would also become acquainted with raw emotion. My dilemma is obvious. To fulfill my quest, I will need a . . . willing participant in the endeavor." Her violet gaze lifted. "Could you? Would you, Lord Burton, be my mentor?"

His lordship felt as if he had taken a direct hit to the bread basket. While he prided himself on being worldly-wise, the implications of what Miss Delafield had just suggested floored him.

"You want me to . . . you want me and you to . . ."

In spite of being a country girl, Gowland's knowledge of the physical side of love, coming as it did from romantic novels, was surprisingly sparse. She hung her head, her cheeks flushed with shame. "I am so sorry, Lord Burton. I should not have asked such an intimate favor, but never having been kissed—"

Startled, Lord Burton leaned forward and firmly cupped his beloved's chin, obliging it upward until their eyes were level and locked. "You think a *kiss* is the ultimate physical expression between a man and a woman?" he asked incredulously.

She tilted her head. The Bellefleur nose had never looked so delightful. "Is there more?"

At this evidence of Miss Delafield's innocence, a wave of overwhelming tenderness swept over his lordship. He cleared his throat. "There might be one or two—ahh . . . other things."

She took a moment to consider this, then said, "As enlightening as I am sure those things would be, I think it would be wise for me to start at the beginning, and"—she looked at him beseechingly—"with someone I trust. Will you kiss me, Lord Burton?"

Lord Burton was an honorable man, but a man, nonetheless. His ego had undergone several painful comeuppances in the last week. If Miss Delafield desired to be kissed, he would make sure it was a kiss she would remember for the rest of her days. Of course, he rationalized, he would keep his own emotions in rein. He did not want to cause Miss Delafield any undue consternation; he just wanted to rattle her in her boots a bit.

He sighed heavily as though struggling in the throes of vacillation. "All right, Miss Delafield," he acquiesced, "I will do as you wish."

"Thank you, Lord Burton. I shall prepare myself." She sat up straighter, squeezed her eyes shut and pursed her lips.

Lord Burton suppressed a grin. "There *are* certain preliminaries." He stood, took her hands in his, and gently brought her to her feet. He drew her close until her silken curls rested tantalizingly beneath his chin. Bewitched by her nearness, he breathed deeply of the lavender-scented aura that surrounded her.

"Is this . . . closeness necessary, Lord Burton?" Miss Delafield inquired after a moment. She sounded oddly breathless.

"I have found proximity to be helpful," his lordship responded gravely. "Shall we begin?"

"Very well." She again assumed what she thought was the correct attitude, face raised, eyes tightly shut, lips pursed. His lordship gazed down at the beautiful though puckery features of his beloved. In their midst, the Bellefleur nose seemed to call to him like a siren's song.

He lowered his head, and his lips, as if of their own volition, bestowed a trail of small kisses upon the beguiling arc of the Bellefleur nose. As Miss Delafield relaxed against him, he felt her sigh, as soft as a kitten's breath, against his throat.

He smiled and pressed on. For a long moment he commanded his lips to merely hover over hers. He breathed against them, watched them part in expectation. He kissed her then, feeling the innocent promise of her response. Slowly, he deepened the kiss.

Like a spark to tinder, Gowland's passion suddenly ignited. Her arms wound around Lord Burton's neck in a convulsive grip of possessiveness. He was her trusted teacher, and she his willing pupil. When his tongue gently parted her lips and demanded more response, she met the challenge with an abandonment that brought a groan of pleasure from his lordship.

The depth and ferocity of Miss Delafield's desire knocked his lordship back on his heels and made him momentarily insensate to such things as honor and good intentions. All he knew was that he wanted more of this golden-haired creature whose lips gave him such pleasure, such warmth, such confusion. . . .

Gowland also wanted more. Somewhere in the inner recesses of her body, she knew the burning promise of his lordship's lips was but the first step down the path to the creativity for which she longed. She wanted the kiss to go on and on; she wanted the promise fulfilled; she wanted—

The gods of lovers and fools, sternly influenced by the Bellefleur nose, decided enough was enough. Together they delivered a solid kick to his lordship's conscience. He came to his senses at once. What in blazes was he doing?

With massive self-control, he broke the kiss and commanded his arms to drop to his sides. He looked down at Miss Delafield. Her lips were still parted, her skin as fevered as his.

Neither said a word. They stared at each other in wonder, as if their buried wants, the very longings of their souls, had been revealed, one to the other.

He took a step back. "Did the kiss fulfill your requirements, Miss Delafield?" His voice sounded like a croak.

"Most decidedly, Lord Burton." Her voice was no smoother. "Thank you."

His lordship bowed. "My pleasure, Miss Delafield." He turned, opened the window and hauled himself out into the frigid night.

With her fingers pressed against her telltale lips, Gowland watched as Lord Burton traversed the ledge to his own chamber as if the hounds of hell were on his heels.

Then, closing the casements to the chill night air, she took a deep breath and sank down upon the cushioned window seat. She felt boneless, light as air, adrift in wonderment. His lordship's kiss had successfully aroused her raw emotions and several others as well. There could be but one reason for this heady feeling. She was in love with Lord Burton!

The momentous implications of the situation brought her back to reality with a thud. But what of her dream of being a great artist? What of her promise to Wombwell to endow the Wombwell School for the Arts?

Mr. Delafield sat upon the ledge one floor up, his brow furrowed in deep deliberation. He had gotten to his elevated perch in time to see Lord Burton's agitated entrance into Gowland's bedchamber, and his equally agitated exit.

Would his lordship attempt an assault on the locked studio later this evening? The thought was disturbing. The ledge was particularly treacherous, and in his present state, Lord Burton might very well suffer a misstep and fall to his demise. Something had to be done to prevent such a disaster. The Bellefleur nose demanded much of its chosen one, but Lord Burton had proven himself beyond a doubt. As a father, it was time for Mr. Delafield to act!

He turned, crawled back through the open window and hurried to his desk. There was a length of twine in the top drawer that should do admirably for his purpose.

Effortlessly, Lord Burton walked the icy ledge on legs made buoyant by love. The memory of Miss Delafield's kiss burned like a signal fire, making him impervious to even the biting wind.

He recalled the feel of her lips, the warm honey of her mouth, the subtle taste of her desire. Surely her response was an indication that she returned his love.

He pushed open the window of his chamber and bounded in. He had but one thought in mind. He would go back on the ledge and smash his way into the studio.

The rock was on the bedside table where he had left it, but he would need something to protect his hands from the breaking glass. A moment of rummaging in the clothes-press yielded results. Pulling on a pair of heavy leather gauntlets, his lordship picked up the rock. He was ready.

Dramatically he flung open the casements and prepared to step out. He stopped cold. Directly in front of him dangled a key. It was suspended on a length of twine.

As his lordship stared in amazement, the twine twitched, sending the key on a merry dance. Whoever was holding it was impatient that his lordship take it.

Lord Burton needed no further enticement. He knew it was Mr. Delafield who dangled the key from above, and what door the key would open. It all had to do with what the old gentleman had been trying to tell him that morning in the book room: he, Lord Burton, had been picked by the Bellefleur nose!

With steady fingers, his lordship reached for the length of twine and hauled it to him, untying its precious burden. His heart pounded with pride. He, and no one else, was destined to wed Miss Delafield!

ELEVEN

The key turned smoothly in the lock. Glancing furtively up and down the corridor, Lord Burton opened the door and stepped into the studio. His mind was at ease. Despite what he discovered, it would matter little. Gowland was his. The Bellefleur nose had chosen!

The chamber was pitch dark. The drapes were tightly drawn. Out of necessity, they would have to remain so. The lack of illumination did not concern his lordship. He had come prepared with a light box.

He waited where he stood until his eyes adjusted to the lack of illumination. Gradually, the dim outline of a cloth-draped table materialized directly to one side of him. He went to it, set down the light box, opened its cover and carefully dipped an acid-dip match into the bottle of vitriol. It spat furiously for a moment, then burst into flame. The box contained two small candles. Igniting one, his lordship stood up and surveyed his shadowy surroundings.

On the fringes of the candlelight, he could make out two large easels standing by the window. Holding the candle aloft, he covered the distance with quick strides.

On one easel was displayed an oil painting signed by Wombwell. It depicted a snowy landscape with Chigger Hall looming in the distance.

Lord Burton studied it critically. It was a more than adequate rendition, but no more than that. The painting did not draw the observer's eye into its core, then coax it to move on to more subtle delights, as a great painting should. Wombwell might be an excellent teacher, his lordship concluded, but he would never be a distinguished artist.

The second easel held a block of watercolor paper, half of which had been used and folded over the spine of the block. The uppermost painting, signed by Miss Delafield, was a portrait of Miss Clarke. His lordship gasped in horror. Never had he seen such an abomination!

Gowland had painted her companion with a smear of bright yellow paint for hair, two gray blobs for eyes, and a nose so long it had displaced Miss Clarke's chin, causing that unfortunate feature to find its final repose between the lady's bony collarbones.

Slowly, his lordship brought the used pages, one by one, to the front of the block and held the candle close. He was stunned. Each was worse than the last, if that were possible—

He froze. He had heard a noise. Someone was outside in the hallway. Holding the candle high, he circled the room with light. There was a sofa to his immediate left. He dove behind it, extinguishing the candle's flame as he went.

Seconds later, someone entered the studio and proceeded to fling himself bodily upon the sofa. A lamp was lighted nearby, which meant, his lordship shrewdly concluded, that more than one person had come in and was present.

Suddenly, there came the distinctive rustle of clothing being unceremoniously removed, the sound of shoes being dropped, then a girlish giggle, a gasp. Crouching down, his lordship peered under the sofa. On the other side he saw a pair of bare feet. Large, narrow feet with long prehensile toes and skin the color of newly fallen snow.

Good God! Such appendages could only belong to Wombwell. Another smaller foot, obviously a woman's, and obviously attached to the sofa dweller, suddenly appeared.

Clad in a dainty black kid slipper, it swung lazily back and forth.

The woman started humming a sprightly tune. In horror, his lordship watched as Wombwell's long white feet began a mincing dance.

At the sound of more girlish giggling, Lord Burton's blood boiled. Not only was the drawing master a despicable liar; he was also a foul seducer of young serving wenches.

He had seen and heard all that he could stomach. He rose majestically from behind the sofa and announced in ringing tones, "Enough, I say. Enough!"

A feminine scream and two manly gasps marked his lordship's sudden appearance and pealing pronouncement. Surprisingly, one of the gasps had emanated from Lord Burton himself.

He could scarce believe his eyes! Wombwell was stark naked and fully aroused. Worse yet, he gripped a rose between his teeth! And the girl on the sofa, her bodice undone, was Miss Clarke!"

Wombwell's mouth gaped in shock; the rose fell to his feet. As his arousal faded into memory, the drawing master gave vent to a string of unoriginal curses. "How did you get in?" he then demanded of his lordship.

"I will ask the questions, Wombwell, and you will answer them," Lord Burton snapped back. "And for God's sake, man, put on your clothes."

While Miss Clarke nonchalantly tied the tapes on the bodice of her gown, her mind feverishly questioned why Lord Burton had seen fit to sneak into the studio in the dead of night. There could be only one reason. She regarded him with a cool stare and a slight smile. "I presume you have seen Miss Delafield's paintings, my lord?"

"I have."

"And?"

"They reveal her complete lack of talent, and your and

Wombwell's complete lack of scruples. I demand an explanation of your deceptive motives at once."

Wombwell had pulled on his trousers and shoved his feet into pair of embroidered slippers. He stood holding the rest of his apparel bunched in his arms. He looked to Miss Clarke as if for guidance. When she nodded her head, he made a run for the door.

"Not so fast, Wombwell—"

"Let him go, Lord Burton," Miss Clarke advised. "He will be of no good to you. I will answer whatever questions you have."

Lord Burton pulled up a chair opposite the sofa and sat down. As much as he admired Miss Clarke's unruffled demeanor, he felt sorry for her. He asked gently, "Has Wombwell left you before to explain such situations?"

She sighed wearily. "Wombwell does not bother his head with details, Lord Burton. He is, after all, *an Artiste.*"

The vehemence in her voice surprised his lordship. He leaned back and crossed his legs. "I want to know everything about this scheme, Miss Clarke, from the beginning."

Camilla's gaze shifted. Her outward composure was but a desperate facade hiding a mind that grew more deathly afraid with every passing moment. Had Gowland confided to Lord Burton about the endowment? Had his lordship surmised the rest of their fraudulent scheme? Would it be the convict hulks for her and Wombwell instead of the warm shores of sunny Italy?

Camilla knew she would have to watch her every word until she was certain of what Lord Burton actually knew. Finally she said, "First off, Lord Burton, I am not Miss Clarke. I am Miss Havasham. Wombwell was my drawing master." She laughed mirthlessly. "Can you guess the next part?"

"He seduced you?"

"You *are* clever, your lordship. Yes, Wombwell and I ran off together. Whether or not he actually intended to marry me is now a moot point. My father caught up with us at a small inn on the way to Greta Green. Unfortunately, he was too late; my virtue was gone."

"I am sorry, Miss Havasham. I hope your father used a horsewhip on Wombwell."

Miss Clarke-Havasham shrugged. "He did something much worse. My father disowned me, Lord Burton, and forbid me ever to darken his door again. He cut me off without a cent. Wombwell and I were penniless. Since *an Artiste* cannot soil his hands with labor, I was forced to seek employment as Gowland's companion."

"And, you, in turn, insinuated your lover into the household."

Miss Havasham nodded. "Gowland and I were shopping in the village on a day when I just *happened* to have several examples of her artwork—done under the auspices of her former drawing master—with me. You see, I had pretended to admire several of her paintings, and she had given them to me, insisting that she have them framed and hung in my room."

In spite of himself, Lord Burton shuddered at the prospect of having to face the work of Miss Delafield's brush on a daily basis. Miss Havasham nodded sadly. "The wages of sin, Lord Burton, are bitter to behold."

"What happened then? How did you stage the encounter with Wombwell?"

"It was a boldly enacted scene. While crossing the street, I turned my ankle. The portfolio flew out of my hands, and Gowland's paintings were scattered on the ground. Wombwell gallantly came to our assistance."

"I can guess the rest. He raved over Miss Delafield's paintings and expressed astonishment at her innate talent, talent that needed only the guiding hand of a drawing master trained on the Continent to bring it to its full potential. Is that correct?"

Miss Havasham nodded calmly. She did not have long to

wait for his lordship's next question. She watched his eyes narrow in suspicion.

"What about the announcement that Miss Delafield plans to make at the ball?"

Camilla's stomach sank to her slippers. Damn Gowland, she had told about the endowment! Quickly deciding that ignorance was her best defense, Camilla widened her eyes and raised one slender hand to her throat. "Announcement? I know nothing of an announcement to be made at the ball."

"Do not lie to me," Lord Burton growled. "As you well know, Miss Delafield planned to announce her engagement to Wombwell on the night of the ball."

Engagement, not endowment? Camilla's mind whirled in shock. She did not trust Wombwell as far as she could throw him, but she doubted if he had the brains needed to play her false. To gain time, she assumed an innocent air. "A young girl will often develop a *tendresse* for her drawing master. I am sorry proof of that. Did Gowland tell you herself that she and Wombwell planned to announce their engagement on the night of the ball?"

"No, she did not. She hinted of it, however, in her letter of invitation to Lady Rettinger, who put two and two together. It was she who asked me to intervene. She had suspicions that Wombwell was a fortune hunter from the first."

Camilla exhaled a pent-up breath of relief. Lady Rettinger had set his lordship on the wrong track. Wombwell was a fortune hunter, but not the marrying kind.

His lordship shook his head in disgust. "I do not believe that you knew nothing of the forthcoming marriage announcement, Miss Havasham. How could you do such a thing to one of your own sex? You would encourage an innocent young girl into a marriage that could only bring her shame and grief and a cruel cessation to her dreams of being a great artist. She would be Wombwell's wife, while you remained his mistress."

Since aligning her fate with Wombwell's, Camilla lived by

a new motto: when cornered, prevaricate! In some ways, his lordship was as gullible as Gowland. If she played her cards right, she could gain a needed reprieve for her and Wombwell.

She hung her head. "You are right, your lordship. I am ashamed to say that I knew about the forthcoming announcement. But," she lied glibly, drawing herself up in an attitude of outraged virtue, "Wombwell and I never actually intended for him to go through with the marriage to Gowland. In a matter of weeks, he comes into an annuity that was set up for him many years ago by his grandfather. When the allotment was settled on him, Wombwell and I planned to leave England and live in Italy where he could paint, and I could tend to him."

Lord Burton's lip curled in contempt. "And leave Miss Delafield to be the laughingstock of the county?"

Miss Havasham sighed tragically. His lordship was proving to be a tougher nut to crack than she had thought.

Introducing a tremor into her voice, she whispered, "That was very bad of me, your lordship, but please believe me, I love Gowland like a sister and did not want to hurt her."

She sighed again. "You see before you, Lord Burton, a very foolish girl. I am in love with Wombwell in spite of his faults and cannot live without him. Surely you can understand my feelings? Have you not been in love yourself?"

Lord Burton found himself relating to Camilla's plight. Had he not gone to great heights for the woman he loved? Could he blame this poor wronged woman for like frailties?

Camilla saw from his lordship's expression that she had scored a hit. She dug her nails into the palm of her hand until tears came to her eyes. "I hope you will find it in your heart to be merciful, Lord Burton, and perhaps intercede with Gowland for us?"

His lordship was not an abuser of women, quite the opposite. To be the cause of tears in the fairer sex cut him to the quick. Wearily, he got to his feet. "It is out of my hands,

Miss Havasham. I will go to Mr. Delafield in the morning and tell him everything. What becomes of you and Wombwell will be his judgment, and his alone." He paused, "I will, however, put in a kind word for you."

When he closed the studio door behind him, Miss Clarke-Havasham was weeping piteously.

Fifteen minutes later, when Wombwell joined Camilla in her chamber, there was no sign of tears upon her face. Instead, her gray eyes glittered with anger as she told him all that had transpired between her and Lord Burton.

"We must leave the Hall at once." She stressed the words by pulling a portmanteau out from under the bed and tossing it upon the coverlet.

"Tomorrow morning, when Lord Burton learns the truth of the announcement Gowland planned to make at the ball, he will surmise the rest. He is no cods-head, unlike Mr. Delafield. If we do not flee, we will find ourselves at the Old Bailey before the week is out."

The drawing master's face turned the color of blue chalk. "But where will we go?" he questioned.

"As far from the Hall as we can possibly get. Go to your chamber and pack only what you can carry. We must travel light."

Wombwell's mouth puckered in a childish pout.

"But I cannot leave my clothing or my paintings."

Suddenly, Camilla had had enough of his whining. She whirled on him. "Stop your sniveling, you spineless ninny. Either you travel light or you will find yourself in the hulks with nothing but your choirboy good looks to recommend you. I am leaving, with or without you. Suit yourself."

Wombwell trembled with fear. He could not take even a day of confinement in the hulks; he was much too delicate for such a milieu. He would have to go with this suddenly cold-hearted Camilla. Once again, he trembled with fear.

TWELVE

Lord Burton wasted no time when he left the studio. In spite of the lateness of the hour, he went directly to Lady R's bedchamber. While not a vindictive man, the thought of knocking Lady R's "keen powers of perception" into a cocked hat gave wings to his heels.

At his muffled knock, she opened the door a crack and peered out at him. She wore a huge, beruffled nightcap from which peeked an array of knotted curling papers.

Averting his eyes from the monstrosity on her head, his lordship whispered, "Allow me to come in, Lady R. I have news that will not wait. I have successfully breached the studio."

With surprising strength, she grabbed his arm and all but yanked him into her chamber. "Tell me at once what you have found!"

"It is as you suspected. Miss Delafield is void of talent."

"I knew it!" she crowed. "My keen powers of perception are never wrong—"

"There is more," his lordship said with a smile. He told all, not sparing Lady R's delicate sensibilities one iota. He was unprepared for the results.

She stared at him, seeming to wilt before his very eyes. "Miss Clarke and Wombwell?"

"*Miss Havasham* and Wombwell," Lord Burton corrected glibly. "It seems your keen powers of perception—"

Lady R let out a croak and collapsed into a chair. "I was wrong?" she whispered incredulously.

Lord Burton was about to do a little crowing of his own, until he took a good look at his nemesis. This defeated-looking woman was not the frustrating Lady R he had come to know and—yes, admit it—grown fond of. This was a little old lady wearing a ridiculous cap, a little old lady slumped in the protective arms of the wing chair, a little old lady so tiny her feet did not touch the floor.

His heart melted. He went down on one knee beside her. "You were not *wrong*, Lady R; you were led by the Belletleur nose to do what was *right*. It is a proboscis of great wisdom and powerful persuasion. I, too, am its happy victim. Miss Delafield and I were destined for each other. For the first time in my life, I am truly in love, and I have you to thank for it."

Lady R sat up straighter. "Then, I was not wrong, but merely led in the wrong direction!"

In a twinkling, the fire returned to the dragon's eye. "Of course," her ladyship triumphed, "I was destined to be the instrument of your marital salvation, Lord Burton. I sensed at once that you and Gowland . . ."

Lord Burton patted her hand. She was still talking when he slipped from the room.

His next stop was Mr. Delafield's book room. The window was open; his host sat upon the ledge staring intently at something out on the grounds. He turned and smiled. "Do join me on the ledge, Lord Burton."

Why not? his lordship thought. As he crawled out the window, his host obligingly moved over to give him room.

When they were settled companionably, side by side, legs dangling over the edge, Lord Burton said, "I have distressing news to tell you, sir, most of which, I feel you are already aware of. You were the one who suspended the key, were you not?"

"I was, your lordship. I have a spare key to every room

in the Hall. As a gentleman, I would never invade my guests' privacy, but as a father, I did make use of the key to the studio. What I observed of my daughter's drawings one evening several months ago confirmed the suspicions I had had of Wombwell from the beginning. Speaking of that rascal, I have just watched him and Miss Clarke sneak from the Hall. Wretched night for absconding."

Lord Burton peered into the darkness, but saw nothing. "Should we not send someone after them?"

"Let them go. They are not important."

Lord Burton sighed. "Mayhap then, I can tell you something you do not know. Gowland planned to announce her engagement to Wombwell at the Valentine's Day Ball."

Mr. Delafield seemed unimpressed. "I doubt the truth of that, Lord Burton, but no matter, it would not have come to pass. The Bellefleur nose chose you to be Gowland's husband."

Lord Burton gave Mr. Delafield an exasperated look. "May I ask why did you not say something to me earlier and spare me a lot of grief?"

"I could not. It was the Bellefleur nose that dictated my action or lack of it. Let me tell you something, Lord Burton, that will put you in good stead for the future. Women who possess the Bellefleur nose must be given free rein. To force them to do anything would break their spirit. They have to be gently led to what is best for them."

"Led by the Bellefleur nose, so to speak?"

"Exactly, Lord Burton. As the nose led you to Gowland."

"You are a very wise man, Mr. Delafield."

"I am a man who needs solitude for my studies. Eccentricity assures me that solitude." He smiled. "You, of course, Lord Burton, will always be welcome in my book room." After a pause, he added, "I think you should go to Gowland now and tell her of Wombwell and Miss Clarke's absconding."

"I will wait, sir. At this hour in the morning, your daughter is still asleep."

It was Mr. Delafield's turn to sigh. "I think not, your lordship. I think not."

His lordship hesitated before his beloved's bedchamber. How devastated would Miss Delafield be when told the man she loved and planned to marry had been revealed to be a liar, a coward and a *lecher*?

The situation called for the utmost in diplomacy and patience. Obviously, although chomping at the bit, his lordship would have to wait to press his suit until Miss Delafield had recovered from the shock of her betrayal.

Straightening his shoulders, he rapped upon her door.

She opened it immediately. She still wore her blue silk gown, evidence that she had not been to bed. "Lord Burton! You look distraught. What is it?"

She gasped. "Papa has not fallen from the ledge, has he?"

"No, no, nothing like that." His lordship stepped into the chamber, keeping the door suitably ajar. "It is Wombwell and Miss Clarke. They have . . . they have run off together."

Her face crumpled in bewilderment. "How can that be?"

"Ahh, proximity between a man and a woman often results in unbridled . . . love, Miss Delafield."

Her head lowered; she turned from him and went to the window.

Lord Burton fumed to see his beloved so downcast. He should have beaten Wombwell to a pulp when he had the chance.

After a painful silence, she inquired in a wistful tone, "Are you *sure* they are gone for good?"

With his heart close to breaking, his lordship responded, "Yes, Miss Delafield, I am sure."

She whirled round, her face radiant with happiness. "How perfectly splendid!"

Lord Burton's jaw dropped several notches. "Their absconding does not bother you?"

"No, not at all. Well, a little bit. You see, I had planned to use my inheritance to endow the Wombwell School for the Arts and devote the rest of my life to my artistic ambitions. I meant to announce my intentions on the night of the ball. Miss Clarke swore me to secrecy until then."

Lord Burton felt as if he had been poleaxed. "You planned to announce that you would become Wombwell's *patroness*, not his wife?"

The Bellefleur nose lifted to more rarefied air. "Wed my drawing master? Lord Burton! How could you think that I would marry beneath my station? In fact, recently, most recently, I decided most emphatically that I did not want to become Wombwell's patroness and was in a quandary as to how to tell him. So you see, I am glad that he and Miss Clarke have found true happiness."

His lordship knew he had been duped. Miss Havasham and Wombwell had had a more ambitious scheme than marriage. He would bet a monkey that they had planned to fleece Miss Delafield of her inheritance, then flee to the Continent to enjoy their ill-gotten gains.

He should be incensed, but was not. Mr. Delafield had the proper perspective on Wombwell and Miss Havasham. They were not important.

What was important was that his lordship was now free to press his suit! His senses soared with the ease of an eagle. He strode to his beloved and took her into his arms. She did not appear to mind.

Smiling up at him, she disclosed, "I have had a change of heart regarding my future aspirations, as well, Lord Burton. I have decided to abandon my painting for the nonce and explore a different creative pursuit."

Visualizing a series of lumpy, headless statues desecrating the formal gardens, his lordship asked cautiously, "And that is?"

Her arms wound around his neck. "Babies, your lordship."

"Babies?"

"Mine . . . and yours. I desire to have babies. Could you, would you, Lord Burton, give me babies?"

Gently, his lordship tweaked the Bellefleur nose. "It will be my pleasure, Miss Delafield, my darling Gowland, to give you all the babies your heart desires."

EPILOGUE

The engagement of Lord Burton Dance and Miss Gowland Delafield was announced at the Valentine's Day Ball held at Chigger Hall. In the years that followed, Lord Burton was true to his promise, seven times over.

None of the children, although possessed of fine good looks and splendid minds, received the Bellefleur nose. After the matching of Lord Burton and Miss Delafield, the nose decided it needed a rest and wisely took one.

Lady R visited the Hall so often to see her seven godchildren that she was given her own apartment, and eventually, she left London and moved to the Hall for good.

Mr. Delafield conducted a thorough study of Lady R's mental processes, but remains baffled to this day as to what makes her tick.

As a grandfather seven times over, Mr. Delafield does not have too much time to ponder these days. His book room mostly resembles a nursery with hobby horses in the corners, and dolls and toys upon the floor. He could not be happier.

In spite of her claims, Lady Burton did not entirely abandon her Art to motherhood. She painted a portrait of each of her darling babies and presented it to her husband as a symbol of her devotion. That his lordship hung the portraits in his study, for all the world to see, remained an undisputed symbol of his.

FROST FAIR

by

Carola Dunn

The number of letters sent on Valentine's Day,
makes several additional sorters necessary
at the Post Office in London.
—Robert Nares, *Glossary,* 1822

ONE

As the door of the cloth merchant's office closed behind them, the two girls exchanged a look.

"Couldn't we, Miss Ros?" begged the shorter of the two, a plump blonde in a warm cloak of blue duffel and woolly mittens. "We're not likely ever to get another chance. Just think on it, froze solid all the way from Blackfriars to London Bridge!"

"Mr. Braithwaite said it's the first time in living memory," murmured the tall girl in the ruby red velvet cloak trimmed with white satin. She pulled the white-lined hood over her raven black hair as the icy air nipped at her ears after the warmth indoors. Burying kid-gloved hands in her muff, she went on, "But if we stay out so long, your hands will freeze, Betsy."

"Oh, no, I'll stick 'em in my pockets, see. Do let's."

"It does seem a pity to miss the Frost Fair," Rosabelle admitted, "and I expect *maman* can spare you for an extra hour or so. All right, let's go."

They turned off Cheapside down Queen Street toward the Thames.

When they reached the wharf, they found the steps down to the ice guarded by watermen swathed in colourful mufflers. Robbed of their usual livelihood by the great freeze, they were charging a fee to allow fair-goers past. Betsy's face fell.

"I shall pay for both of us," said Rosabelle, taking her purse from the reticule dangling from her wrist.

"Good on you, miss," said the boatman who took her coppers, standing aside. "Go careful now, ladies. 'Ang onto that there rope. Them steps is sanded but they's still slicker'n a mollisher's knickknack."

His fellows guffawed at this touch of wit.

Blushing, Rosabelle hurried past. Not that she understood the man's words, but she could tell by the way the others laughed that her ignorance was fortunate. Besides, the Thames watermen were notoriously almost as foul-mouthed as Billingsgate fishwives.

Betsy at her heels, she started cautiously down the stone stair, grasping the rope looped through iron rings set in the wall of the wharf. All along the riverside quays and docks, as far as she could see, barges, wherries, and a few merchant ships were tied, becalmed by the ice.

A few steps down, Rosabelle stopped to look out over the Thames. The sound of barrel organs, fiddles, pipes and drums floated across the ice in the sparkling air, punctuated by the shouts of barkers. Flag-bedecked tents, stalls and booths were laid out in two main streets, crossing in the middle.

"Oooh," sighed Betsy in ecstasy, "a merry-go-round, and swings! And look, Miss Ros, donkey rides! Could I? Not all of them, I mean, just one?"

Continuing down the stair, Rosabelle smiled at her companion's childish delight. "If I have enough money on me. They may charge exorbitant prices because of the setting. Which will you choose?"

"I'll have to look closer afore I make up my mind. What about you? What d'you fancy?"

"Oh, the donkeys, I think. I still remember being sick on the swings at Bartholomew Fair when I was a little girl, and why ride a wooden horse when you can ride a real, live donkey?"

"I will, too, then," Betsy decided.

Rosabelle had not really intended to participate, but she did not want to disappoint Betsy, who had few enough pleasures in life. Stepping cautiously across the ice, she wondered how long the Thames would remain frozen. Perhaps she could bring one of the other girls to the Frost Fair tomorrow, and enough money to buy fairings for the rest. Papa would grumble, but he would give way in the end.

A fingerpost stuck in a barrel of stones, pointing toward Southwark on the south bank, announced Freezeland Street. The first tent, a hastily erected shelter of sailcloth over a rough wooden frame, was a tavern. On the benches within, men sat quaffing ale and bantering with serving wenches bundled up in warm wraps. Opposite was a skittle alley, and next to it a barker invited passersby to step up and try their luck at the Wheel of Fortune.

"Oysters! Fresh oysters, sixpence a dozen," cried a woman carrying two buckets on a yoke.

"Hot chestnuts, roasted on ice!" called a man sitting by a brazier full of glowing coals. Though it was raised on iron feet, it stood in a puddle.

"I hope the ice is good and thick," said Betsy.

"Let's have some chestnuts," Rosabelle proposed. "They'll warm your fingers."

She bought two-penn'orth. They strolled on, peeling off the charred, crackling skins and munching the sweet insides.

There were toy shops and a Punch and Judy show. Rival printing presses tried to top each other's ballads celebrating the Frost Fair. Dogs barked at small boys sliding on a smooth patch of ice, and fiddlers sawed away while young men hopped and swung with their sweethearts on an improvised dancing stage.

"Fry your own sausages! Take 'em 'ome pipin' 'ot."

"Lapland mutton, roasted right 'ere on the river, shilling a slice!"

"Prick the garter! Try your skill and win a vallible prize!"

"Buy my brandy balls!"

"Cut and a shave," shouted a barber, his chair set up in the open with the striped pole stuck in the ice. "Cut and a shave. Razors sharper'n icicles!"

Rosabelle stopped to glance over the wares of a book-stall, while Betsy admired the gaily painted swings next door. The attendants, their breath puffing out in clouds, pushed the gondolas higher and higher, while the girls seated inside with their swains squealed and giggled.

"Changed your mind?" Rosabelle asked.

"It does look like fun, but it'd be better if you've got a young man. No, let's find the donkeys."

"Over that way, I think."

As they turned right on the Grand Mall, which ran down the middle of the Thames from Blackfriars Bridge to London Bridge, Rosabelle glanced back down Freezeland Street. Beyond tents and booths, behind the wharves and warehouses of the City, the spires of churches rose, and over to the left, St. Paul's great dome towered high above the rest.

She would have liked to sketch the panorama. If the freeze held, she could bring paper and pencil tomorrow, but it was too cold to sit still for long. Even if she escaped frostbitten toes, chilled fingers would be too clumsy to do the scene justice.

The very thought made her shiver. She was sure her nose must be red from the nip of the glacial air, and the chill of the ice was beginning to seep through the soles of her smart boots. Her velvet cloak was elegant, but even though she wore a spencer underneath, on top of her kerseymere gown, Betsy's duffel was probably warmer. How horrified *maman* would be if she said she wanted a pelisse of the coarse woollen cloth!

"There they are." Betsy pointed to where a string of patient donkeys plodded across the ice toward a space marked with hoofprints and other unmistakable evidence of a less mentionable nature. "Aren't they sweet? I hope I can ride that one with the red and yellow ribbons, the one with a side saddle. I wish I had a lump of sugar to feed it."

"Perhaps the stall next door will let us have some, that one with the 'Dibden, Pastry Cook' sign. Look, they are selling hot chocolate, so they must have sugar. I'll tell them we shall buy chocolate after our ride, to warm us."

"Can we really? I'm ever so glad it was my turn to go with you today, Miss Ros!"

Rosabelle went up to the counter beneath the slapdash, hastily painted sign. On it were laid out trays of tarts and biscuits and gilt gingerbread shapes. From the back of the stall came the mouthwatering aroma of hot meat pies, mingling with the sweetness of the fragrant steam from the chocolate pot on its spirit lamp.

A young man with curly brown hair peeking from beneath his hat was serving a customer with a crisp, golden, hot apple turnover, redolent of cinnamon and cloves. He took the money and turned to Rosabelle.

"What can I do for you, madam?" he enquired, an appreciative light in his sparkling blue eyes.

Though she was not unaccustomed to admiration from the opposite sex, Rosabelle felt a blush rise in her cheeks. No doubt they matched her nose and her cloak, she thought ruefully. But there was nothing to take offence at in his merry gaze, so she smiled back.

"We would like hot chocolate after our donkey ride," she said, perhaps a trifle primly. "I wondered if you might let me have a lump of sugar or two now, to feed to the donkeys. Only if your master will not be angry," she added.

"Not he." The young man grinned, showing white, even teeth. "You want to bribe the beasts not to toss you, do you?"

"Oh!" Betsy's eyes widened in alarm. "Do they throw people off?"

"He's teasing, Betsy," Rosabelle assured her, glancing

back at the stolid animals as they stopped in a circle to let their present riders dismount.

The Pastry cook's assistant chuckled. "Better safe than sorry. If you were bucked off, you might slide all the way to the open river and take a ducking, and that would be a great pity. Here you are, ladies." He handed each of the girls a piece of lump sugar.

Thanking him, they turned away just as a skinny youth with a tray suspended from his neck rushed up.

"More pies, Mr. Rufus," he cried.

"Coming up!"

"Mr. Rufus is a shocking saucy fellow," Betsy said severely. "Teasing, indeed! Are you sure he was teasing, Miss Ros?"

"Would you prefer a wooden horse after all?"

"N-no. Oh, come quick, before someone gets my donkey." Her qualms forgotten, Betsy rushed to take possession of the steed with red and yellow bows in its tufted mane.

The donkey boy took Rosabelle's fourpence and showed them how to offer the sugar on the flat of the hand. The soft lips of Rosabelle's green-ribboned mount whuffled across her palm, tickling. She jumped as the donkey behind it in line hee-hawed its envy.

Looking round, she saw that Mr. Rufus had finished loading pies onto the tray and was watching her. He gave her a wave of encouragement.

She half raised her hand in response; then the donkey boy came to help her up into the sidesaddle. With no train to hide them, her ankles were exposed, but so were those of the other female riders. No one who knew her would see her, she told herself, nonetheless very conscious of Mr. Rufus's vantage point nearby. Studiously she avoided looking that way.

"It's not so very high off the ground," Betsy said with a touch of anxiety, and she squeaked as her donkey set forth in leisurely pursuit of the tail of the one in front.

As Rosabelle's mount ambled conscientiously after its fel-

lows, its warmth thawed her cold feet. The motion was
soothing. She wondered whether riding a horse would be
as pleasant; having lived all her life in London, she had
never learned. Horses were much taller, though, and apt
to move much faster. Best be satisfied with the present en-
joyable experience, she decided, and patted the patient
donkey's neck.

They had a good tuppence-worth, going as far as Blackfriars Bridge before turning back. The great rounded
arches of the bridge looked very odd from below, with no
water rushing through. Like the water stairs, they were
guarded by boatmen exacting their toll of those who approached the fair on the ice from upstream.

The donkey-train returned toward its starting point. Rosabelle glanced across to the pastry cook's booth, half expecting to see the saucy young shopman watching her
again. But Mr. Rufus was busy serving customers, along
with another youthful assistant who had joined him.

Rosabelle found herself ridiculously disappointed that
he did not notice her approach. No doubt he had flirted
with at least half a dozen pretty girls since her departure,
she told herself. He was friendly by nature, and doubtless
it was good for business.

The donkey boy led his charges around into a circle and
stopped. He came round to help the women dismount.
Rosabelle tipped him a ha'penny and shook out her skirts
as he moved on toward Betsy.

Impatient, Betsy slid down without waiting for his hand.
As she landed on the ice, her feet shot out from under
her, and with a squawk of alarm, she fell heavily.

"Betsy!" Rosabelle started forward to raise her. "Are you
hurt?"

The girl scrambled cautiously to her knees. "I don't
think so, 'cepting a bit bruised." With Rosabelle's hand
beneath her elbow, she rose to her feet, then collapsed

with a whimper. "Oh, Miss Ros, my ankle! It hurts so, I must've broke it." Tears trickled down her cheeks.

"Oh, dear!" Rosabelle glanced round the crowd of by-standers which had quickly gathered, looking for a helpful face.

"You wants to stop it swelling," said a burly fellow in a frieze jacket. "Put ice on it!" He roared with laughter, and several others tittered.

The donkey boy was growing annoyed at the interruption to his business. "You gotta move 'er, miss," he said roughly. "Come along, now, I'll give you a 'and to slide 'er out o' the way o' my beasts."

For want of anything better, Rosabelle was about to accept his offer, when Mr. Rufus pushed through the circle.

"What's the trouble?" he asked, his face full of concern. "The young lady's hurt herself?"

"It's her ankle," Rosabelle explained. "I fear she has broken it."

"Very likely just a sprain," he said reassuringly, "but deuced painful all the same. Up you get, Miss Betsy, put your weight on me—that's right—and hop along, and we'll soon have you somewhere more comfortable."

Sniffling, Betsy made her painful way, leaning on his strong arm, toward the pastry cook's. Rosabelle picked up her muff, which she had dropped, and followed.

"How'd you know my name?" Betsy asked.

"I heard your mistress address you. I've a good memory for names; it's useful in my line of business. Customers like one to recall their names. And I never forget a pretty face." As he said this last, he turned his head to smile back at Rosabelle, apparently addressing the compliment to her.

Which was all very well, but she was clearly only one of many fated to clog his memory. Still, he was only a shop assistant, however charming. The galleries of female countenances adorning his mind were no concern of hers.

TWO

The pastry cook's shopman assisted Betsy into the booth and sat her down on a bench near the cast-iron oven where the pies and turnovers were baking.

"Ooh, it's lovely and warm," she exclaimed.

From the "doorway" where she stood, Rosabelle could feel the radiating heat. "I'm surprised it has not sunk through the ice," she said.

"The legs of the firebox are set on bricks." Mr. Rufus moved aside to let her see. "And the bricks on thick planks laid across more bricks. We've scarcely even made a puddle. My own notion," he added modestly.

"Ingenious." Rosabelle advanced into the booth. "Betsy, how does your ankle feel now?"

Betsy warily turned her foot from side to side, and winced. "It hurts like anything, Miss Ros."

"If she can move it, it cannot be broken, can it?"

"I think not, ma'am."

"Thank heaven. Pray turn your back, while I see if it is swelling."

Mr. Rufus obliged, stepping forward to the counter to help his busy colleague serve a new rush of customers. Rosabelle sat down on the bench beside Betsy and stooped to examine the injured joint.

"It seems a little swollen," she said doubtfully. "We had

best take your boot off, I suppose. How I am to get you off the river, I cannot conceive."

"I'm ever so sorry, Miss Ros," Betsy wailed. "Don't leave me here!"

"Of course not, you goose." Rosabelle found herself gazing pleadingly at Mr. Rufus's back, as if she expected him to come to the rescue again.

Even if Betsy was able to hop as far as the bank, which seemed unlikely, he could not be expected to risk his employer's wrath by leaving his work for long enough to support her. Perhaps he would be kind enough to find a couple of men willing to carry her for a fee. Rosabelle looked in her purse. A shilling, a threepenny bit, some pennies, and a few farthings—and once ashore she still had to pay for a hackney to take them home.

Mr. Rufus finished with his customer and, a moment later, turned with a steaming mug in each hand.

"Your chocolate, ladies."

"I . . . I don't think I can afford it now. I didn't bring much money with me, and I shall have to hire someone to help Betsy ashore, and a hackney . . ."

"It's on the house." He put a mug into her hand.

"Oh, but your master . . ."

"Trust me," he said with a grin, "I shan't be turned off without a character. Call it my treat if it makes you feel better."

Blushing, Rosabelle persisted. "Can you afford it?"

"A ha'penny-worth of hot chocolate will not break the bank, ma'am."

"He gives you a discount? I beg your pardon, I don't mean to pry."

"Your concern for my solvency does you credit," he said gravely, but with a twinkle in his eye. "Pray believe I shall not suffer for the expense of two cups of chocolate. Now drink up, and then we shall see about getting you both safe to dry land. We have the handcart we used to transport everything here. I daresay Miss Betsy will contrive to perch on it while I wheel her across the ice."

"Oh, yes," Betsy assured him.

Rosabelle did not venture to protest any further. He knew his own affairs best, and the temperament of his employer. "You are very kind," she said gratefully.

She sipped her chocolate. Somewhat to her surprise, it was excellent, as good as she had ever had at home or at Gunter's, the grand confectioner in Berkley Square. Perhaps Dibden's was in a better way of business than their presence among the mostly tawdry hawkers at the Frost Fair suggested.

Mr. Rufus's appearance ought to have given her a clue, Rosabelle thought, eyeing his back as he helped at the counter again. Those broad shoulders were clad in good Bath cloth, and the boots below his fawn stockinette pantaloons had the high gloss held only by the best leather. His high-crowned beaver was glossy, too. His neckcloth, she recalled, was snowy white, starched, tied in an exuberant knot which matched what she had observed of his character, and stuck with a gilt pin.

She hoped he was not living above his means. Altogether, he was almost as smart as the Cheapside mercers' assistants, who were notorious for lounging on their masters' doorsteps, prinked up to the nines.

Mr. Rufus was better-spoken than most of those jackanapes. Maybe he had studied elocution with an eye to bettering himself—which might explain his attentions to a well-dressed young female. Rosabelle was more elegantly clad than many a blue-blooded damsel with a house in Mayfair and an estate in the country.

No mere shopman could aspire to such heights, however. She preferred to believe he was simply chivalrous by nature.

He turned, and caught her gazing at him. His amused air made her lower her eyes in confusion.

"Are you ready to . . . ? Oh, just a moment." He swung round as the hot-pie lad dashed up to the booth entrance.

"More pies!" He handed over a jingling purse.

"They won't be ready for a few minutes yet," said Mr. Rufus, emptying the coins into a cash box beneath the counter. "You're selling too fast for me. Sit down and catch your breath, Jack."

"I'm not tired, honest. It's fun running around crying, 'Hot pies.' It was a prime notion to set up on the ice."

"Makes a change, eh? All right, you give Oswald a hand here and keep an eye on the pies in the oven, whilst I help these ladies ashore."

The youth had not noticed the girls in the shadowy depths of the booth. He tipped his hat with a grin and a wink. "Sure you can manage without me, Mr. Rufus?"

"Quite sure," said Mr. Rufus dryly. Pulling on leather gloves, he gave Betsy his arm.

The handcart was quite clean, but Rosabelle was glad it was not she who had to undergo the decidedly undignified ride in it. Betsy giggled, enjoying it almost as much as the donkey ride. Mr. Rufus made nothing of the weight as he pushed her along, bumping over the ruts in the ice.

"You came from the City bank, ma'am?" he asked Rosabelle, walking at his side, as they came to the crossroads.

"Yes, down the steps at Three Cranes Wharf, but it doesn't matter where we go up. I haven't a carriage waiting. My mother needed ours today, so we came in a hackney."

Rosabelle at once regretted speaking of the carriage. It was quite unnecessary, since she had already mentioned taking a hackney, and he was bound to think she was boasting.

But his friendly manner did not change as he manoeuvred the cart around the corner into Freezeland Street, saying cheerfully, "Three Cranes Wharf will do very well. It's straight ahead, and rough as the ice is in these makeshift streets, it is worse where wheels and feet have not tamped it down. Besides, we are more likely to find you a hackney in Queen Street than in some of the lesser by-ways."

We, he said, so he did not mean to abandon them at the edge of the river. Rosabelle wished she had enough money in her purse to give him a big tip.

Or would it offend him? She had never met anyone quite like him before. Whatever his station in life, he seemed to have more gentlemanly instincts than many who went by the name of gentleman.

"There are more stalls setting up all the time," said Mr. Rufus as they passed a couple of men struggling to spread canvas over a wooden framework. "Business has been good today. By tomorrow word of the fair will have spread, and we shall have the crowds out in force if the freeze holds."

"Was it your idea to bring Dibden's to the Frost Fair?" Rosabelle asked.

"Yes, though more for the fun of it, as young Jackie said, than because the company is in need of the custom."

"And you were put in charge?"

He laughed. "None of the older men wished to exchange the warmth within doors for the chill outside. Jack and Oswald are volunteers, and there are two or three other young fellows eager to take their turns. I let them off for half an hour now and then to explore the fair."

"I thought I might bring another of the girls tomorrow," Rosabelle said tentatively. "It doesn't seem fair that only Betsy should see the fun."

Mr. Rufus turned his head to look at her, with a warm smile in his blue eyes. "I wager your servants are happy to work for you, ma'am."

"I hope so, though they are not exactly—"

"Miss Ros," Betsy interrupted in a tone of deep foreboding, "how'm I going to get up those stairs?"

The wharfside loomed before them. Several people were

coming down the steps, and nearby one of the cranes was
lowering a heavy load in a sling.

"We'll get the crane to hoist you," Mr. Rufus proposed
straight-faced. "Just remember to hold on tight to the
hook."

"No!" Betsy squeaked in horror.

"He is quizzing you again, goose. All the same, I cannot
quite see how it is to be done. You surely cannot carry her
up alone, sir."

"Do you impugn my strength, madam? But you are
right," he admitted with a sigh. "I might manage it, but
it would be risky. No, I believe I shall have to persuade
those fellows at the top to labour a little for their fee. One
of those hulking brutes will make nothing of it."

Recalling the waterman's earlier comment, undoubtedly
lewd, Rosabelle was doubly glad it was not she who had
hurt her ankle. She had rather be lifted in a sling, swaying
in midair, she thought, than submit to being carried by
any of the uncouth boatmen.

As soon as the last newcomer set foot on the ice, Mr.
Rufus ran up the stair. Rosabelle could not hear what he
said, but she watched closely to see whether money
changed hands. She could not repay him now, but it would
give her an excuse. . . . That is, when she came tomorrow
she would bring funds enough.

No payment appeared to take place, however. The men
all laughed, and one slapped Mr. Rufus on the back in an
amicable gesture which visibly rocked him. He came back
down the stair, a waterman lumbering after him.

"All settled," he announced.

His burly companion picked up Betsy as if she weighed
no more than a meat pie. He slung her squealing over his
shoulder, in a flurry of flannel petticoats, and set off upward. Anxiously, Rosabelle hurried after, not wanting to
leave Betsy alone at the top at the ruffians' mercy a moment longer than necessary.

"Take care." Mr. Rufus was close behind her, his hand at her elbow to steady her. The warmth of his touch seeped through the barriers of leather and cloth to envelop her in a glow from the tips of her toes to the crown of her head.

Trying to explain away the flustering phenomenon, Rosabelle assured herself it was just because he was heated from the baking and his exertions with the handcart.

They reached the top to find Betsy perched on a barrel, pink-faced but none the worse for her unorthodox ascent. The watermen were by now noisily engaged in fending off a band of nine or ten urchins without the means to pay the toll. The men had the size and strength, the boys the numbers and agility. Foul language appeared to be shared equally between them.

Mr. Rufus seemed scarcely to raise his voice, but it cut through the babble: "I'll pay the fee for whichever boy is first to bring a hackney carriage for these ladies."

The urchins raced off, now calling insults to each other.

"I only hope they don't bring back half a dozen hackneys!" said Mr. Rufus, laughing.

"If they do," Rosabelle retorted, "I shall leave you to deal with the squabbling jarveys. What is the toll for a child?"

"A penny, I believe." He held out his hand to stop her as she felt in her purse. She looked up. His face was serious, with a half-smiling question in his eyes. "You may repay me tomorrow," he said softly.

Rosabelle nodded, and busied herself with tightening the strings of her reticule.

The ragamuffins returned in short order. Half of them clung to various parts of the hackney they brought with them; the rest cavorted around it. All of them came, and as the carriage stopped on the wharf, they clustered together. In silence they regarded Mr. Rufus with doubtful hope.

"Sixpence the lot," he said to the watermen.

"A tanner it is, gov'nor."

Whooping, the boys scampered toward the stair.

While Mr. Rufus paid their toll, lifted Betsy down from the barrel and helped her to hop to the hackney, Rosabelle spoke to the driver.

"New Bond Street, Number 36."

"Yes'm." He saluted with his whip.

She climbed in, wrinkling her nose at the musty smell. Suppressing a twinge of jealousy at the sight of Mr. Rufus's hands clasping Betsy's waist, she caught the girl as he lifted her in, and settled her on the shabby seat. He closed the door.

Rosabelle lowered the window. "Thank you," she said. It seemed inadequate, but what more could she say? The jarvey was already whipping up his sorry nag.

"It was my pleasure," said Mr. Rufus emphatically, and he bowed as the hackney moved off, rattling over the cobbles.

"How is your ankle now, Betsy?" Rosabelle asked.

"It aches a bit, Miss Ros, but it only hurts really bad if I put my weight on it."

"That's good. *Maman* will know whether we need to send for an apothecary." She hesitated. "Betsy, we'll tell *maman* a kind man helped us, of course, but I see no need to mention what a . . . a *personable* young man he was."

"No," Betsy promptly agreed, with a giggle and a sly look. "Nor there's no need to tell *Madame* Mr. Rufus is a *young* fellow, even."

"We shall just say he was most amiable, polite, and obliging."

"That he was, Miss Ros, that he was. And for all it was me he gave a hand to, if you ask me, it wasn't me he fancied!"

THREE

Dusk was already drawing in on that last day of January, 1814, when the hackney stopped in New Bond Street. The new gas street lamps had not yet been lit, but peering through the grimy carriage window, Rosabelle made out the house number.

"Home at last!"

Here were no bow windows such as displayed the wares of Hookham's Circulating Library, just up the street, and many of the other fashionable shops. Number 36 looked like an ordinary town house, built of brick, five stories from semibasement to attics. On the ground floor, next to the pilastered door, it had a single white-painted sash window. This was veiled in the sheerest of white muslins, concealing the interior while admitting daylight.

Even as Rosabelle descended from the hackney, lights sprang up within the front room, and a silhouetted figure closed heavy brocade curtains.

"Don't try to step down, Betsy. I'll just pay the fare; then I'll summon Jerry and Philip to carry you in."

She was opening her reticule when the front door flung open and two tall footmen in corbeau-coloured livery burst out.

"Miss Ros, where've you been? Madame's in quite a taking!" cried Jerry.

"I'm afraid we have been gone longer than I intended," Rosabelle said guiltily.

"I'll pay the jarvey, miss," said the quieter Philip, reaching into his pocket.

"Thank you. What a nodcock I am, worrying about whether I had enough money left! Mam'selle Betsy has hurt her foot, Jerry. You'll have to carry her in."

Amidst good-natured teasing, Betsy was borne into the house. As Rosabelle followed, the nearest gas lamp flared into brilliance. Its light gleamed on the discreet sign above the door, flowing gilt script on glossy black, so familiar she rarely noticed it: *Madame Yvette, Modiste.*

From the front room emerged Madame herself, short and slim, the essence of Parisian elegance in her midnight blue poplin gown. She shut the door behind her with a firm click echoed by the click of the front-door latch as Rosabelle closed it.

"Enfin, chérie! Where have you been?"

"I'll explain later, *maman.* You have a customer, have you not?"

"Two. Business continues excellent for the time of year, thanks to the weather." Madame noticed Betsy, whom the two footmen had deposited upon a chair in the entrance hall. "What is amiss?" she asked sharply.

"Betsy has sprained her ankle. It's quite swollen. I wish you would take a look at it."

"Poor child! I expect it just needs an arnica compress and a supportive bandage. In a few minutes I come, when Lady Withers leaves and Mrs. Bowditch goes to a fitting room to have her measurements taken. Every year a little plumper, that one. Jerry, Philip, carry Mam'selle Betsy up to the drawing room, if you please."

Rosabelle went first up the stairs. At the top, she poked her head round the door of the office to say, "I'll bring you Mr. Braithwaite's bills in a minute, Papa."

"I hope he doesna expect to be paid before the goods

are delivered," complained her father, a lanky Scot with a long face and sandy hair touched with gray. .

"He never has yet, Papa," Rosabelle reminded him with an affectionate smile.

"Och, they'll all take advantage if they can, and don't you forget it, lass, or ye'll end up in the poorhouse when your mither and I are gone. 'Many strokes, though with a little axe, Hew down and fell the hardest-timbered oak.' "

"Henry VI, Part 3," said his daughter pertly. It was one of his favourite quotations.

She went on, following the footmen and Betsy into the elegant drawing room. The upper floors of the house, invisible from the street, had been knocked into the house next door. Thus, the first floor afforded a comfortable dwelling for Madame, her husband, Kenneth Macleod, and her daughter.

On the second floor were a spacious workroom and four storage rooms, for finished goods, work in progress, bales of cloth, and sundry sewing necessaries and trimmings. The garrets comprised living quarters for the servants and such of the seamstresses as chose to live in, while the basement contained the usual domestic offices.

Cook must have observed Rosabelle's return from the bitter cold outdoors, for she had scarcely settled Betsy on a comfortable sofa when one of the maids appeared with a steaming pot of tea. Rosabelle sent her for a second cup. After sitting in the draughty hackney, she and Betsy were both thoroughly chilled, though the room was warm.

"I ought to get back to work," Betsy fretted. "My ankle won't stop me sewing. We're busy upstairs, what with everyone wanting new pelisses against the cold."

It was true. Those ladies who resided in or near the metropolis were ordering warm mantles, cloaks, and pelisses in heavy velvets and woollen cloth, often lined and trimmed with fur. Though difficult to sew, these brought a correspondingly high profit.

Many established customers also took advantage of discounts, carefully calculated by Mr. Macleod, to order part of their wardrobes for the Season in advance. They ran little risk of finding their gowns already *démodé* when spring brought the rest of the Ton to London. Madame Yvette's creations had a timeless elegance which acknowledged the brief fads and fancies of fashion with at most a distant bow.

So the seamstresses in the workshop above were well occupied, though by no means stretched to the limit, as they would be at the height of the Season.

"You can go up as soon as *maman* has bound your ankle," said Rosabelle. "And I'll come and lend a hand shortly."

Between them, her mother and father had taught her every aspect of the business, from dress design and dealing with clients to keeping accounts and dealing with merchants. That afternoon's outing to the City had been made, with swatches of material and a list of measurements, to order the fabrics chosen by customers to be made up. It was one of her favourite tasks. She was as good at haggling as Papa, and understood silks and velvets, muslins and worsteds, almost as well as *maman*. She loved the warehouses piled with bales of cloth in a rainbow of colours, some still exuding exotic odours from foreign climes.

Another favourite task, and one she was better at than *maman*, was sketching designs, both ideas for gowns and specific gowns as they would look on specific people. Banking on her talent, Papa had started a small, monthly *Journal de Modes*, which had subscribers all over the kingdom.

Rosabelle also enjoyed short stints in the workroom, whither she repaired after discussing Mr. Braithwaite's bill with her father.

A low buzz of conversation filled the long, light and airy room, warmed by a Dutch stove at each end. Papa often grumbled about the price of coals, but *maman* pointed out, quite rightly, that cold fingers were clumsy fingers. Yvette

Macleod prided herself on her practicality as well as her flair.

"Me, I am a hard-headed shopkeeper in your nation of shopkeepers," she was wont to say, "and comfortable, cheerful employees work far more efficiently than downtrodden slaveys."

As a result, never had Madame trained an apprentice only to see her defect to a rival, taking trade secrets with her. Her employees rarely left except to marry. Even then, they often returned once their children were grown.

Such a one was Madame Blodgett, who was in charge of the workroom. Rosabelle asked her for a job to do, and settled at one of the long tables to apply jet beads to a disembodied bodice marked with an embroidery design in French chalk.

Betsy had arrived before her. Her injured leg raised on a spare chair, she was chattering about the Frost Fair as she stitched a seam.

"It was fun, wasn't it, Miss Ros? Being in the middle of the river on the ice, and all the stalls and everything."

"Weren't you afraid of sinking through?" someone asked.

"Not me. I told you about the printing presses, putting out ballads about the freeze and such, and the taverns with tuns of beer. I reckoned if the ice was strong enough to hold them up, it wasn't going to break up under my weight, not even on a donkey. I liked the donkeys 'specially, even though I hurt myself. That Mr. Rufus who rescued me was ever such an obliging fellow, wasn't he, Miss Ros?"

The question, and the look that accompanied it, seemed to Rosabelle full of innuendo. She hoped none of the others noticed it, and that the warmth in her cheeks was invisible as she bowed her head over her work.

"Most obliging," she said composedly.

As Betsy continued her description of the fair—avoiding any details about Mr. Rufus, Rosabelle noted with relief—

Rosabelle took herself to task. All there was between her and the young man was a brief flirtation, amusing while it lasted but nothing to be sensitive about. *Maman* and Papa would never countenance a closer relationship with a mere shop assistant, even if Mr. Rufus desired it, which Rosabelle had no evidence he did.

Her busy days allowed little leisure for dreams of marriage. Her parents took no apparent thought for finding a husband for their daughter, concentrating on preparing her to run the business successfully when eventually she inherited it.

At twenty she felt herself competent in every branch of the trade, wanting only the polish which practice would bring. What would *maman* and Papa say if Rosabelle announced that it was time she was wed?

More important, what would they do?

The occasional dinner parties would become more frequent, she supposed, with the guests chosen from those of the Macleods' wealthy business connexions who had sons of the right age. Perhaps they might raise their sights to the banker, and even the lawyer, who handled their affairs.

With a respectable dowry and the prospect of inheriting a flourishing business, Rosabelle was unlikely to suffer a dearth of suitors.

She had met a few of the young men concerned. More than one had shown signs of interest, due—she thought she could claim without flattering herself—as much to her personal charms as to financial considerations. She was quite pretty to start with, and her mother had taught her to make the best of herself. Madame Yvette's daughter must not be less elegantly dressed than her clients.

The trouble was, not one of those suitable young men lit a spark in her as did the ineligible Mr. Rufus. Not that he was particularly handsome, though his countenance was pleasing. He was lively, cheerful, and intelligent—wit-

ness the contrivance he had rigged up under the oven—
besides being. . . .

"A most obliging person," Betsy reiterated, chiming
with Rosabelle's thoughts. He had voiced his approval of
her kindness to Betsy, she recalled.

And he was without doubt a shocking flirt.

"He laid out a whole sixpence so that every one of the
good-for-nothing brats could go to the fair!"

Rosabelle owed him that sixpence. She had to go to the
Frost Fair tomorrow to repay him. More than likely she
would discover she had grossly exaggerated his attractions
in her mind. Finding him an ordinary, impudent jackanapes of a common shopman, she would be cured.

At dinner that evening, she told her parents all about
her and Betsy's adventures at the Frost Fair. "I don't know
what I'd have done if the pastry cook's man had not come
to the rescue," she said. "He even laid out his own money
for us. I promised to pay him tomorrow."

"How much?" growled her father. "How do you know
he's not cheating you?"

"I saw and heard the transaction, Papa. You would not
have me default on a debt, would you?"

Glumly he shook his head. "Nae, lass. 'No legacy is so
rich as honesty.' "

With a teasing smile, she continued, "Especially a debt
for the excessive sum of . . . sixpence!"

Papa's laugh was a trifle sheepish.

"Of course it must be repaid," her mother said. "Sixpence is no small sum for a shop assistant who has, perhaps, a family to support, and it was *très gentil* on his part
to help you. But there is no need for you to go, *chérie*. I
must send one of the footmen on several errands tomorrow. It will not take him far out of his way."

"I'd like to go, *maman*, if you have no pressing need of
me. I'd like to see more of the fair. And if you can spare
one or two of the girls, I should like to treat them as I did

Betsy. There may never be another Frost Fair in our life-times. It would be a pity if they all missed it."

Madame Yvette pursed her lips consideringly. "We are well beforehand with the work. Yes, it will not do to single out Mam'selle Betsy for such a treat. Take the next two on the list to go with you to the City, so no one can complain of injustice."

Accompanying Rosabelle on her forays to the wholesal-ers' was a jealously guarded privilege. "That will be fairest," Rosabelle agreed. "Thank you, *maman.* Fortunately, tomor-row is the first of February, so I shall have my whole month's allowance."

"Mais non, chérie, this is a business expense, to keep the employees happy."

"We's'll all end up in the poorhouse!" Mr. Macleod groaned. "How long is this Frost Fair to continue?"

"Weeks, Papa," Rosabelle said saucily. "There is no sign of a thaw."

"And if there were," he grumbled, "I'd no be letting my lass venture onto the river ice, for all she's a wicked tease. Verra weel, then, a business expense it shall be."

Rosabelle blew him a kiss. "And I want to buy fairings for the rest, those who can't go," she coaxed. "Just in case the ice doesn't last much longer. Nothing expensive. Gilt gin-gerbread, perhaps, so as to give my custom to the kind pas-try cook."

"An excellent idea," her mother approved.

Outnumbered, Papa gave in, as usual. He kept a tight hold on the purse strings, but once persuaded that an ex-penditure was reasonable—or would please his womenfolk for a reasonable sum—he was no nipfarthing.

So Rosabelle would see Mr. Rufus next day, and be re-leased from her infatuation. He could not possibly be as wonderful as he had seemed. Could he?

FOUR

Well before the landau reached Three Cranes Wharf, it was forced to a halt by the crush of carriages and pedestrians. As Mr. Rufus foretold, news of the Frost Fair had spread, and half the world was heading for the river.

Which made him prescient on top of his other qualities, Rosabelle thought quizzically.

"We shall get down and walk," she decided, "or we'll hardly have any time there."

Mary and Anna eagerly agreed. They were both young enough to be excited, for the older seamstress whose turn it really was had denied with a shudder any desire to spend more time out in the cold than strictly necessary.

Rosabelle told the coachman to pick them up in two hours' time. "Do you know any stairs west of here, Peters?" she asked. "This is probably the most crowded spot."

"There be Queen Hithe stair, Miss Ros. You can't miss it, acos there's a great dock cut into the bank."

"We'll meet you there, then, when the church clocks strike four. If there is a great crush, leave the carriage as close as you can drive, and walk to the top of the stairs, or we may never find you."

"Right, miss."

As the three girls walked on down Queen Street, Rosabelle noticed several exceedingly smart vehicles, accompanied by liveried footmen. One or two even had crests on the doors. The Beau Monde was turning out along with the common people to enjoy the wonders of the Frost Fair.

With real ladies to compare her against, Mr. Rufus would soon realize Rosabelle had no claim to gentility. If he hoped for some advantage from flirting with someone above his station, he would quickly transfer his attentions to an aristocratic damsel likely to be of more use to him.

Naturally Rosabelle would not care a rap. She would be a little disappointed in him—but she expected that anyway. She just hoped he would not think the worse of her for inadvertently misleading him.

Well, almost inadvertently. She could have disabused him if she had tried, when he had spoken of her servants, instead of letting Betsy interrupt.

Still, what did it matter to her if he believed she had deliberately deceived him?

Recognizing that her thoughts about Mr. Rufus were growing hopelessly muddled, Rosabelle concentrated on navigating through the crowd. They reached the top of the stairs, where several very happy watermen were collecting in tolls far more than they could have earned by toiling at their oars. Anna and Mary were thrilled at the sight of the fair spread out below. Rosabelle was astonished at how much it had grown since yesterday.

Freezeland Street now stretched all the way from bank to bank, and all the gaps along it and the Grand Mall had filled. In the four quadrants between them, a number of stalls were set up higgledy-piggledy, clustering close to the crossroads where the greatest throngs might be expected.

Rosabelle wondered if she would be able to find Dibden's booth, or get close to it if she found it. Starting down the stair, she shaded her eyes against the pale but glaring winter sun and looked for the donkeys.

"There they are," she exclaimed in relief. She glanced back at her companions. "Do you want to take a donkey ride?"

Anna, close behind, glanced back in turn before replying, "We'd like the swings better, if you don't mind, Miss Ros."

"Of course not, but I shan't join you. I daresay Betsy told you of my one experience in a swing."

Their giggles were answer enough.

"Ooh, look!" Mary exclaimed breathlessly, eyes round, as they reached the bottom of the steps. "He must be freezing."

A black pugilist pranced upon a stage, clad in no more than breeches and a sleeveless singlet. Rosabelle hastily averted her eyes from his bulging muscles as he waved his fists, bellowing a challenge to all comers. Below the stage swirled a group of well-dressed youths, some egging on one of their number to answer the challenge, others holding him back.

"He'll be made mincemeat of, silly young chub," said Anna. "Look there, Mary, there's a hot-chestnut man. I wonder if it's the same one Betsy told us about."

In response to this broad hint, Rosabelle purchased a paper of chestnuts. Nibbling, they wandered on, passing a large tent with a barker outside.

"Walk up, ladies and gemmun! See the wonders of naycher, only fourpence, can't be beat. Bearded lady, ape-boy, two-'eaded calf, tattooed savage, dozens more. 'Ad to leave the mermaid at 'ome; didn' want 'er getting froze to death. Walk up!"

The barker outside the smaller tent next door advertised his single attraction in an even louder voice: "Come see the counting pig! On'y fruppence and 'e'll count your pennies right afore your eyes. Sir Francis Bacon, the on'y counting pig on ice, fruppence a show!"

Mary and Anna were tempted, but they decided to stick with the swings. Rosabelle paid for their ride and gave them directions to the pastry cook's stall.

"Join me there, or if I'm not there, wait for me. At least,

if you wander off, listen for the church clocks and come straight back when they strike half past three, or we'll never find each other. Here is money for hot chocolate."

She left them and hurried off around the corner into the Grand Mall, then slowed her steps as Dibden's booth came into sight. She did not want to appear too eager.

Since yesterday the booth had been improved. Before it now stood two benches for customers to sit on while imbibing their chocolate. The slapdash name board above had been replaced with a new one, neatly painted in green on white:

DIBDEN PASTRY COOK
at the sign of the Pie and Pipkin
Cornhill.

At one end was depicted a golden-crusted pie decorated with cut-out pastry leaves and a fluted rim; at the other a brown earthenware pot.

The stall was besieged by customers. Reluctant to wade into the crush, and to transact her business so publicly, Rosabelle hesitated.

The crowd was for the most part composed of solid citizens, tradesmen and their wives and children taking a holiday from the demands of commerce to enjoy the Frost Fair. Among them Rosabelle saw the caped greatcoats of two gentlemen, and a footman's livery. As she watched, three young ladies took possession of one of the benches.

All three were expensively dressed in fur-trimmed pelisses. From the cut and ornamentation, Rosabelle guessed which rival modiste had designed and made up two of the three. She was more expensive but less exclusive than Madame Yvette, who was in a position to pick and choose her clients, and to dictate to them.

That plump redhead should never have been rigged out in coquelicot, Rosabelle thought disapprovingly, nor with horizontal bands of fur around the full skirt of her Russian mantle. Worse, the short cape of fur made her shoulders almost as broad as those of the black pugilist.

In contrast, the equally plump brunette, who was one of *maman's* customers, looked almost slim in a close-fitting pelisse, narrow-skirted, with vertical stripes from neck to hem. The rich amber colour flattered her, too. Rosabelle knew the Honourable Miss Abernathy had wanted modish Pomona green, which made her look sallow, but Madame Yvette had not permitted it.

The third was a fair beauty who would have looked lovely in rags. She was the most animated of the three, chattering and laughing with endearingly mischievous glee. They had probably slipped away to taste forbidden pleasures after telling their mamas they were going to walk in Hyde Park.

Rosabelle found herself smiling in sympathy.

A woman pushed free of the throng at the counter and approached the young ladies. Dressed in black, she appeared to be an abigail. She bobbed a curtsy and said something, then moved to stand behind the bench.

A moment later Mr. Rufus emerged from the booth. He carried a tray with three cups of steaming chocolate, which he presented to the three on the bench. He bowed, and through the din of the fair Rosabelle picked out the timbre of his voice. She could not hear what he said, but whatever it was, it made the three ladies blush, bridle and giggle.

Sympathy vanished as a dart of pure jealousy shot through Rosabelle. In vain she reminded herself that she had known him for a flirt.

For a moment she watched as he continued to speak to them. Cures were usually unpleasant, were they not? But this was too painful. She need not torment herself with meeting him face-to-face—she could send Mary and Anna with his blasted sixpence and find something other than gingerbread for fairings.

She was about to turn away when he glanced around,

searchingly, a slight frown creasing his forehead. He saw her, and his face lit.

Without another word to the aristocratic young ladies, he strode toward Rosabelle. Her heart felt ready to burst. Afraid of what he might read in her face, she looked down and fiddled with her reticule, suddenly clumsy fingers striving to take out her purse.

"Miss Ross! I was afraid you wouldn't come."

Shyly she raised her eyes to his face. The warmth in his gaze brought a rush of warmth to her cheeks.

In self-defence, she made a joke of it. "Fie, Mr. Rufus, you thought me the sort of person who doesn't pay her debts? I came to return your sixpence."

"Forget the sixpence." His hands clasped around hers, stilling the struggle with the obstinate reticule cords. "Or no, I'm very glad you remembered it, but I don't want it."

"But you said I could repay you tomorrow. Today."

"How else was I to make sure you returned? My dear Miss Ross, your honesty must surely be obvious to the meanest intelligence. I knew a debt would bring you back."

Again she concentrated on inessentials so as to avoid commenting on his eagerness for her return. "My name isn't Ross. They call me Miss Ros, short for Rosabelle."

"What barbarism! It's by far too pretty a name to deserve shortening. May I call you Miss Rosabelle?"

"If you wish," Rosabelle said with reckless abandon. After today—or at least once the Frost Fair was ended—she would never see him again, so what did it matter what he called her? Her name sounded sweet upon his lips.

Nonetheless, she withdrew her hands from his and said firmly, "I want to buy fairings for everyone at home, and I thought gilt gingerbread would serve very well, but you *must* let me pay the proper price."

He smiled. "If you insist. How many?"

Seamstresses, including the assistants in the show and fitting rooms, cook, coachman, maids . . . "Oh, and the footmen. I'd better take two dozen in case I've forgotten anyone."

Mr. Rufus's eyes widened. Two dozen servants made a substantial household. Rosabelle nearly told him that most of those, including the footmen, were employees of the business, not household staff, but she held back. If he still had not guessed that she was not a real lady, she did not want to disillusion him.

He must be aware no family of the aristocracy, or even the gentry, would accept him as a son-in-law, despite his obviously excellent education. As long as he believed her one of them, he would expect no more than a brief flirtation with her, to be laid to the magic of the Frost Fair, so he would not be hurt when it ended.

Between the owners of a prosperous, fashionable establishment and the employees of a commonplace small shop the gulf was narrower but just as deep. Mr. Rufus might hope to jump it, not realizing how determinedly it was maintained by those on the far side. Better that he should continue to imagine the gulf as wide as it was deep. Rosabelle did not want him to suffer the double pain of a snub and dashed hopes.

Of blighted love she did not let herself think. He could not possibly have fallen seriously in love upon such brief acquaintance. And nor could she.

"Two dozen of gingerbread," he said. "Any particular shapes?"

"I don't know what you've got. I didn't really look yesterday."

"Just the usual, I'm afraid. Diamonds and circles, stars and crescent moons, that sort of thing, and of course men with currant eyes." He laughed. "I experimented a bit with cutting out icicles and snowflakes, but by the time they came out of the oven they were unrecognizable."

"What a pity! Anything will do, a variety."

"Very well. I'll have a neat parcel made up for your maid

to carry." He glanced around, raising his eyes from her face for the first time since he had spotted her. He frowned. "But where is Miss Betsy? Is she still incapacitated?"

"She is much better, but not able to walk."

"You haven't come alone, have you? There are some rough characters about."

"Oh," said Rosabelle doubtfully, remembering numerous taverns and the rowdy youths by the pugilist's stage, "perhaps I ought to go back to Anna and Mary. I brought two others, as I said yesterday I would, and I left them on the swings."

"They'll be all right together. You arranged to meet?"

"Yes, I gave them money for hot chocolate and told them to wait here if I had left to look at the sights."

"Then will you allow me to escort you to see the sights?"

A sudden stillness fell between them. Even the hubbub of voices and music seemed to Rosabelle to come faintly to her ears.

Until his last question, all their interchanges could be seen as related to his work, or Betsy's accident, or friendly funning. To wander off with him, alone together though in the midst of crowds, would be an open acknowledgement of the attraction between them.

"Can they spare you?" Rosabelle temporized, gesturing at the booth.

His elated look told her she had inadvertently given away her desire for his company. "I brought three fellows today," he said jubilantly, "expecting a crowd. They will cope between them. Come over here for a minute while I give your order and put on my topcoat, and then, Miss Rosabelle, I shall be entirely at your service."

FIVE

Along the Grand Mall they wandered, toward Blackfriars Bridge. Rosabelle heard herself exclaim, laugh, comment on the stalls and entertainers they passed, but a moment later she could not have said what she had just seen. Her consciousness was concentrated entirely on the man at her side.

Mr. Rufus walked with an easy stride, his pace adjusted to hers. The two or three inches between their elbows seemed to Rosabelle to be filled with the tension that comes before a storm. When, inevitably in the crush of people, his sleeve brushed hers, the discharge of lightning made her head spin, her pulse race, and her knees tremble.

At one such moment she stumbled. Instantly he steadied her.

"The ice is slippery in places. Won't you take my arm?"

"Y-yes. Thank you."

Rosabelle slipped her hand through his arm, half expecting the contact to make her lose her balance altogether. Instead, she was enveloped in a sense of safety.

As she relied upon his strength to save her from falling, she trusted to his honour not to take advantage of the favour she showed him. Wondering how to express these feelings, or whether they were better not put into words, she looked up at him.

He was smiling down at her. "I shan't presume," he said

softly. "At least, not much. I should like to buy you a fairing, something to remind you of this day. May I?"

"I . . ." No, she must not tell him that nothing could make her forget. Yet she could not deny him. "If you wish. Not something expensive."

"Nor anything as ephemeral as gingerbread! Would you like a ballad? They all seem to mention the Frost Fair every other line, so you will never mistake it for a memento of any other occasion."

She realized they were standing in front of one of the printing presses set up on the ice by competing booksellers. This one had hired a singer to perform his latest publication, to a tune from *The Beggars' Opera*. Thus advertised, the broadsides were selling fast.

Rosabelle listened for a minute. The words struck her as high-flown nonsense, rhyme and rhythm both stretched to the breaking point, or beyond. They must have been hastily scribbled by a Grub Street hack—in fact, a lean, gray-haired man was seated at a table to the rear of the press, busy at his next composition.

Mr. Rufus was also listening, and he forestalled her. "No," he said decidedly, "such rubbish would in time make a travesty of your memories."

"It's quite dreadful, isn't it?"

"Appalling. We shall seek further."

But Rosabelle noticed that the ballad seller was also disposing of prints at a great rate to purchasers attracted by his singer. "Let's just take a look at those pictures," she proposed. "I was thinking yesterday how I should like to draw the scene, if only it were not too cold to sit still."

Though the pictures must have been created in almost as much haste as the ballads, among the mere scrawls was the lively work of a close observer and expert sketcher and engraver. Rosabelle chose one that showed fair-goers and booths against a background of London Bridge and St. Paul's Cathedral.

Mr. Rufus paid for it, and a bit extra to have it rolled

up in a protective sheet of blank paper. He presented it
to Rosabelle with a bow.

"*Thank* you. I shall have it framed and hang it on my
chamber wall." She bit her lip, which had suddenly developed a distressing wobble. "I'll treasure it forever."

He looked at her gravely. "For as long as the remem-
brance brings happiness."

Rosabelle nodded, unable to speak for a moment, then
said with a gasp, "I want to give you something!"

"There is something I should treasure forever, if you
don't think it an impertinence to ask."

"W-what?"

"This morning I saw an artist taking likenesses. I
thought his work quite good. It would be an honour and
a joy to possess your portrait."

"Oh!" Rosabelle exclaimed, flustered. "Well, I daresay,
if that is what you really want . . ."

"It is," said Mr. Rufus positively. "The fellow works
swiftly. You would not have to sit with the frost nibbling
your toes for more than a few minutes."

"Oh, the time!" Though the chimes of the church
clocks on both sides of the river rang clearly through the
sounds of the fair, she had paid no attention. Turning to
the print seller, she asked, "Do you know the time, pray?"

"The half hour struck about ten minutes ago, miss."

"I must go! Anna and Mary will be waiting for me, and
the coachman, too." Rosabelle started back toward the
pastry cook's stall.

Mr. Rufus fell into step at her side, offering his arm.
When she took it, he laid his hand on hers. "You will come
again? Yes, you always pay your debts. This time you owe
me a portrait, and that I will accept."

"I promised to bring two more of the girls, if the freeze
holds."

Contentedly he assured her, "It looks set for a sennight.
I shall see you tomorrow."

* * *

The parcel of gingerbread, when Rosabelle opened it at home, turned out to contain not twenty-four but twenty-six pieces. Twice a baker's dozen, she thought. Six stars, six crescents, six crosses, seven men with currant eyes—and a heart.

Hastily she wrapped the last in a handkerchief and hid it in a drawer of her dressing table.

Wednesday morning. Frost flowers bloomed on Rosabelle's chamber windowpanes, and the rising sun glistened on frosted roof tiles across the way. Down below in the street, the breath of men and horses rose in clouds of steam.

Rosabelle spent the morning attending customers downstairs while her mother supervised some complicated cutting-out up in the workroom. In general, Madame Yvette's clients were easy to deal with, since they knew she would not hesitate to dispense with their custom should she decide they were more trouble than they were worth.

Today the worst was a spoiled young lady about to embark upon her first Season, who wanted a flame-coloured ball dress. Her mama, Lady Warburton, had failed to convince her that only white and the palest pastels were acceptable for girls making their come-out.

"I declare, I do not know what to do with the child, mademoiselle," she whispered, wringing her hands, while Miss Warburton glanced through a book of fashion plates. "I am at my wits' end. Pray make her see reason!"

Thanks to her mother's training, Rosabelle succeeded with a mixture of firmness and persuasion in diverting Miss Warburton's yearnings to silver net over pale blue satin.

Lady Warburton was lavish with her thanks. "We shall both order the entire Season's wardrobes from Madame

Yvette," she promised. "And Elizabeth's next year, and Marianne's two years after that."

"Madame will be honoured to serve you, my lady," Rosabelle assured her.

"You may be sure I shall highly recommend your tact to your mother, and to all my friends with willful daughters," whispered her ladyship. "Naturally I should never venture to tip Madame, but will you be offended if I offer you a little something extra for yourself, my dear?" She pressed three sovereigns into Rosabelle's hand.

Rosabelle smiled and curtsied.

At last her mother came down and Rosabelle was free to go. She had to return to Braithwaite's a length of mismatched rose sarsenet delivered in error, and obtain a replacement, and there was a haberdashery order for Lowe's in Gracechurch Street.

"And then I may go to the Frost Fair, *maman?*"

"Oui, chérie. They talk of nothing else upstairs. I hope you find some amusement there, as well as giving pleasure to *les demoiselles?*"

"Oh, yes, maman," said Rosabelle, willing herself not to blush, "it is very amusing, and I don't believe I've seen half of it yet."

"Enjoy yourself then, *ma petite.*" Madame reached up to pat her tall daughter's cheek.

On her way up to the workroom, Rosabelle looked in on her father. "I'm off to the fair, Papa."

He groaned and reached for his cash box.

She laughed. "It's all right, I don't need any money. I have a little left from yesterday, and a customer tipped me this morning. I'll bring you a fairing."

"Don't you go spending your bawbees on fiddle-faddling rubbish, lass!"

"Papa, you don't want a broadside ballad rhyming 'ice' with 'nice' and 'hot pies,' and printed right there on the Thames?"

"I do not!" he said emphatically.

"What about a portrait of your loving daughter? There is an artist taking likenesses."

"Aye, that I'd like fine, if it looks like you. And if it doesna, ye'll no pay the fellow."

"No, Papa." Rosabelle would see what the artist produced for Mr. Rufus before deciding whether to buy a second portrait for her father. She did hope it would be a likeness worth treasuring. "I daresay he draws a flattering picture, to please his customers," she said.

"No need to flatter you, lass, and that's enough o' fishing for compliments!"

She pouted at him, kissed his forehead, and went on to fetch her companions of the day from the workroom. While Eliza and Jenny put on their outdoor clothes, Rosabelle went back down to her chamber to don her cloak. It was the same ruby velvet she had worn yesterday and the day before, the only one she had. "All verra weel being elegant," as Papa said, "but more than one at a time is pure extravagance."

Rosabelle didn't mind. Supposing Mr. Rufus forgot her face—not yet having a portrait to remember her by—he would recognize her by her cloak.

The carriage took them to Braithwaite's, but then it had to return to Bond Street to carry one of the showroom assistants to a customer's house for a fitting. Eliza and Jenny were in a fever of impatience to get to the fair. Rosabelle relented and took a hackney to Gracechurch Street, though she would rather have walked.

Not that she was any less impatient, but the way from Cheapside led up Cornhill. She had hoped to take a look at the establishment where Mr. Rufus usually passed his days. The windows of the hackney were too grimy to see anything without peering, which the girls would have thought very odd.

By the time Rosabelle had transacted her business at Lowe's, the afternoon was well advanced. The three girls walked at a brisk pace down Gracechurch Street and Fish Street Hill toward London Bridge.

Mr. Lowe had directed them to Old Swan stairs as the nearest access to the river. Rosabelle paid their tolls, and they descended to the ice.

The bridge loomed to their left. Ahead lay the beginning of the Grand Mall, with half its length to go before the intersection with Freezeland Street. Jenny and Eliza dawdled along, oohing and aahing over everything, unable to decide what particular treat they wanted. Rosabelle began to despair of reaching Dibden's stall in time for more than a brief exchange of words with Mr. Rufus.

They paused outside a tent advertising a Grand Chinese Masque. From within came the delicate sound of plucked strings.

"Show about to start!" cried the inevitable barker. "Shilling a head, see the mandarins and their dancing girls, see the emperor on his golden throne. Walk right in, only a shilling a head!"

"That's an awful lot," said Jenny wistfully. "The swings Mary and Anna went on yesterday were only sixpence, weren't they, Miss Ros?"

"I can't remember." Rosabelle urged the pair toward the tent. "It doesn't matter, anyway. You may never have another chance to see the Emperor of China."

"Aren't you coming, too, Miss Ros?" Eliza asked.

"No, I'll meet you at Dibden's pastry cook's for hot chocolate." Quickly she explained how to find the stall and arranged a meeting time.

Jenny and Eliza disappeared into the tent as cymbals clashed, and Rosabelle hurried on.

Dibden's was as busy as the day before. Rosabelle hovered on the outskirts of the throng, wondering how to attract Mr. Rufus's attention. She didn't like to be so bold as to go to the booth's side entrance.

"Looking for Mr. Rufus, miss?" enquired a breathless voice at her side. The lad with the empty tray slung before

him was the one who had so enjoyed selling hot pies on
Monday.

"It's Jackie, isn't it? I . . . I would like just a word with Mr.
Rufus."

Young Jack gave her a knowing look. "Step back here,
miss, and I'll tell him you're here."

It seemed an age before Mr. Rufus came out, already
wearing his greatcoat. He frowned at her. "Alone again!"

"Would you rather I had brought a chaperon?" Rosabelle
asked saucily.

"No," he admitted, lips quirking, "but I cannot think it
safe for a beautiful young lady to walk alone here. I should
never forgive myself if you were to come to any harm."

"I shan't." Did he really consider her beautiful? Pretty,
attractive—but his eyes confirmed his words: to him she
was beautiful. And he was worried about her. "Men rarely
bother a female who walks briskly and with determination,"
she averred. "It's when one stops and loiters, as I did when
I arrived here . . ."

"Someone accosted you?" he demanded, fists clenched.

"Only Jackie," she soothed him. "With kind intent."

"Be careful," he ordered sternly.

"I need not, now, for I have you to protect me. Let us go
and get your fairing. Where is the artist?"

"On Freezeland Street, over toward the Southwark bank.
The fellow had better do you justice, or I'll make him start
over."

"I already have instructions from Papa not to pay him if
it's not a good likeness," Rosabelle told him, laughing, as
they set out, "and if it is, to sit for a second."

"For your father?"

"I promised him a fairing, too."

"Did all the gingerbread arrive unbroken?" he asked
with studied casualness.

"Yes, I . . . Thank you for the baker's dozens. I had
enough to spare for the laundrywoman and her daughters."

"You gave them all away?"

"I kept one."

To her relief, he did not press her. Turning right into Freezeland Street, he pointed out a juggler keeping a dazzling array of spangle-covered balls spinning through the air. Glittering in the sunlight, they emitted a constant, whispering tinkle.

Rosabelle and Mr. Rufus stopped to watch for a few minutes, then dropped a few clinking coins into the man's hat and moved on. A nearby tent offered a performance of *The Tempest* (abridged), acted by marionettes so lifelike as to be indistinguishable from living, breathing players. Judging by the thunderous roar, either they had reached the storm scene or the audience was applauding with extraordinary enthusiasm.

"I should like to see that," Rosabelle sighed.

"There will be another performance, I daresay," said Mr. Rufus eagerly. "I'll find out when it starts."

"I cannot stay so long."

"Tomorrow?"

"Perhaps."

He stepped up to the doorman, returning a moment later to report, "Tomorrow they perform *A Midsummer Night's Dream,* every hour on the hour. They cut the plays short, he says, for fear of their patrons' freezing."

"Very short! But I should like to see the puppets acting."

"And I have been racking my brain for an enticement to bring you to the fair again tomorrow. There's no knowing how much longer it will last."

Their eyes met. In his, Rosabelle read an acknowledgement of the fleeting nature of their relationship.

"I shall try to be here—at your stall—at the proper time," she said softly.

SIX

"Tolerable, tolerable," Mr. Macleod allowed grudgingly. "He's caught the look o' ye, lass. 'Tis no sae bad, considering."

"Considering what, Papa?"

"Considering 'twas drawn by a fellow wha sells his skills for a shilling at a fair."

"Half a crown, Papa."

"Wheesht, the mon robbed ye!"

"Pas du tout," maman disagreed. Leaning on the back of the sofa, she peered over his shoulder at the portrait. "It is excellent, *mon cher.* We must have it framed."

Her husband sighed and nodded. For a moment, all three studied the picture in silence. Somehow, in a swift sketch in black and white, the artist had not only accurately delineated Rosabelle's features; he had brought them to life. There was a glow in her eyes and a breathless expectancy in the tender curve of her mouth.

"Ma foi, one would say a girl in love!"

"It must be a trick he has," Rosabelle said hastily as both her parents turned their gazes from her image to her face. "I daresay many of the people who ask for likenesses are girls wanting portraits for their sweethearts, so he draws them that way to please them. He didn't know the gentleman I wanted mine for was my own dear papa."

"I'll take it to be framed tomorrow," said her father
gruffly.

On Thursday, Madame Yvette could only spare one of
her seamstresses to go to the Frost Fair. Esther was a thin,
shy, perpetually worried girl, the sole support of her crip-
pled mother. She offered to give up her turn to one of the
others, but Rosabelle was determined to give her an hour
or two of fresh air and recreation.

"But, Miss Ros," Esther whispered timorously, "I can't
afford to take time off."

"You won't lose any pay," Rosabelle promised. "I have
to go to the furrier to choose some ermine trim first, and
you know Madame doesn't let me go to the City alone."

"You can borrow my cloak, Esther," called Betsy from
the other side of the workroom. "It's ever so warm, and
you'll need it. Colder than a miser's heart it is out there on
the ice. Brrr!"

Esther gratefully accepted Betsy's offer. Her own pelisse
must be thin and threadbare, Rosabelle guessed, ashamed
of herself for not noticing last time they went out together.
She would have to have a word with *maman* about that. She
would point out that Esther was one of the best embroider-
ers, and if she took a chill, it would cause no end of diffi-
culties.

Maman always preferred to disguise her kindness and
generosity as businesslike common sense.

The carriage was in use, so Jerry summoned a hackney
for Rosabelle and Esther. Neither of the footmen had had
a chance to go to the Frost Fair. One must always be at hand
to open the door and usher in customers, and one to run
errands to the great houses of Mayfair and St. James's.

"Sunday's my half day, Miss Ros," Jerry said, handing her
into the hackney with as much ceremony as if she were a
duchess entering a crested coach. "D'you reckon the
river'll stay froze till then?"

"It certainly doesn't feel like a thaw at present," she said with a shiver. "It's as cold as ever."

How much longer? Every time she met Mr. Rufus, she found the prospect of never seeing him again more painful. Already what was supposed to be a brief, lighthearted flirtation had deepened into genuinely tender feelings. What if the present weather continued for another week? A fortnight?

But well before the end of a fortnight Rosabelle would run out of seamstresses to give her an excuse to go to the fair. Then she would have to decide whether to break the connexion deliberately, or to continue her visits brazenly, with no excuse. Either way, she saw heartbreak ahead.

Mr. Rufus seemed to accept that she was beyond his reach, but if he had any hidden hopes, with time they would grow. Perhaps the apparent cruelty of putting an immediate stop to their meetings— regardless of freeze or thaw— would be kinder in the end.

As the hackney made its way along the Strand, Rosabelle tried to persuade herself good fortune had given her Esther as her sole companion today. The girl could not be left on her own; she would have to attend the marionette play with Rosabelle and Mr. Rufus. With her retiring nature, she would not intrude, but her very presence must put a brake on the intimacy of sitting together in a darkened tent.

"I hope you have not set your heart on the swings or the donkeys, Esther," Rosabelle said. "There is to be a performance by puppets of *A Midsummer Night's Dream* which I should rather like to attend."

"A real play, Miss Ros? Not just Punch and Judy?" Esther heaved a beatific sigh. "I'd like it best of anything."

Yes, Esther was the ideal companion. She never joined in the workroom gossip, so she was not likely to mention Mr. Rufus. The others were bound to ask her what she had done, but the play would provide plenty to talk about.

Everything had fallen out perfectly—if only Rosabelle

could ignore the hollow feeling that filled her whenever she contemplated the inevitable goodbye.

The business at the furrier's diverted her for a while. She didn't know ermine, sable or chinchilla as well as she did silks and cambrics, but Mr. Jacobson, the wealthy Jewish fur importer Madame Yvette always dealt with, was teaching her. He always assisted Rosabelle personally, recognizing her mother's eminence among dressmakers to the Ton. Naturally, whenever Madame Yvette's customers wished to purchase furs on their own account, she directed them to Jacobson's.

The intricate give and take of commerce interested Rosabelle, though not as much as the actual process of creating beautiful clothes. Bookkeeping and accounting, on the other hand, she found dull. The beauty of harmoniously balanced numbers escaped her, however eloquently Papa spoke on the subject. She knew *maman* was glad not to have to manage that side of things.

Suppose Mr. Rufus had a flair for numbers, and business in general, Rosabelle thought as she and Esther approached the river. Would *maman* and Papa look more kindly on him, overlook his humble situation, if he proved competent to help their daughter in future?

There was no way to find out, she concluded dispiritedly, blenching at a vision of her parents interviewing Mr. Rufus for the position of husband and finding him wanting.

"What dreadful, rough men!" Esther whispered, nervously eyeing the watermen on the wharf.

"Their manners and appearance are rough, but they mean no harm."

"The others said they won't let you go through without paying."

"The freeze has interrupted their usual livelihood, so they must charge a toll to feed their families. You should sympathize with that." Rosabelle paid the fee, and they descended to the ice.

Esther gazed about with interest, and was pathetically

grateful for a handful of hot chestnuts, but she showed no disposition to linger along the way. Rosabelle hurried her along. It had taken longer than she expected to get there. They would only just be in time to catch the beginning of the next performance if Mr. Rufus was ready to go at once.

He was watching for her, standing in the booth entrance in his greatcoat.

Coming to meet her, he said with a grin, "I've wrapped myself up in anticipation of your arrival at a quarter to every hour since noon."

"That's only twice."

"Including noon. Three times. Let's go, we'll just make it before the curtain rises."

"I hope there will be room for all of us. This is Esther."

Mr. Rufus blinked as if, with no eyes for anything but Rosabelle, he had not even noticed the other girl's presence. "How do you do, Miss Esther," he said courteously, and offered each an arm. "I'm glad you have come with Miss Rosabelle. I've warned her against walking about here alone."

Throwing a scared look around her, Esther grasped his sleeve as if it were her only chance of safety and scurried alongside. He gave her a kind but dismissive smile, then turned to Rosabelle.

"I trust they have not mangled the play too badly. Are you familiar with it?"

"Yes. My mother is not interested in the theatre, but Papa is a devotee of Shakespeare's works. He has taken me to every new production since I was quite small. This is one of my favourites."

"There's no knowing what they have made of it," he cautioned. "Not only are the actors puppets; it has been cut to less than an hour, remember."

"I hope they've kept all the funniest bits," Rosabelle said. She felt in need of cheering up. The joy of being with him was overshadowed by the coming parting.

As if he read her mind, there was a sadness behind his

smile. "I believe you can count on that. I've strolled past the tent twice today, and each time I heard great merriment. Here we are." He freed his arm from Esther's grip and reached into his pocket.

Hearing the jingle of coins, Rosabelle said quickly, "I'm paying for this," as she loosened the strings of her reticule.

"Let me treat you."

She didn't want to hurt his pride, yet she could not let him spend his meagre wages on her. "I might," she said in a low voice, "but I cannot allow you to pay for Esther. And it will look . . . most particular if I pay for her and you pay for me."

" 'Urry up, ladies an' gent! Show's beginning."

"As you will," said Mr. Rufus resignedly, "but I pay for myself."

The doorman accepted their shillings impartially, and they went in.

They found seats on a bench to one side, with a good view of the stage. Rosabelle sat between Esther and Mr. Rufus. Though the tent was not really full enough to justify the way his elbow pressed against hers, she made no attempt to move away. Soon enough, his touch would be no more than a painful but precious memory.

Thank heaven the marionettes were not to perform *Romeo and Juliet*. Rosabelle could not have kept her composure through that tragic romance. She was not sure she'd be able to laugh at the comedy ahead, no matter how well done.

It was very well done. The puppeteers' version of *A Midsummer Night's Dream* concentrated on Bottom's adventures. Rosabelle simply could not help laughing, especially as Esther lost all her diffidence and chortled like a gleeful child at the antics on stage. Mr. Rufus's mirth was transmitted to Rosabelle as much through the contact between them as by sound. His ribs must be aching with laughter.

At the end, they all emerged into daylight with tears of merriment in their eyes.

"Oh, Miss Ros," Esther gasped, "I never seen anything like it in all my born days. I can't wait to tell Mam all about it."

"Hot chocolate all round first," said Mr. Rufus, "before you go anywhere. My treat," he added with a meaningful glance at Rosabelle.

"I'd like to bathe my feet in hot chocolate," she said with a smile of acquiescence. "They are two blocks of ice. The show was so funny I didn't even feel them freezing till now."

"I expect they quickly went numb. We'll go in and sit by the oven and you'll soon thaw."

The word "thaw" sobered both of them. Esther did not notice, prattling away as she rehearsed the tale she would tell her mother about flying fairies, the man with an ass's head, and the talking wall in *Pyramus and Thisbe*.

They drank their chocolate. Rosabelle bought Esther a meat pie. Shyly the girl asked to have it cut in half so that she could take half home. She ate her half hungrily, and Mr. Rufus gave her a gingerbread man to take to her mother.

All the while, he and Rosabelle exchanged scarcely a word. Their eyes met often, but in the dim interior of the booth Rosabelle found it impossible to read what his were telling her.

At last she could prolong her stay no longer.

"We must go."

Mr. Rufus accompanied them outside. "Tomorrow?" he asked.

"I . . . I'm not sure."

After a moment of shock, he nodded. His face was bleak as he took the hand she held out to him. She thought he was going to kiss it, but he raised it to press the back briefly against his cheek.

Wordless, he bowed. Turning away, Rosabelle blinked back tears that had nothing to do with merriment.

SEVEN

That night, a gusty wind blew in from the west. Along with premonitory puffs of cloud, it brought a mellow dampness to the air, a hint of spring, a promise of snow-drops and crocuses and violets.

Rosabelle yearned for frost flowers.

"Ye'll no go on the ice today, lass," her father said at breakfast on Friday morning. " 'Tis too risky wi' the change in the weather."

"Yes, Papa," she acquiesced, subdued. "What do you want me to do today, *maman*?"

They discussed the day's work.

"It may sleet tomorrow," said Madame Yvette, "but to-day everyone will be thinking of muslins. You had best go to Braithwaite's this afternoon for samples of the newest muslins. And we need seed pearls for the embroidery on Lady Vanessa Seagrave's Presentation gown. How I wish the good Queen would stop insisting on hoops at Court!"

"Van Biederbrok in Hatton Garden for the pearls?"

"*Oui, chérie*. Make sure they are all of a size. You may take the carriage, but have the pearls delivered. It is for the seller to bear the risk of carrying them through the streets."

That word again: risk. Did Mr. Rufus realize the danger of going on the frozen Thames with a balmy breeze blow-ing? Very likely rain was already falling in the west, feeding the river with warmer water. How long would the ice hold up to that insidious assault?

Throughout the morning, tension built in Rosabelle until she felt she might explode at any moment. When at last she set out for the City, with Fanny as her companion, she ordered the coachman to drive down to the riverside first. She had promised Papa not to venture onto the ice, but if she saw the Frost Fair still in full swing, she would have to do *something*.

Peters drove them to the top of the Queen Hithe stairs. Rosabelle stepped out of the carriage. To her dismay, the river was still covered with the gaily flagged booths and tents.

"Can't we go, Miss Ros?" Fanny begged.

"No, it's not safe. Oh, what am I to do?"

A trickle of people, much reduced from the past few days' flood, was passing the toll-collecting watermen and descending to the ice. Among them, Rosabelle picked out a pair of lads of twelve or so, and called them over.

"I'll give you a shilling to take a message for me to someone at the fair."

"An 'ole shilling, miss?" asked one.

"Yes. Find the booth of Dibden's, the pastry cook, on the Grand Mall just west of Freezeland Street. Near the donkey rides. Ask for Mr. Rufus and tell him Miss Rosabelle is waiting for him at the Queen Hithe stairs. Can you remember that?"

The other boy gave her a cheeky grin. "Dibden's, Mr. Rufus, pretty Miss Rosabelle waitin' at Queen 'Ithe. Reckon 'e'll come straight, miss!"

"There's a crown for you if you come with him," said Rosabelle, partly to ensure her message's reaching its destination, partly from a pang of conscience at sending the lads into danger. They were going anyway, but if they came to harm on an errand from her. . . .

"Miss Rosabelle?"

At the sound of that beloved voice, she swung around.

Mr. Rufus strode toward her, the worried creases smoothing from his brow as he saw her face. He held out both hands.

"It *is* you! I was not sure."

Today, instead of the ruby cloak, she wore a fitted pelisse of *gros de Naples* in a rich green shade, and a bonnet with a curling green ostrich plume. Yet he had recognized her from behind.

She put her hands in his, speechless with relief.

"Thank heaven I've caught you in time!" he exclaimed. "I've been walking up and down the wharves, just in case you came today. It's not safe on the river."

"This 'im, miss?" queried one of the boys, disappointed. "No crown for us, then."

"I'll give you a crown to stay away from the fair, off the ice. You heard Mr. Rufus. It's not safe."

They consulted each other with a glance. "Done, miss. We was there yes'day anyways. Ta, miss."

"What was all that about?" Mr. Rufus asked as the pair ran off, each with a half crown clutched in his grubby hand.

Rosabelle explained. "I hoped to persuade you not to go back," she added. "You won't now, will you?"

"We went out there first thing this morning to dismantle the stall and haul everything ashore. Dibden's wouldn't imperil its people for the sake of profit."

"Your notion turned out profitable?"

"Extremely, for an enterprise of that size and duration," he told her with a complacent smile. Then the smile faded, and he turned to look out over the Thames. "A few cautious ones have already left, but with money to be made there's a general air of bravado. One or two of the printing presses are turning out ballads proclaiming their defiance of 'Madame Tabitha Thaw.' "

"Do you think the ice will melt soon?" Rosabelle asked.

"I fear it is already melting from below. The chief danger, though, is not sinking through as it melts, but that it will break up. I've talked to people coming off who speak of creaks and groans underfoot. It isn't only that the air is too warm. Today is a spring tide, with high tide a little while ago. In winter the sea is always warmer than rivers, and salt water freezes at a lower temperature than fresh."

"So the ice is being undermined? I wondered about the effect of warmer rainwater flowing in from the west."

His glance was admiring. "I hadn't thought of that." He turned to gaze westward. Dark banks of clouds were building beneath the haze which had spread across the sky during the morning. "A good point. But the main factor, I believe, is that as the tide continues to ebb, the ice is left unsupported. When it fails, it may collapse very suddenly."

"Any moment now?" asked Fanny, who had been listening with a bemused expression. "Eh, Miss Ros, I'm that glad we didn't go to the fair. Can we leave now? I don't want to see all those people drownded!"

As one, Rosabelle and Mr. Rufus turned to stare with dread out across the river.

"What can we do?" cried Rosabelle.

"Nothing, now. I've tried to explain my reasoning to everyone I've spoken to. Some listened. Some didn't."

Rosabelle listened, trying to hear the creaks and groans of the overburdened ice. All that came to her ears were the merry notes of barrel organs, fiddles, pipes and drums, the shouts of barkers, the hum of the crowd's myriad voices.

"I can't—"

With a crack like a thousand coachmen's whips snapping in unison the ice split. The music ended in a horrid jangle, and screams rent the air. The watchers on the wharf saw jagged channels open, dark, toothed mouths gaping for their prey.

The prey fled, those who could, swarming across the remaining ice toward the banks, leaping the widening gaps. Some made it. Some did not.

Rosabelle closed her eyes in horror. When she opened them, Mr. Rufus was gone, as were the boatmen. In less

time than seemed possible, from stair after stair, the
Thames wherries pulled out into the stream. Boat hooks
reached, caught, dragged the hunted from the hungry current into the frail cockleshells dodging between the floes.

Mr. Rufus appeared at the top of the stairs, soaked to the
waist, a dripping child in his arms and a weeping woman
clinging to the skirts of his coat. Rosabelle ran to him.

He thrust the child at her. "Take care of them. There's
not much more I can do from here. I'm going out in a
boat, to wield the boat hook so that the rowers can concentrate on their oars."

He leaned forward, over the wailing child's head. His kiss
was warm on Rosabelle's mouth. Then he was gone again.

Rosabelle cast a last glance at the dreadful scene, then
set about helping the woman and child. They were soaked
to the skin, and beginning to shiver convulsively. She sent
Fanny to the carriage to fetch a lap rug, while she stripped
the little girl naked and her mother to her shift.

As Rosabelle wrapped the child in her own pelisse,
Fanny came back with the rug. Before the woman had
been enveloped in its folds, another dozen drenched fu-
gitives reached the wharf, with more behind.

Peters was close on Fanny's heels, his heavy, caped topcoat already half off. Fanny—rather unhappily—took off
her cloak. They were but the first.

As word spread of the disaster on the Thames, the people of London rallied round. The poor brought ragged
sheets and blankets; rich merchants sent bales of woollen
cloth and cartloads of clothes; charitable institutions set
up soup kettles all along the wharves. Dockside warehouses
were opened to shelter the victims from the wind, which
no longer seemed benign.

Rosabelle had no time to think. More and more of those
the boatmen saved had to be carried ashore and into the
nearest warehouse. Chilled to the bone, they were incapa-
ble of stripping off their own sodden clothing. Her fingers

numb, Rosabelle worked alongside whores and dock labourers, tapsters and jarveys, fishwives and chimney sweeps, struggling with buttons and tapes and hooks and pins. She undressed women and men alike, for modesty was an unaffordable luxury when frigid death lurked close at hand.

And then suddenly the influx ended. Swaying with weariness, Rosabelle stumbled toward the great door of the gloomy warehouse to make sure no one else was coming.

Peters caught up with her and took her elbow. "Time to go, Miss Ros. There's others'll tend 'em now. You done your bit, and more, and you need to get home and change your clo'es."

A gust of wind blew in through the door, making Rosabelle aware that her own gown was damp. She shivered. The coachman was in his shirtsleeves, and the knees of his breeches showed wet patches where he had knelt. Fanny, joining them, was also damp and weary.

"Fanny, have you seen him? Mr. Rufus?"

"No, Miss Ros. Likely he ended up at one of the other stairs and went home by now."

"Yes, I suppose so."

As cold inside as out, Rosabelle let Peters lead her to the carriage. She slumped in one corner, her head resting back against the squabs. Her eyes were closed, but branded on the lids was the last sight she had seen on her last glance at the river.

Just as Mr. Rufus had run down the stairs to embark in the first wherry available, one of the little boats out on the swirling water had been struck by an ice floe and overturned. He had gone out onto the perilous stream, among the deadly floating islands. Had he come back?

Between the tales told by Fanny and Peters, and the newsboys already crying scores drowned—though hundreds were saved—Madame Yvette and Mr. Macleod did not wonder at their daughter's low spirits. Clucking, Madame hustled Rosabelle to bed and plied her with *tisanes* and broth.

"It will not do to fall ill with the Season almost upon us," she scolded gently as Rosabelle pushed away the cup of broth, silently shaking her head. "Hot drinks will help to warm you thoroughly. Shall I send for *chocolat* instead?"

Rosabelle burst into tears. *Maman* rocked her in her arms as though she was still a little child.

"A *crise de nerfs* is natural after such an experience, *chérie.* Tomorrow you shall stay in bed."

But lying in bed gave her all too much time to think, so on Saturday morning she got up as usual. She found it impossible to present the necessary cheerful face to clients downstairs, and the chatter in the workroom was unbearable. In the end, she took some embroidery to the drawing room to work on in peace. It was a complicated task which demanded her full concentration.

If now and then Mr. Rufus's face floated between her and her work, she fiercely blinked it away. Dead or alive, he was lost to her forever, so what did it matter whether or not he had survived unscathed?

By Sunday, that argument had worn itself out. Rosabelle bitterly regretted not having sent to Dibden's yesterday to discover Mr. Rufus's fate. Now she had to wait until Monday. Filled with restless energy, she would have liked to go for a long walk in one of the parks. Rain poured down all day, and *maman* refused even to consider letting her go out. She paced the drawing room, back and forth, back and forth, like a caged tiger at the Tower.

Monday, the seventh of February, a whole week since she first met Mr. Rufus, was merely damp and dreary. However hopeless her love, she had to see him.

If he was still alive.

Growing impatient with her fidgets, her mother hurried to make up the list for Braithwaite's. "Take the carriage," she said. "You must go to Van Biederbrok's, too, to select the seed pearls, since you did not get them on Friday. Lady Vanessa's gown cannot be made up until the embroidery is done. I shall have to put off her first fitting appointment."

"I'm sorry, *maman*. I'll go there first."

At the jeweller's, Rosabelle managed to give her attention to choosing matching pearls. She found it more difficult at the cloth wholesaler in Cheapside, which had none of the interest of rarity. Fortunately her companion, Mam'selle Fogarty, was one of the older and more knowledgeable seamstresses. Between them, they settled on the needed materials.

Bidding Mr. Braithwaite a hurried goodbye, Rosabelle led the way out to the waiting carriage and went to speak to the coachman.

"Peters, there is a pastry cook's shop in Cornhill called Dibden's. At the sign of the Pie and Pipkin. Do you know it?"

"Aye, Miss Ros, I seen it often. Halfway up on the left, just past the Royal Exchange. Hungry?"

"I didn't eat much breakfast." Which was true. She had lost her appetite last Friday and it had yet to return.

"Have you there in a jiffy, miss."

The carriage seemed to crawl the quarter mile, through the busy traffic of Cheapside and Poultry and past the vast pillared portico of the Mansion House. There was the still vaster Bank of England, off to the left in Threadneedle Street, and the Royal Exchange with the Stock Exchange just beyond it. Here was the financial heart of the City of London, of England, of the world.

And, half a dozen houses farther up Cornhill, there was Dibden's.

The carriage stopped. "Wait here, I shan't be a minute," Rosabelle told Mam'selle Fogarty. She stepped down, her gaze on the pastry cook's premises.

Shop was too meagre a word. Over the double façade

with its sparkling windows on either side of the door, the
sign—gold on dark green—read

PASTRY COOK DIBDEN CATERER
established 1679
Caterers to the Lord Mayors of London

with a golden pie on one side, a golden pipkin on the
other. Beneath, in smaller script, was a list of further distinguished customers, from the Directors of the Bank of
England to Merchant Taylors' and Grocers' Halls.

Dibden's was no commonplace small shop. If Mr. Rufus
was no more than a shopkeeper's assistant, at least he
worked for one of the best.

Had worked?

Heart in mouth, Rosabelle pushed the door open and
went in.

EIGHT

Though Rosabelle's heart was in her mouth, her mouth began to water as she stepped into the pastry cook's. The mingled aromas almost awoke her appetite, but her anxiety was too great for that.

No one appeared to notice the jangle of the bell as the door swung shut behind her. The large room was abuzz. Customers stood and waited their turns at the counter which ran down one side and across the back; more sat at the small tables to the right, where waiters in striped aprons hurried to and fro.

Rosabelle scanned the faces of the waiters and the counter assistants. The one face she wanted was missing. Perhaps he was working in the kitchens today. The shopmen were dashing in and out through a swinging door to the rear of the premises. Mr. Rufus might appear at any moment.

The bell jangled behind her, and she hastily moved forward into a gap at the back counter.

A harried assistant turned to her. "Yes, miss?"

"I'll take two of those and two of those," Rosabelle said, pointing at random. As he wrapped her purchases in a paper, she asked urgently, "Is Mr. Rufus here?"

His hands stilled, and he looked at her. "No, miss, he's at home in bed with an inflammation of the lungs. That'll

be ninepence, miss, if you please." Swiftly he completed
the wrapping.

Her head in a whirl, Rosabelle paid and took the neat
parcel he thrust at her. She had expected to hear "alive"
or "dead," not something in between. Before she could
think what to ask next, he was serving someone else.

It had not dawned on her that Mr. Rufus, so vital and
vigorous, might succumb slowly and painfully to his icy
wetting. Inflammation of the lungs! She had no experience of the malady, but she was sure she had heard of it
as frequently fatal. Was he getting proper care? Had he
seen a physician, or at least an apothecary? Was someone
looking after him, buying medicine for him, feeding him,
keeping him warm?

Her stomach clenched at the thought that he might be
lying alone and shivering in some squalid garret.

She had turned away from the counter, and the press
of customers had hustled her several steps farther toward
the door. Now she swung round, desperate to find out
more. Everyone was busy. If she stopped one of the rushing
waiters to ask Mr. Rufus's whereabouts and circumstances,
very likely he would not know or be willing to tell her. She
didn't know what to do.

"Miss Rosabelle!" It was Jackie. "You look ill, miss. Come
and sit down."

She let the boy usher her to a just vacated table. Sinking
into a chair, she said in a trembling voice, "I'm not ill, but
I just found out Mr. Rufus is. Jackie, do you know how bad
he is?"

"Pretty bad, I heard, miss, but the doctor says he has a
chance to pull through, being in general strong and
healthy."

"A chance? But at least he has seen a doctor. He is getting proper care?"

"I'm sure he is, miss, what with his ma and two sisters."

"Do you know where he lives, Jackie? I should like to enquire after him, to send a message."

"I dunno the exact direction, miss. It's one of them big houses in Russell Square. I can ask the number, or you c'd leave a message for Mr. Dibden to take home this evening."

"Mr. Dibden?" Rosabelle said, surprised.

Jackie gave her an odd look. "His pa. Mr. Rufus's. Most days he goes home 'bout six or. . . . Hi, miss, don't faint!"

The room whirled about Rosabelle's head. Mr. Rufus Dibden, of Russell Square, of Dibden's Pastry Cook's, caterers to the Lord Mayor of London! Why hadn't he told her?

Anger restored her enough to take the glass of water Jackie anxiously pressed upon her. A few sips enabled her to thank the worried lad with tolerable composure.

"Pray don't tell anyone I came," she added, rising.

"No, miss. D'you want me to find out that house number for you, miss?"

"No, thank you. I must go."

As Rosabelle reached the door, Jackie ran after her with her forgotten parcel. He opened the door and bowed her out.

With quick steps she crossed the pavement to where the carriage awaited her. "Home, Peters." She climbed into the gloomy interior and handed the paper of pastries to Mam'selle Fogarty. "Here, eat what you wish. I'm not hungry after all."

As the carriage moved off, Rosabelle cast a last, hurt glance through the window at the pastry cook's flourishing establishment. Mr. Rufus Dibden's deceit had cost them any chance of happiness. *Why hadn't he told her who he was?*

"Don't tell anyone I came," her own instruction to Jackie echoed in her head. Unnecessary, since he knew her only as Miss Rosabelle. He didn't know who she was— any more than Mr. Rufus Dibden did.

The realization shocked her. So certain of her own imagined superiority, she had let him believe she was a highborn lady. To a blue-blooded damsel, a wealthy trades-man's son was of no more account than a shop assistant. Rufus could only have stamped himself as a coxcomb had he asserted his higher status, and he was far too sensitive not to know it.

Rosabelle screwed her eyes shut to keep back the rising tears. It was all her fault. If only she had been honest with him from the first!

Had he known who she was, he could have sent a message warning her not to go to the Frost Fair on Friday. Then he would not have been on the wharf when the ice cracked. He would not have risked his life to rescue those rash fools who had ventured onto the river despite the plain signs of a thaw.

Had he known who she was, even if he had viewed the disaster, the prospect of their future happiness together might have held him back. Had her smug conceit made him so miserable he *wanted* to die?

By the time the carriage reached New Bond Street, Ros-abelle was so miserable *she* wanted to die.

As the carriage door opened and light fell on Rosabelle's face, Mam'selle Fogarty exclaimed, "You're ill, Miss Ros!"

"No," Rosabelle said wearily. "I have the headache a little."

"You go on up, dear, and I'll tell Madame you're not well."

Too downhearted to argue, Rosabelle dragged herself up the stairs and sank onto a sofa. A moment later her mother came in.

"What is the matter, *chérie?*"

Rosabelle buried her face in her hands. "Oh, *maman*, he is Rufus *Dibden*," she wept, "and he is dying, and it's all my fault!"

Under *maman's* gentle probing, the whole story came out. "So you see," Rosabelle finished, "if he dies, I'm to blame."

"Nay, lass," said her papa, who had come from the office in time to hear most of the tale, "dinna fash yoursel'. 'Men have died from time to time, and worms have eaten them, but not for love.' "

"*Zut alors,* Kenneth, this is not one of your most helpful quotations! Rosabelle, *chérie,* consider how you slight your *amant* in suggesting such a motive. Is it not possible that he rushed to the rescue because he is a brave and compassionate man, a true hero?"

"Oh, yes, *maman,* he is, he is. But he is still dying!"

"That remains to be seen. You were told he is very ill. Now it is up to you to give him a reason for living. If you are correct about his feelings . . ."

"Of course she's correct," said Papa indignantly. "Any man in his right mind must love my lovely lass."

"If you are correct, *chérie,*" *maman* repeated, "then knowing who you really are and that you are concerned for his health may be all the medicine the young man needs."

Rosabelle sprang up. "I'll write to him at once."

"For a young woman to correspond with a young man is *peu convenable*—not proper. You will not wish to offend his parents."

"Write from all of us," Papa suggested. " 'Mr. and Madame Yvette Macleod and Miss Rosabelle Macleod beg to enquire. . . .' That will tell who ye are, without much tiresome explanation. All the world knows of Madame Yvette."

Both his wife and his daughter kissed him, and his long face broke into a beam.

Madame returned below to a waiting client. Rosabelle and her father repaired to the office. The note was written, rewritten, folded, and sealed, and then Rosabelle despairingly remembered she didn't know the Dibdens' house number.

"The post man will know," said Papa. "I daresay they'll be getting enquiries by the dozen."

"Then, if he's too ill to read them himself, perhaps they

will not tell him about our note. Papa, let me take it myself!
I'll find out the number when I reach Russell Square."

"Your mama wouldna like it," he said, frowning. His face
cleared. "So I'll go wi' ye, and we'll no tell her till after."

They took a hackney. Rosabelle had never been to
Russell Square before. There was a garden in the centre
which must be beautiful in spring and summer, and the
houses were finer than many in Mayfair, especially those
on the west side. Among them, the Dibdens' betrayed itself
by the straw spread on the cobbles in front to deaden the
sound of hooves and wheels.

The sight banished Rosabelle's excitement. Now she felt
only dread.

A sombre footman opened the door. "The ladies aren't
receiving," he said.

"Oh, no, I wouldn't expect . . . ," Rosabelle stammered.
"Pray give this to . . . Oh, *pray* make sure *he* knows I enquired!"

"I'll give it to the mistress, miss." The footman gave her
a curious but kindly look. "And I'll say the young lady
brought it personal, but I can't promise Mr. Rufus'll be
told."

"How . . . how is he?"

"Desp'rate ill, miss, but not quite despaired of."

Rosabelle swung round blindly and buried her face in
her father's waistcoat.

His arms around her, he spoke over her head. "Tell your
mistress, laddie, that it might do Mr. Rufus some good to
hear what's in yon paper."

"Very good, sir." The footman bowed, and closed the
door as Mr. Macleod supported Rosabelle down the steps
and into the hackney.

On their return, *maman* shook her head reproachfully
and put Rosabelle straight to work.

"Be thankful you are not *en vérité* a young lady of leisure," she said, "with no occupation to keep you from

moping yourself into a decline. I have heard this morning
from several ladies already come up to London from the
country to order their gowns in plenty of time for the
Season. There is a great deal to be done."

Maman kept Rosabelle busy all day. Her misery receded
to a dull ache, always there in the background. She realized,
distantly but with gratitude, that everyone was particularly
kind and attentive to her, without being intrusive. Between
them, servants and employees had apparently put the clues
together and worked out more or less what was going on.

No news of Rufus Dibden arrived until the last delivery
of the twopenny post. The postman brought a formal note
written in a round, careful schoolgirl hand: Mr. and Mrs.
Dibden thanked Mr. and Mrs. Macleod and Miss Macleod
for their obliging communication. Mr. Rufus Dibden was
presently too ill to be informed of all the kind enquiries
about his health.

"He doesn't even know I care!" cried Rosabelle, deso-
late.

"Write again this evening," said her mother. "Jerry or
Philip may take it in the morning."

"Can't I . . . ?"

"No, *chérie*. To send by a footman instead of the post
gives sufficient particularity. To go yourself would be not
at all *comme il faut*. That sort of persistence will offend, or
give rise to contempt. Consider, to his family you are quite
unknown."

Her father gave her a wink. Later he whispered, "Your
mither's ay richt, but if we don't hear tomorrow that yon
lad's been told of your enquiry, I'll go mysel' the day after."

Rosabelle hugged him.

On Tuesday afternoon she was in the office, helping her
father prepare the *Journal de Modes* to be sent to the printer,
when Philip brought up the post. Papa flicked through
the small pile and handed one to her. He watched as she
slit the seal.

The note began like yesterday's. Mr. and Mrs. Dibden thanked the Macleods for their obliging enquiry after the health of their son. But below, in a hasty scrawl, Rosabelle read:

Dear Miss Macleod, I just told Mama that Dennis (our footman) told me you came yourself on Monday and Particlarly asked for poor Rufus to be told you had called and she said who? so I told her you are Madame Yvette's daughter (she knew at once who Madame Yvette is though I confess I did not) (you see I have been opening and answering all the letters as Mama is busy Nursing poor Rufus) She said she will mention your Name to him when next he wakes up. He is *very* ill. Your obedient servant (I hope that is the Right Ending, it looks a bit Odd) Sarah Dibden (Miss) (Rufus's sister) (younger) Oh dear, I hope you can make sense of this scribble I haven't time to rewrite it. SD.

Rosabelle had to turn the page to read the last part of this missive, which was squeezed in around the edge.

Finishing, she glanced back over it, her eye at once caught by the underlined word. "Papa, he is *very* ill."

"We knew that already, lass." He took the sheet from her and read it. " 'Twas written before he was told you had called. That'll set him well on the road to recovery."

"Suppose he's delirious?" Rosabelle fretted. "Or if he's told 'Miss Macleod,' it won't mean anything to him. He only knows me as Miss Rosabelle. Oh, Papa, how could I have been so dreadfully puffed-up, when I love him?"

" 'If thou remember'st not the slightest folly
" 'That ever love did make thee run into,
" 'Thou hast not lov'd.' "

Rosabelle sighed. "I must answer Miss Sarah's letter. She sounds a very amiable girl, don't you think? I'll mention about 'Miss Rosabelle,' just in case."

The next news did not arrive until Wednesday evening. Miss Sarah Dibden informed Rosabelle that Rufus had taken an immediate turn for the better on hearing her name, and she thought it was excessively romantic.

Rosabelle was elated. The very sound of her name had cured him!

Then it dawned on her that he might have recovered anyway, that his improvement did not necessarily mean he loved her. She struggled to be unselfishly glad as Sarah's daily letters chronicled his convalescence.

Monday dawned again, two weeks since the first day of the Frost Fair. Drawing back the curtains at her chamber window, Rosabelle saw a pair of pigeons on the sill. The male puffed out his neck feathers, iridescent green and purple, and cooed as he bowed and bobbed to his mate. It was Valentine's Day, Rosabelle recalled, the day when birds—and maids and men—chose their mates.

And she still had not received a single word from Rufus himself, either in his own hand or reported.

Though the twopenny post delivered on Sundays, yesterday had brought no note from Sarah. No doubt Rufus had at last recovered enough to warn his sister to drop the correspondence. He must be so disgusted with Rosabelle's behaviour, he couldn't bear even to hear her name. If he had ever loved her, she had killed his love.

A tap on the door. "Miss Ros, you awake?"

"Just a moment, Jerry!" She put on her dressing gown and went to open the door. "What is it?"

"The post came early, acos they're extra busy Valentine's Day." The footman handed her a letter.

For a moment hope flared; then she saw Sarah's writing. "Thank you." Better than nothing, unless it was to tell her this would be the last.

Her feet were almost as cold as her heart, so she went back to bed to open it. It was thicker than usual, she realized, her heart beginning to pound. She ripped open the seal.

Inside was a second sheet, folded in four. On the front, a pie was painted in watercolours, with a verse in shaky handwriting beneath it. Rosabelle's sight blurred, and it was a moment before she was able to read:

"Sing a song of sixpence,
"A pocket full of rye,
"Just one loving, hopeful heart,
"Baked in a pie."

Through the yellow paint, the outline of a heart was faintly visible. Half laughing, half crying, Rosabelle opened the first fold.

Another pie, with a slice missing. Above it flew a crimson heart with wings, surrounded by musical notes.

"When the pie is opened,
"Make sing this heart of mine!
"Tell me to expect a call
"From my dear Valentine."

Beneath was more wobbling writing, "Dreadful doggerel, bad as the Frost Fair ballads, but penned with love."

Maman made Rosabelle wait until eleven o'clock to call in Russell Square. She went, too, for propriety's sake, and Papa came along, saying, "Never too early to start discussing marriage settlements."

"Papa, you wouldn't!"

"Not until Mr. Dibden mentions the matter," he assured her with a smile.

"He'll be at his business."

But he wasn't. Mr. and Mrs. Dibden greeted the Macleods and presented their two daughters. Rosabelle heard scarcely a word. Rufus was not there in the drawing room with his family.

Mrs. Dibden nodded to the younger girl. Sarah took

Rosabelle up a pair of stairs, sighing on the way, "Oh, it is more romantic than a novel, I vow. And how very fortunate that today is Valentine's Day! Here she is," she announced dramatically, opening a door.

Bundled in rugs, Rufus lay on a sofa near the window. Rosabelle paused on the threshold, suddenly uncertain, shy as she had never felt with him before.

"Your face is thinner," they both said at the same time.

He grinned, and her shyness vanished. "We shall both have to live upon gingerbread and hot chocolate for a while," he said with a chuckle, "and perhaps the odd hot pie."

"Oh, Rufus!" she cried, and ran to him.

As she knelt by the sofa, he caught her hand and raised it to his pale, hollow cheek. "I was afraid you were only a midsummer night's dream," he said lovingly, "but when I regained my senses, I knew you couldn't be. After all, we met at the Frost Fair."

CUPID'S ARROW

by

Alice Holden

ONE

Sarah Buchanan squirmed on the blue silk seat of the straight-backed chair in the anteroom where Mr. Bertram, Lord Darnay's valet, had directed her to wait some twenty minutes before until his lordship was free to receive her. She had counted the stripes in the silver and blue French wallpaper and admired the finely turned legs of the rosewood table where a gentleman caller to Thornystone Manor could divest himself of his hat and cane. Mr. Bertram had draped Sarah's second best hooded cape across the antique table with more care than she believed the much worn black garment warranted.

Not able to sit still any longer, she rose and peered into the distorted glass of a gilt-edged mirror above the small table. She spent a minute tucking in the unruly dark brown whisps of hair that had escaped from their pins while confined under her hood. One more quick check of her appearance left her satisfied that she had tamed the offensive strands. She turned from the mirror and looked down at her bare hands. She had placed her black woollen gloves inside the pocket of her cape. Hadn't she read somewhere that real ladies kept their gloves on during an audience with a titled aristocrat? She wrinkled her nose. But not serviceable woollen gloves, she was sure.

She began to pace back and forth in the confined space and wondered if she should be having second thoughts about her impulsive visit. But Papa had died over a year ago, and still the village of Thorn did not have a doctor to replace him. No, she was doing the right thing. It was her duty to help the villagers by setting her plan before Lord Darnay, who had recently bought the estate from Baron Ramshaw. And, if she was successful, it would also mean that she could fulfill her own long-held dreams.

Suddenly contentious male voices exploded from the adjacent sitting room where Mr. Bertram had indicated that Sarah would be meeting with his lordship. The occupants apparently had entered from a door on the opposite side, bringing their argument with them.

Sarah sat down again, not wanting to be caught hovering. But the door to the anteroom did not open to admit her. The quarrel continued unabated, and she inadvertently became privy to the private debate.

"Damn it, Rollie, what possessed you to think I wanted company? I have work to do, and I need to get it done fast and be back in London in a matter of days. This is not a pleasure jaunt, you know. I want you and every one of your rackety friends away from here before noon." The male baritone was deep and beautifully forceful and so masculine that it touched a chord in Sarah's heart. She leaned toward the closed door wishing she could see through the panel and discover if the speaker was as grand as he sounded.

Had she been gifted with such powers, she would not have been disappointed, for Lucien Sutter, the Viscount Darnay, known to his friends as Luke, was a tall, exceedingly handsome man with black hair and fascinating hazel eyes of that odd shade that changes color with mood. At the moment, those eyes looked very dark indeed, but did not seem to intimidate his sandy-haired companion, Sir Roland Kirkwood.

"Not too many years ago those rackety creatures were your cohorts as well," replied Sir Roland blandly. "Luke, you have turned into a veritable sobersides. You just aren't fun anymore." He reached out to help his friend as he hobbled his final steps toward a man's oversized leather chair.

Lord Darnay swatted Sir Roland's hand aside, took the few steps, unassisted, and eased himself down onto the cushion.

"You have a warped memory, Rollie," he said. "I never was fun, but neither am I twenty-one anymore. Do you realize you are talking about things that happened nearly eight years ago?" He stretched a long leg in front of him and stared at his tightly bandaged ankle. He had stepped down from his carriage when he had arrived late yesterday afternoon, and his foot had twisted awkwardly, sending him down onto one knee. "Now look at that. How the deuce am I supposed to get around? I planned to survey every inch of the estate before returning to the City."

"I trust you are not blaming me for your clumsiness?" Roland said. He leaned one shoulder of his modest stature into the side of a large bookcase, crossed his ankles, and folded his arms over the lapels of his stylishly cut tan coat.

Luke knew he could not justifiably lay his unfortunate accident at Roland's door, but he intended to hold his friend responsible for everything else that had caused his own testy disposition.

"Why is Isabella Leighton here? I despise amorous females who throw themselves at men."

Roland smirked. "If I am not mistaken, it was not so long ago that you and she spent a night in a bed at my estate in Richmond."

"Nothing happened that night. I had just had a business deal go sour on me, had been drinking off and on since mid-afternoon, and was odiously foxed by midnight."

"And she battered down your door and attacked you," Roland said, grinning.

Luke gave him a fulminating glare, his hazel eyes glowing almost black. "All right, we were gropingly amorous for a time. But if you must know, I fell asleep. She was gone when I awoke in the morning, and I was still in my evening clothes."

Roland let out a loud whoop. "You can do better than that, my friend. Isabella is not a lady who needs protecting. We all know her morals. She isn't going to leave you alone, Luke. It is essential to Bella's pride to be the one to end an affair."

"Damn it, Roland, there was no affair, but think what you like. I still must have Isabella and those others gone before luncheon. I cannot function with partying going on around me. It's too distracting." He weighed his next words, but decided to say them anyway. "I hope when you and Jane are married, you will spend less time with this crowd."

"Come now, Luke, surely you don't intend to run my life once we are brothers-in-law, because I won't have it," Sir Roland said, straightening, his expansive smile fading. "We have been bosom beaus since we were in short coats. I think we know each other pretty well. I have bowed to your family's wishes and not offered for Jane until she turned eighteen; but I have not been with a woman since I fell in love with her, and I intend to be a faithful husband."

"I know you do, Rollie," Luke said, wishing he could recall his imprudent words. Jane was so innocent, and Rollie's friends were too sophisticated for her. But he had been preached at enough by his own family to know better than to be unfairly sermonizing to his old friend.

The door from the adjacent library opened, and Bertram came into the room. "Have you seen Miss Buchanan, yet, my lord?" the valet asked.

"Miss Buchanan? Oh, yes, the doctor's daughter. Where the devil did you stash her?" Luke asked.

Bertram looked toward the anteroom door. "Out there."

"You could have warned me," Luke muttered. He and Roland had had some loud moments. He hoped they had not been overheard.

The valet ignored the mumbled rebuke. "Should I show her in?"

"Give me a minute before you do, Bertram," Roland intervened. He walked to a handsome cherry desk between the large windows and pulled out the desk chair, sat down, and scratched a message across a sheet of stationery with a quill pen.

"Find a groom to ride to my Richmond estate and deliver this to the housekeeper there," he instructed Bertram as he handed him the paper.

He walked over to Luke. "I have alerted my staff to expect our little party late this afternoon. Now I better break the news to the others before they become too comfortable. Poor Isabella will be devastated."

"What made you invite her?" Luke asked, his irritation giving way to his curiosity.

"I didn't. She got wind of my plans and invited herself and young Havercole."

"I wondered what he was doing here when I was introduced to him last night, before I used my ankle as an excuse to make an early escape," Luke said.

Roland shrugged. "I couldn't very well tell Isabella not to come, even though I know you abhor her. It would have looked uncommonly strange. Not only is she the wife of one of our leading diplomats and received everywhere; she has always been included in our doings. As for Havercole, I know he's a loose screw, but his family is good Ton."

"I'm sorry if I came down hard on you, Rollie, but I am here on business, not pleasure. I want to meet with the bailiff and the staff and go over the books and tour the grounds. Guests would get in the way."

"I know. But you are mired so deep in business these days, I thought I might be able to surprise you with an impromptu house party. You rarely go into society these days. I miss your company, Luke."

"In a few weeks, you and Jane are to announce your betrothal at my mother's Valentine Ball," Luke said amiably. "Soon after, you will be wed and too busy sitting in Jane's pocket to be concerned about me, Rollie."

"Gad, Luke, you don't really believe I intend letting your sister lead me around by the nose," Roland said dryly, as Luke laughed, but he was clearly mollified and left the room with a good-natured grin on his face.

Luke turned to his valet. "Show Miss Buchanan in, Bertram, and then deliver Sir Roland's note to the stables."

A moment later, Bertram ushered in the most beautiful woman Luke had ever seen. He forgot Roland, Jane, Isabella, and every concern that weighed on his mind.

Using the arms of the chair for leverage, Luke pulled himself erect, favoring his injured leg. She was slim and graceful, of medium height, not too tall, not too short, perfectly formed, and all woman. Her hair was a rich dark brown, and her large eyes were a deep mahogany. So sudden was his desire to possess her that Luke was tempted to search the room for Cupid to see if the chubby Eros had unleashed an arrow into his heart, but to do so would have forced him to take his eyes from the vision before him. He could not bring himself to look away and stop drinking her in.

He dispensed with the obligatory greetings in short order and apologized for receiving her in his carpet slippers.

"I twisted my ankle in a careless misstep," he said with a self-deprecating grin.

"I am sorry to find you indisposed, my lord. Perhaps I should come back at another more propitious time," Miss Buchanan offered. Her voice was angelic, sweet and soft.

His smile sensual, Luke said, "I wouldn't think of it, ma'am. I would be the worst kind of clunch if I sent you packing when you have been so patient."

Sarah found her heart was suddenly unmanageable. He was so magnificent that she wondered why some enterprising young woman had not captured him long ago.

Luke motioned her to a comfortable chair directly opposite his, which Bertram had earlier placed in a position conducive to conversation, and eased himself once again down into his own lounger.

Her clear, bright eyes reflected the wonder Luke himself felt. Emotional currents crackled between them. He sensed that she could not resist him any more than he could resist her. Who would have guessed that he would find himself instantly in love? But civilized people did not fall into each other's arms and lock lips without some preamble.

"So, Miss Buchanan, you are seeking a replacement doctor for the position vacated by your father's death, is that correct?"

Sarah was relieved to hear him get down to business, for if she were allowed to gaze at him much longer without speech, she would be simpering.

"I hope to convince you, my lord, to fall in with a plan of mine," she said, matching his efficient tone. "Let me explain. You have the living to dispense for a vicar for the church. I would like you to consider setting up a like arrangement for a doctor."

Lord Darnay's face became attentive. "Are you asking me to finance a physician on a permanent basis the way I do a churchman?"

"Not quite. My late father was the village doctor for thirty years. Baron Ramshaw made futile inquiries for some months in hopes of filling the vacancy left by his death, but he became engrossed with his own troubles and abandoned the project when his problems became overwhelming. But I think," she said, "that securing a doctor for a poky little village like ours will be impossible unless we can offer an incentive."

"Yes, I can see how that could be true," Luke said, stroking his chin. "What sort of incentive do you have in mind?"

"A rent-free house," she replied. "What I would like you to do, my lord, is to buy my house and offer it as a permanent residence for the use of a doctor as long as he maintains his practice in the village. I would leave the books and instruments in my father's office and some of the furnishings for the use of the new physician." Sarah was suddenly embarrassed by her own audacity and looked up at him through lowered lids.

Luke pursed his lips, feigning deep thought, for he had already made up his mind that he would give her whatever she wanted, even if it were the moon.

"Interesting concept, Miss Buchanan," he said. "I think you are on to something. Of course, I would have to examine your house to ascertain a fair market value."

Sarah nodded, unable to believe that it had all been so simple. "You will find the house in good repair, my lord," she assured him.

"And where do you plan to relocate after I buy the house?" he asked. Was it possible that she might be betrothed and planning to wed?

But she quickly eliminated his dread. "Well," she said, "I have my eye on a snug little cottage at the edge of the woods. It is on your land, Lord Darnay, but the forester who lived there until a few months ago was old and decided to give up gamekeeping and moved in with his son in the village. Baron Ramshaw never replaced him. I would be pleased to lease the cottage from you for my aunt and myself, if you are willing, my lord."

"I can see no impediment to such an arrangement," Luke said. "Your aunt lives with you?" he asked to prolong her stay, for she had edged a little forward in the chair as if she were preparing to rise.

"Yes," she said, sitting back again. "I have only a vague

memory of my mother, who died when I was very young. Mrs. Matilda Drayton, my father's sister, was widowed near the same time and came to live with us. My aunt and I have plans to travel once the house is sold . . . to you, I hope, my lord." She gave him an elfin grin that caused his heart to flutter like that of a lovesick schoolboy.

"You can count on my buying your property, Miss Buchanan, as well as helping to procure a physician. I like your sensible plan. So you plan to travel," he said, as a means of detaining her further.

"Yes, I have never gone more than a few miles from the village. I would like to see London first, I think. Then, perhaps, someday my aunt and I can travel to Paris and Rome, as well."

With the exception of her few brief encounters with Baron Ramshaw, Sarah had never conversed with a titled gentleman before. She had fallen for Lord Darnay with a love sudden and sweet and impossible. Though she was all but certain that his heart spun with hers, rank and fortune determined relationships in his world.

Both of them looked up when Sir Roland came through the anteroom door, which Bertram had earlier left ajar in the interest of propriety.

Luke introduced the two. "Your servant, Miss Buchanan," Roland said with a proper bow. He sized her up as pretty enough to carry on a flirtation with, but definitely not one of them, for hadn't Luke mentioned that she was a doctor's daughter?

"Miss Buchanan has solicited my assistance in finding a much needed replacement for her late father, who was the village doctor," Luke said, corroborating Roland's recollection.

Roland put his hands behind his back and rocked back on the heels of his shiny Hessians. "No offense, Miss Buchanan, but from what I have seen of your backwoods village, you have your work cut out for you. No young man with any ambition is going to want to bury himself here."

"Ordinarily I would agree with you, sir. But Lord Darnay has promised to purchase my house and allow the doctor to live in it gratis as long as he remains in Thorn. For a young man without means just starting in practice that could prove to be quite an irresistible carrot."

Roland raised his sandy eyebrows fractionally and turned to Luke. "I thought you bought Thornystone as an investment and didn't mean to keep it long. How do you know the new owner will want to finance a doctor in perpetuity?"

Obviously daunted by Roland's observation, Miss Buchanan looked at Luke searchingly. But Luke had no intention of allowing any sort of wedge to be driven between him and this angel.

"My plans for the estate are unsettled, Sir Roland," he said smoothly, "but my covenant with Miss Buchanan is unbreakable. Her house will be mine, and I shall endow it to the village and set up a trust to insure that there will always be funds to maintain it as a doctor's residence."

"How splendid and generous, my lord," Miss Buchanan said with such adoration in her brown eyes that Luke almost thanked Roland for compelling him into yet another involuntary decree. Since his little beauty's arrival, he had abandoned all business sanity and, without his usual calm, cool circumspection, had made long-term financial decisions for no better reason than to see a woman's eyes light up. And it did not bother him one bit.

Sarah decided, much as she would like to, she could linger no longer. She rose to leave, and Luke stood up with her, regretting that he would have to let her go.

"I am exceedingly grateful to you, my lord," she said. "I look forward to receiving you at my house when your ankle has mended, so you may make your appraisal and set a price."

"Shall we say tomorrow at two?" Luke said, knowing he could not let a day pass without seeing her again.

"Why, yes, my lord, if you feel up to it. I very much want to make you known to my aunt," she replied. Her heart lifted, for she did not know how she would have borne not seeing him again for several days while his foot improved.

Sarah clutched her reticule and made a semblance of a curtsy to Luke as she said goodbye, but failed to offer her hand to him. He was crushed, for he had been anticipating pressing his lips to her ungloved skin.

"Sir Roland, would you escort Miss Buchanan to her conveyance," he said, masking his disappointment at not being able to touch her. "Bertram has not returned from executing your errand to the stables, and I am unable to manage the front steps."

Sir Roland said, "My pleasure." He followed Sarah into the anteroom and placed her cloak over the shoulders of her navy woollen gown, which was raised modestly just to the tops of her black boots. She retrieved her gloves from a pocket and pulled them onto her hands.

The two made their way to the entrance hall and stepped through the front door onto the portico. Sarah clutched her hood close against the wind. Her gig was parked at the edge of the brick-paved drive with her horse tied to a decorative iron post.

"I say, Miss Buchanan," Sir Roland said, "surely you did not drive yourself."

Sarah laughed. "How else would I have gotten here? If it were a fair summer's day, I might have walked the mile, even though it is all uphill from the village; but we are still in January, and there is a brisk wind today."

"But . . ." He seemed at a loss for words. "I suppose rules here for females are more lax than in the City."

Sarah caught his meaning. Even though her aunt had assured her that being a lady had less to do with the accident of birth and more to do with kindness and goodness, the upperclasses to which Sir Roland and Lord Darnay belonged did not subscribe to such a loose interpretation.

But she knew who she was and what she was, and she saw no reason to justify her habits to this aristocrat who had nothing better to do than to plan each day's pleasures.

Sir Roland helped her onto the box, untied the horse for her, and handed her the reins. Before she set the horse in motion, Sarah said, "Sir, you mentioned that his lordship might sell Thornystone. Why would he have bought the estate in the first place if that was his intention?"

"Lucien Sutter is an astute businessman. He acquired the estate for a song because the baron had dug himself into a ponderous financial hole. His lordship will make the improvements he deems necessary, fix things so the estate pays again, and sell Thornystone sometime in the future for a nice profit."

Sarah looked down at him from her perch with a sinking feeling. "He is not going to do that with my house, is he?"

"Oh, no," Sir Roland said. "Lord Darnay's word is as good as gold. Whatever he promised you, Miss Buchanan, you can accept as fact. Regardless of his plans for Thornystone, he will buy your house for a doctor's residence and endow it, so your village will always be able to entice a physician here to Thorn."

Sarah gave him a revitalized smile before snapping the reins and clattering down the drive.

Walking back toward the house, Roland was more than a little surprised that Luke went along with Miss Buchanan's scheme. His friend was a hard-nosed businessman, not famous for being overly altruistic. He was nearly to the porch when he noticed Lady Isabella Leighton framed in the doorway. He took the steps two at a time. "Gad, Bella, shut the door. It's the middle of winter," he said, brushing past her.

Obeying him, and with the door closed, she chafed her

bare arms and said, "I was too intrigued by the tableau on the drive to notice the chill. Coming from the breakfast parlor, I caught a glimpse of you through the window. I thought I would get a better look from the doorway. Who is she, Rollie?"

"A girl from the village," he replied.

"Lud, you did not waste a moment, did you? Whatever would dear Jane say to know you are still taking lightskirts to your bed?" Her assumption put an idea into Roland's head.

"Oh, the young woman was not here for me. She was with Luke," he said, hoping Isabella would draw an improper conclusion. He would be doing Luke a favor if he got Bella off his back.

The blond vixen did not disappoint him. Jealousy leapt into her blue eyes. "I never dreamed that Luke found pleasure in bed with the lower orders. It seems he has not only a disgustingly plebian penchant for business, but for his women as well."

"You know Luke. He thrives on doing the unconventional," Roland said nonchalantly.

Isabella moved the cashmere shawl she carried draped over a shapely arm onto her shoulders. The fashionable, low-cut yellow satin gown set off her lush figure quite nicely for admiring male eyes, but was hardly the dress for a cold winter's day. She wrapped the embroidered shawl tightly around her full breasts.

"Just what does dear Lord Darnay think he is doing throwing us out?" she asked. "I do not appreciate having to make two tedious carriage trips within a day of each other."

"Luke is not giving us the heave-ho, Isabella. It is all my fault," Roland said, taking the blame onto himself. "I should have consulted him before I foisted seven ladies and gentlemen on him. Luke is going to be up to his ears in business. He wouldn't be able to play cards or set up a riding party or play the host."

"So we are to get out of his way and remove to your Richmond house," Isabella said.

"Exactly," he confirmed, ignoring her snideness. "Are you packed? I would like to leave in an hour."

"When I came down to breakfast, my maid had nearly finished filling my cases, and from the general conversations at table while we ate, I think everyone is ready to leave. Roland, don't think any of us are reluctant to put paid to this place. You would think with this battalion of servants one could expect better service."

"Yes, one would think so." Sir Roland maintained a serious mien until Isabella had flounced a safe distance down the hall. Only then did he allow a cheeky smile to animate his moderately handsome features.

TWO

Sarah stepped down from the box of the rig onto the drive beside the stone house and handed the reins to Jem, a sturdy youngster who worked for her as a stableboy and odd-job lad. She exchanged some light banter with the boy before he led the horse to the small gray barn behind the house. Unlatching the gate, she walked through the dormant garden to the back entrance, climbed the three stone steps, and opened the door into the spotless kitchen, the smell of baking bread assailing her nostrils.

"Aunt Matilda, what are you doing working in here?" Sarah asked, pulling a small brown paper parcel tied with twine from the pocket of her cape and setting it on the table. "Here is the thread you wanted," she said. She removed her cape and hooked the long garment over a wall peg.

The short, plump woman in her late fifties, her brown hair flecked with gray, slipped a loaf pan from the oven and placed the freshly baked bread onto the table. She hung up the pot holder before speaking. "Mrs. Goodings took a turn for the worse, and Jilly was called home to attend to her mother. I finished the baking she started before she left."

"Poor Mrs. Goodings," Sarah said, clicking her tongue against her teeth. "She has suffered for so long. If the end is near, I would not be surprised if Jilly and Ben Briggs might decide to wed immediately to avoid having to wait a year until Jilly was out of mourning."

"That would mean we would lose Jilly," Matilda said. "What would we do then? Not many girls are willing to work for slim wages these days. I am afraid we will not find another as industrious as she."

Sarah's eyes twinkled, anticipating the shock she was about to unleash on her unsuspecting aunt. "We shall miss Jilly, of course," she said, "but haven't we proven this past year that women can do perfectly well on their own?"

"Humph," Matilda grumbled. "I am not at all certain I want to do perfectly well on my own, especially in this big house."

"We might not have to worry about this house much longer. Before long we just might be in a cozy cottage." Sarah laughed and seized her aunt's hands in hers and performed a gay little jig.

"What have you been up to, Sarah Buchanan?" her aunt said, suspicious of the radiant smile illuminating her niece's face. "Oh, Sarah, tell me you didn't?" She disengaged her hands and fell back onto the kitchen settle, fanning herself with her oversized apron. "I wondered what had kept you. It shouldn't have taken so long to buy a few spools of thread."

Sarah sat down next to her aunt on the hard bench. "Auntie, Lord Darnay is so kind, and very tall and terribly handsome with hair as dark as a blackbird's wing," she gushed. "He said yes. Not only will he buy the house, but he is going to help to find a doctor for the village. Moreover, he promised me the let of the cottage at the edge of the woods that we have had our eyes on."

"Lud, child, you sound positively smitten with him. I do wish you would be less impulsive. You get an idea into your head, and before I even have a chance to digest it, you are off and running."

"When I heard at the dry goods store that his lordship

was in residence, I felt I should seize the moment. He might have escaped back to London if I had procrastinated," Sarah said. "Who knows when I would again have had an opportunity to speak with him?"

Matilda grasped Sarah's chin and looked deep into her niece's bemused eyes. "I hope you acted in a proper manner. You didn't give him notions that your virtue was not all that it should be?"

Sarah giggled. "I'm afraid even if Lord Darnay meant to ravish me, he would have been at a decided disadvantage, for he has sprained his ankle. I would have been able to outdistance him easily if he had attempted to chase me."

"I do not appreciate your levity, Sarah," Matilda said, pausing for effect. "This is a serious matter. Your reputation could be in question. You know how people talk."

To placate her aunt, Sarah gave her a glossed-over account of her visit. At the end, Matilda had nothing to say about his lordship's conduct, but showed concern for Sarah's garments. "You should have come home and changed into your Sunday clothes," she said. "The Quality sets great store in dressing fashionably."

"Auntie dear, haven't you told me since I was little more than a toddler that those gildings are not what makes a lady, but what is in here," Sarah said, tapping her chest in the vicinity of her heart.

"And rightly so. But, unfortunately, the aristocracy have their own queer ideas of what is proper."

Sarah looked pensive. "There is no doubt that his lordship is very different from the young men of the village."

"Of course he is. Some of the village boys are very nice, but they have rustic manners. Your father was an educated man, and your mother the daughter of a learned clergyman. You inherited their cultured ways. But I have often despaired because there is no man in Thorn worthy of you."

Sarah gave the older woman a considering look. "Yet,

Aunt Mattie, if I had fallen in love with Simon Jones or
Peter or Geoffrey, each of whom showed an interest in me,
I would have gladly accepted his suit, no matter how rustic
he was. But I didn't fall in love, and each of them married
one of my friends instead. So now here I am on the shelf
at four-and-twenty."

Matilda patted Sarah's hand. "I did not dream you
would be content with one of those young men. You were
always so quick to dismiss them. Yet thinking back, I must
admit that Peter was a good prospect. He has made something of the farm his father left him. He of all the others
I would have advised you to keep dangling until you were
absolutely sure of your feelings. After all, love does not
happen suddenly, Sarah, it has to grow."

Grow? Sarah chewed on her aunt's word. She had top-
pled head over heels in love with Lord Darnay in one
glance. Was her love for the viscount, then, just an illusion?
Tomorrow she would see him again and put to the test
her sudden passion.

Reminded of his impending visit, she said, "Lord Darnay is to call tomorrow afternoon to inspect the house."

Matilda's brows knit in consternation, and she forgot
Sarah's lost loves. "Tomorrow? But with Jilly away who will
answer the door and serve the tea? What will his lordship
think of us if we cannot produce even a single servant?"
She worried her lower lip.

Sarah covered her aunt's fidgeting fingers with her own
calm hand. "It will be fine, Aunt Matilda. I will show his
lordship through the house and answer all his questions
about what stays and what goes and then serve the tea.
Have you thought of anything else you want to keep in
the way of furniture other than the things we have already
decided on?"

"No, dear. The cottage is so much smaller than this
house. We must be very selective."

"I'll make a final inventory this afternoon to be cer-

tain," Sarah said. "I don't suppose Jilly baked any tea cakes
yesterday that I can serve to his lordship?"

Her aunt shook her head. "I could fetch something
from the confectioner's," she offered.

Rising from the settle, Sarah said, "No, we need not go
to the added expense. There are still some walnuts in the
larder. I'll bake a pan of those little nut cakes that everyone
likes so much."

Recalling Sarah's verve when speaking earlier about the
lord of the Manor, and her niece's unexpected reflections
on old beaus, Matilda grasped her hand and held Sarah
beside her. "Lord Darnay is way above us in station, child.
Men in his class don't marry doctors' daughters."

"Ninny, I know that! Who said anything about marriage?
It is just that he has a magnetic personality, and every
woman who meets him must dream a little. You'll see."

Sarah removed a pad and pencil from a kitchen cupboard
drawer, gave her aunt an impertinent wink to cover her
deep feelings for Lucien Sutter, and set off to take inventory
of the furniture that would be sold with the house.

Sarah opened the door to Lord Darnay at exactly two
the following afternoon, showed his lordship into the parlor, and made the appropriate introductions between him
and her aunt. He was elegant in the browns and tans and
tweeds of expensive, but casual, country clothes.

Limping to a straight-backed chair, he waited politely
for Sarah to sit down beside her aunt on the alpaca sofa
before he eased himself into the chair.

For a few minutes the conversation centered on his injury and progressed to the mildness of the day, but when
her aunt Matilda would have sent Sarah to the kitchen to
fetch a tea tray and the cakes she had baked, Lord Darnay
put up a staying hand.

"Ladies," he said, "as you can see I am still somewhat

hobbled. If you will agree, I would like to call my valet inside to appraise the house for me. He will be able to crawl into the attic and check out the cellar as well as go through the lower and upper rooms."

Sarah nodded her assent. "Yes, of course, my lord, that will be satisfactory. I have compiled a list of furniture which I am including with the house."

"I'll call my man," Luke said and rose from the chair, stepped into the small vestibule adjoining the parlor, and opened the front door. Bertram stood outside holding his and Lord Darnay's mounts. Luke motioned to his valet, who looped the horses' reins on two nearby bushes and made for the stone house.

Once inside, Bertram followed Luke into the parlor. "You remember Miss Buchanan, Bertram, and this is her aunt, Mrs. Drayton. If you would be so kind as to point Bertram in the right direction, Mrs. Drayton, I'm sure he will be able to find his way."

Matilda had been impressed with Lord Darnay's easy friendliness and warm smile. She could now understand how Sarah had been so completely charmed by him. His voice was soft, yet she had the feeling that he was used to being obeyed without question. His manservant was now looking at Matilda for instructions, but before she could speak, Sarah said, "I would be happy to show Mr. Bertram around."

"Actually, Miss Buchanan," his lordship interjected, "I would be pleased if you would show me the grounds." He smiled divertingly. "While climbing stairs is tedious, I do quite well on level ground and need to fix a value on the external property."

Sarah's heart soared at the thought of being alone with him. She removed a list from her dress pocket and handed it to the valet. "These are the pieces, room by room, which will remain, if you agree, my lord," she said, looking back at Lord Darnay.

"See if you can put a price on the furniture, Bertram," he said. "If not, I will get a dealer to come down from London later."

The valet took a pad similar to the one Sarah had used the previous day for her tally from his coat pocket and went off in the direction that Mrs. Drayton had pointed out as leading to the stairs to the upper floor and attic.

Outside, Sarah adjusted her light shawl on her shoulders. "What a lovely day," she said, and began to comment on her property. She was keenly aware that Lord Darnay's eyes rarely left her face, exhibiting little interest in the outer buildings as she named them. When she led him behind the barn out of sight of the house to show him the large garden where she grew summer vegetables with Jem's help, he put his hands on her shoulders and turned her to face him.

"I want you to come to London with me," he said, looking down at her with a smile that would melt stone.

The unexpected statement threw her into a fluster. "London? Me? I couldn't. How? Oh, no, my lord, no, definitely no."

His dazzling smile ameliorated into an amused grin. "Hear me out. I am not suggesting anything improper. You told me that your dream was to visit the metropolis. I want to show you the sights."

"Yes, but—" As she began to interrupt, he put a finger to her lips.

"Sarah, my cousin Mary Westlock, who is nearly sixty, lives with me, and with your aunt there as well, you would be adequately chaperoned."

"Still, my lord, yours is a bachelor establishment. I do not know all the nuances of polite society, but I think there would be raised eyebrows at my stopping in your home."

She stared down at the tips of her black boots, which peeked from under the hem of her gray woollen dress.

He said very quietly, "Look at me, Sarah." She raised her brown eyes and met his, which looked emerald green in the full light.

"Who would have dreamed that at one glance you and I would have fallen victim to Cupid's arrow? But it happened. I don't want to leave you when I have just found you, but I planned to stay at Thornystone for only four days. My business is in London, and I must return there. Come with me," he urged. "There will be no disapprobation heaped on you if you put up at my town house. I promise you I will protect your good name."

Sarah shook her head slowly from side to side, although her heart was so full of him that she knew that if he really pressed, she would go with him to the ends of the earth.

His voice took on a rigid edge. "Are you denying the love that I can read all over your face?"

"No," she said with lack of guile. "But I need time to sort out my feelings. I don't even know how one whose emotions have become so thoroughly engaged in so short a time is supposed to behave."

His expression softened. "My dear, you have stolen my heart completely, and I know that I want you; but I can see how the suddenness of these strong emotions might disconcert you. Yet I beg you, give us a chance to become acquainted. Come to London where you and I can spend time together and learn to know each other."

Luke ran an ungloved hand down her cheek. Sarah leaned into his palm. How could a mere mortal oppose Cupid's arrow?

"While I am excited by the idea of seeing London for the first time, particularly with you, my lord, I am not at all certain that my aunt will be persuaded that remaining under your roof would be appropriate for an unmarried female."

"Leave your aunt to me. Just follow my lead, and do not weaken," he said with a faint grin. "Now, do you think you could call me Luke? I fear I lack the proper respect for titles. In business I am known as Lucien Sutter, not Lord Darnay, much to the chagrin of my parents."

Sarah's silvery laugh rippled through the country air. "It would be fine with me, but I think Aunt Matilda would fall into a decline if I addressed you by your nickname. Perhaps, it would be more prudent for me to confine the familiarity to the times when we are alone."

He laughed heartily and made to reach for her, but shoved his hands behind his back. He looked down at her with longing. He would have to keep his lips from this enchanting woman's and his hands from her exquisite form and court her with the respect he would a lady of the Ton. It would be an ultimate exercise in self-control, for he wanted to snatch her into his arms badly and do all kinds of deliciously improper things to her, but his patience would be rewarded if she came to him in the end of her own free will and without pressure from him. Then, he would have the rest of his life to make love to her.

Back at the house, Mrs. Drayton was shocked when the trip to London was first presented to her. But Luke was as good as his word.

"Ma'am," he said, "Miss Buchanan will need to be in London to work out the details of the sale of the house and the setting up of the endowment with my solicitor. Also, I know next to nothing about physicians. I am sure she can be of help in selecting the most skilled candidate and the one best suited to being a country doctor. If you do not wish to lodge with me, then, do you have someone with whom you can stay?" He already knew the answer to his question, before she shook her head.

"Then, of course, you must allow me to offer you my

hospitality," he said. "I have an unexceptionable female cousin much of an age with you who lives with me and runs my household. You would not have to lift a finger, simply enjoy yourself, for there are two maids of all work, a butler and a cook and, of course, Mr. Bertram." He inclined his head toward the valet, who sat in a chair by the door, attempting to melt in with his surroundings and feeling very visible.

"Mrs. Drayton insisted I wait inside," Bertram said to explain his unorthodox presence in the parlor where he sat as if he were an invited guest.

Luke's mouth quirked briefly at his correct valet's discomfort, but retained its staid mode while he continued to address Mrs. Drayton.

"I have a close friend in Lady Cheney, who married above her station and is a comfortable person, not high-in-the-instep, who will take you up. I think, ma'am, you will be pleased to know her. She will see that you are entertained royally. And you would, of course, have the companionship of Mary Westlock, my cousin."

Luke could see the older woman's reluctance crumbling at the goodies he was offering.

"Two weeks or perhaps a little more?" Luke suggested. "Miss Buchanan tells me she has long yearned to see the City."

Matilda looked at her niece, sitting beside her. Sarah nodded her concurrence. "Well, two weeks or so, then," Matilda conceded.

"Good!" Luke shot back. "Then, it is settled. When can you be ready to leave?"

Matilda wrung her hands. "There is so much to do. We would need at least a month to get ready."

"Ah, but, dear lady, I must leave in three days," Luke said.

"Three days!"

"I'm afraid so, ma'am." He waited.

"We can be ready by then, Auntie," Sarah said, heading into the kitchen. "We must not inconvenience his lordship."

"No, I suppose not," Mrs. Drayton said tentatively. "But . . ."

"Let's say Saturday, then. My traveling coach will take you up at eight o'clock in the morning."

In the kitchen, laughter bubbled inside Sarah as she prepared the tea and arranged the nut cakes on a platter to take back to the parlor. Luke knew how to seize the advantage. But, then, Sir Roland had said that this intriguing man was a highly successful businessman. Lucien Sutter had not reached that status by being a slow top.

THREE

Luke was much in evidence at the stone house during the next three days. His need to be near to Sarah was so great that in spite of being immersed in every facet of the workings of Thornystone Manor, he still found time each day to spend with her.

Jem had spread the news of the pact Sarah had made with Lord Darnay to entice a village doctor to Thorn. Although most of her neighbors had never been to the City, it did not keep a few from offering her advice on how to dicker with a London solicitor, nor did it inhibit some others from warning both her and her aunt about the perils of the wicked City. Most, however, were kind souls who came to tender their good wishes for a successful trip. A good number of these people had known Sarah since she was born.

How their eyes would have widened if she had confessed her true relationship with Luke, Sarah thought, as the young aristocrat sat in her kitchen the day before their scheduled departure, chatting with her. She was preparing the food for the hamper that would travel with them inside the carriage, a necessity, for there would be no inns available on their route for the midday meal.

Sarah rolled the dough for meat pies, cut the pastry into triangles, added the filling, and sealed the edges with deft motions. Watching her with warmth in his eyes, Luke observed, "You really enjoy cooking, don't you?"

"Yes," she said in her unaffected manner. "I truly do. Jilly, whom I told you about, and I usually share the kitchen chores, with Aunt Matilda pitching in when needed. But my aunt would rather do the sewing. She makes all of our clothes."

Luke did not comment. He found Sarah's dresses neither good nor bad, but different, yet somehow flattering to her. Had he thought to ask, he would have discovered that Matilda Drayton sewed a fine seam and that the economy was in the number of garments and not the quality of the cloth. But both women dressed to suit themselves and their country life-style.

Luke leaned over and pinched a bit of the meat mixture from Sarah's mixing bowl. He savored the taste of the filling and licked his fingers, something he had not done since he was a little boy.

"This is delicious," he said.

"Thank you, my lord," Sarah answered, dropping a playful curtsy. "I often thought that if I ever needed to seek a situation, I would go for a cook rather than a governess."

"Wise girl. I still recall how abominably my mother treated my sister Jane's governess, but the countess is afraid to wound the chef's sensibilities, for she is in a constant state of trepidation that he will give notice just when she has an important dinner party planned."

Sarah was not quite sure if Luke was joking. His mother could not really be so unkind and shallow, but she did not dare ask.

"I don't think Jilly is coming back, so I'll be doing all of the cooking soon," she said. "But once Auntie and I remove to the cottage, we can cope easily with the inside chores. I will keep Jem, though, for those inevitable odd jobs which are best handled by a male."

"You won't have to cook or do housework for a while," he assured her. "I sent Bertram ahead to warn my cousin Mary and allow her time to prepare for your visit. Cook will draw up plans for the daily meals, and the maids will keep your rooms in order."

"My, I never had a whole day completely free of work before," Sarah said.

Luke wondered how he would manage if he had to do all the menial tasks left to his male employees. He decided he had no intention of testing himself on that score. There was a lot to be said for having money. Which reminded him. . . .

"I wish you would accept the bank draft for the sale of your house, Sarah," he said.

"No, Luke, we have been over this before. Not until we definitely secure a doctor do I want to be paid. I would feel that I was cheating you if no physician agreed to set up his practice and live here."

"Rest assured, we will find someone," he said.

She gave him a wily grin. "When we do, I will accept the money."

"Stubborn woman," he said lightly as he reluctantly rose from the kitchen chair where he had been sitting for the past hour. He no longer limped. Sarah slipped an arm through his and walked to the door with him. His heart filled with love for her, but he dared do no more than press a kiss into her floured palm.

On Saturday morning, Luke's carriage arrived promptly at eight. The luggage was strapped to the boot, and the ladies joined Luke inside the plush interior. The groom sat beside the coachman on the box.

Sarah found that even a modern coach with the latest innovations was not immune to the ruts and washboard roads. There was much jostling and holding on to the seat. But when at last the driver turned onto a smooth road, he sprang the horses and flew over the countryside with its fallow fields and winter-barren trees.

Before long Mrs. Drayton curled into a corner of the coach. Her eyes closed, and she soon snored softly.

Luke patted the seat beside him. Sarah moved across the aisle and sat next to him. The two spoke in muted tones, their heads close together.

Occasionally, Matilda awoke and listened to their conversation while feigning sleep. She heard the familiar use of first names and the tenderness of tone. Forgotten was her warning to her niece that Lord Darnay was of the privileged class and far above Sarah's touch. Matilda's waking dreams conjured up a scene where the earl's son proposed to her beautiful niece, and she and Sarah were launched into a fabulous social life where the two of them moved in the best circles.

At dusk, the coach pulled up to Lord Darnay's town house in Berkeley Square. The door to the house was thrust open, and a tall man in the livery of a butler came hurrying down the steps. He opened the carriage door, set the steps in place, and handed down the ladies. When Luke disembarked, he said, "Welcome home, sir."

"Thank you, Billings," Luke replied, introducing his guests to the servant, who bowed politely before turning and assisting the groom with the luggage.

Mary Westlock waited in the vestibule, clasping her restless hands before her. She was a timid woman, and the prospect of entertaining house guests for the first time at the Berkeley Square residence had caused her to feel almost faint with nerves. But her fears were soon eased, for she found that Mrs. Drayton was unassuming, and Miss Buchanan was as pleasant as she was pretty.

Two girls in their late teens came down the hall dressed in dark frocks and spotless aprons.

"Since Lord Darnay has informed me that you were not bringing your own maids, I took the liberty of assigning Mollie to look after you, Miss Buchanan, and Chloe for you, Mrs. Drayton," Miss Westlock said, explaining the girls' presence.

Neither Sarah nor Matilda had ever had a personal maid before. But the well-trained young women escorted their respective ladies to their bedrooms without overt curiosity, helped them unpack, and made them comfortable in the unfamiliar surroundings.

In the drawing room after dinner, Luke read the *London Times* while Miss Westlock embroidered a pillowcase. Sarah and Matilda sat on a sofa paging through a picture book with drawings of London landmarks which Luke had given them.

"Look through this," he had said, "for attractions that you might want to visit."

After a time, Miss Westlock stifled a yawn and announced that she was retiring, and Matilda decided she would do the same.

Sarah kissed her aunt's cheek and thanked Mary for her hospitality.

As soon as the older women were gone, Luke put down his newspaper. "I must go to my office for a few hours in the morning, but I am freeing the afternoon to be with you."

Since Lady Cheney had sent word that she would like Mary Westlock and Matilda to spend the afternoon with her, Luke and Sarah would be alone. The dowager duchess had been sympathetic to Luke's plight when she had read the letter that Luke had entrusted to Bertram and had agreed to help him by keeping Luke's cousin and Sarah's aunt entertained. She, herself, a shopkeeper's daughter, had captured her duke in a love match. But after twenty years, her inglorious beginnings had receded into the background, and her place in the Ton was no longer an issue.

"There are so many choices in this book," Sarah said, "but could we go to see the Elgin Marbles which have just recently gone on display?"

Luke pulled a face. "Rather a dull and insipid beginning to your holiday," he said. "We should leave the Marbles until later. I have a more exciting and inspiring suggestion."

"But all the papers have been writing about Lord Elgin's find," Sarah pointed out.

"Do you know what the Marbles are? Some battered stones of classical Greek sculpture of interest to no one but erudite scholars and would-be students of antiquity."

"Sounds exactly like something I would revel in," Sarah said with a careless grin. "But I am open to suggestions. What did you have in mind, my lord?"

"That's my girl," he replied. "You, of course, have heard of Sir Humphrey Davy?"

Sarah furrowed her brow. "Isn't he a scientist who was recently knighted by the Prince Regent for his work? He developed the safety lamp for miners, if I'm not mistaken."

"One of his many accomplishments. Sir Humphrey is a brilliant man with a voluminous output of important scientific findings to his credit. It happens that tomorrow afternoon he is giving a lecture at"—Luke leaned over and picked up the newspaper he had discarded at his feet and turned to an inside page—"at two o'clock." He let the newspaper fall to the floor. "Bertram secured two tickets for me earlier today."

"A lecture?" Sarah said, an eyebrow arching upward.

"Oh, yes," Luke answered. "The City is a veritable universe of culture."

Sarah sighed. "I don't know, Luke. Articles I have read of a scientific nature, more often than not, bore me."

"But, my dear," Luke protested, his eyes golden brown with excitement, "seeing the experiments is not like wading through a treatise. Davy brings them alive."

"If I choose not to accompany you, will you take Bertram?" Sarah asked.

"No, what sort of odious creature do you think I am? I would give the tickets to Bertram and Billings, and you

and I would be off to see the Marbles. But this is a rare
opportunity for us. Sir Humphrey seldom gives public talks
these days. We may never have a chance to see the great
man again."

Sarah was certain her life would be complete if she never
sat in on a lecture by the chemist, but Luke's handsome
face shone with such unbridled enthusiasm that she could
not deny him.

"All right," she said, her cheeks dimpling.

Luke clapped his hands together in a prayerful attitude.
"Thank you, Sarah. You are top of the trees. I was unaware
that Davy was speaking here until Bertram reminded me
when I returned home. I have been waiting for nearly a
year for the opportunity to see him."

The look of sheer gratitude he gave her was worth her
small sacrifice. And what did it matter, after all? She would
be with Luke and that was what was really important.

During the morning while Luke was at his office, Sarah
read the *Morning Post* and learned that Humphrey Davy
was known as a popularizer of science. His sensational lec-
tures, it seemed, were filled with bangs and smells and
bright lights. Reviewing the listings, she saw that as Luke
had said London fairly hummed with discourses on everything from mesmerism to the analysis of poetry.

By the time Luke arrived from his office to share a cold
collation with Sarah, she was not at all adverse to attending
Sir Humphrey's lecture, and by the time they reached the
hall, she was looking forward to the show.

Inside the auditorium Luke led Sarah to their seats on
a long bench in the fourth row. The room was noisy with
the loud drone of male voices.

Sarah became aware that she was sitting in what appeared
to be an exclusively male audience. She pasted herself
against Luke and whispered, "There are no females here."

Undismayed, Luke scanned the hall and looked over his shoulder, picking out two women. "Not a preponderance," he understated. "But you will not be alone. These male things always attract a number of bluestockings."

"It is hardly comforting to me to be classified as a bluestocking," Sarah said. "I feel like an oddity. You should have come with Bertram or Sir Roland or some other male."

Luke squeezed her hand. "Now, my dear, how could I have left you to your own devices when my whole purpose in bringing you to London was to keep you near to me?" He pulled her arm through his. "If you are truly uncomfortable, Sarah, we can leave right now."

She was certain that if she said, "Yes, let's," he would get up, lead her from the hall, and never hold it against her.

"If we left," she said in a more positive tone, "I would never discover what all those bottles and tubes and glass hoses on the table up there on the platform are for. I don't believe my inquisitive nature would allow it. We better remain."

Luke brushed his lips over Sarah's cheek, but when Sir Humphrey stepped from the wings onto the stage, he loosened himself from her and joined in the thunderous applause.

Luke became totally engrossed in Davy's lecture and the illustrative experiments, leaning forward and occasionally nodding his head in silent agreement with the great man.

A sudden explosion caused Sarah to scrunch her shoulders and grimace. Luke grinned and snaked a protective arm around her waist, drawing her closer. Humphrey Davy could have magically vanished in the puff of smoke that wreathed his receding hairline and Sarah would not have noticed. During the next fifteen minutes she was aware of nothing but the bliss of having that strong male hand warm on her waist.

After the performance, Luke directed his coachman to drive to Gunther's, a popular confectioner's. The tea shop was filled with customers, but a waiter, who addressed Luke by name, found them a small table for two near the window and took their order.

"How did you like the lecture?" Luke asked.

"It was . . . enlightening," Sarah answered a little hesitantly.

"You hated it."

"No, not really. Some of the experiments were quite dramatic, but I am more the Elgin Marbles type. Greek myths and stories of the gods and the Trojan War are more intelligible to me than nitrous oxide."

A quick grin dented Luke's mouth. "You are a good sport, my sweet. Most women, I know, in your situation would have kept up an incessant salvo of whining and complaining. Tomorrow, you shall have your reward . . . the British Museum and the Marbles."

The waiter arrived with cups of hot chocolate and a platter of butter cakes, and soon the two were lost in each other and unaware of anyone else in the restaurant.

At a corner table Lady Isabella Leighton sat with her friend, Lady Bernice Capens, taking tea.

"Who is the woman with Darnay?" Bernice asked, drawing Isabella's attention to Luke. "His latest flirt, do you suppose?"

"Her conservative clothes are not at all in the style of a ladybird," Isabella replied, sweeping Luke's companion with an all-encompassing glance. "Hmm, you know, there is something decidedly familiar about her." She put a gloved finger to her chin.

"An odd choice for Lord Darnay," Bernice said. She was a plain woman who lacked the striking good looks of her blond friend. "When Darnay does deign to squire someone about, she usually has more style than this creature, but he is a strange one." She gave a small titter. "You

know, he is perching on the brink of social disaster. My
husband says Lord Darnay is occupied in numerous business interests that are definitely not good Ton."

"Your husband has the right of it. But it is nothing new.
It has been going on for years. Lord Covington found himself in dun territory the year his son reached his majority.
His father was about to face ruin when Lucien took over
the family finances. Unfortunately, within a year he had
turned his back on all the pleasures of the Ton and had
become a businessman to the family's horror."

"I can well imagine their anguish, although Capens ad-
mits that were it not for Darnay's business acumen, Lord
and Lady Covington would not have a feather to fly with,
and Lady Jane would not be about to become betrothed
to Sir Roland."

"I wouldn't go that far, Bernice," Isabella said with
authority. "I have known Roland Kirkwood quite well for
years. I think he is truly fond of Jane. But while Darnay
may prosper and flourish in both his personal finances
and in those he handles for his family, his eschewing his
title and turning down bids to the better clubs does harm
to his consequence among the high-sticklers of the Ton.
Lord and Lady Covington, however, manage to stay respectable by virtue of loyal friends like my husband."

"Aren't you ever concerned, Bella, that Lord Leighton
will catch you out when you cuckold him?" Bernice asked,
for Isabella had never been shy about discussing the shocking habits of the fast crowd to which both she and Sir
Roland belonged.

Isabella shrugged. "If he truly wanted to trap me, he
could have any time these nine years. He has his heir from
his first wife. Leighton needs an ornament to grace his
table when he entertains others in the government. I serve
my purpose."

Isabella sipped her tea. She still smarted from Luke's
having passed out the one time she might have slept with

him. He had never bothered to apologize, nor had he
given her the opportunity to reignite the passion she was
sure he had felt for her that night. She had hoped for a
second chance when Sir Roland put together the house
party at Thornystone. But things had gone awry when
Luke had put business before pleasure. Yet, she was certain
that he could not hold out against her beauty and charms
forever. She would step up her campaign, and by the night
of his mother's Valentine Ball, Luke Sutter would be back
dancing attendance on her.

FOUR

The following day Luke took Sarah to the British Museum to see the sculptures from the Parthenon which Lord Elgin had recently sold to the museum. She tried to appear worldly as she viewed some reliefs of nude and seminude muscular men astride powerful horses and chewed her lip thoughtfully to hide her inexperience with the unclothed male form.

"Do you think ancient Greek men were that perfect?" she whispered to Luke, coloring at her own boldness.

Luke's lips twitched with amusement. "I imagine Greeks came in all shapes and sizes, just as males in our modern world. Grecian classical art, after all, portrays the ideal. Not even among the younger men, I would think, would you have found too many with such perfect builds."

"How disappointing," she said without thinking, which evoked a deep guffaw from Luke that was immediately joined by her own unchecked giggle. A devotee of the arts standing nearby raised his quizzing glass and looked down his nose at them. Luke grabbed Sarah's hand, and the two hurried off and spent the next hour wandering through some of the older, less provocative, exhibits.

Sarah's sage comments as they viewed the displayed artifacts surprised Luke. She was better educated than he would have expected for a country girl. When he made this observation, she told him, "My father encouraged me to read. He, himself, ordered all kinds of books from London with some regularity and made them available to me. Of course, when he allowed me to choose for myself, I would pick a romantic novel."

The day was cold, and a brisk wind blew as the two left the museum for home. Luke ordered his coachman to drive the City carriage at a decorous pace to allow Sarah to enjoy glimpses of the London streets and shops.

"Romances?" Luke said, continuing the conversation about books. "From all the learned remarks you made in the museum, I would have thought your literary tastes ran deeper."

"I do read serious works," Sarah said, not put off by his remark. "But for some reason I can't seem to shake my addiction to the popular press."

"I find it rather endearing that so practical a young woman would find that romantic folderol entertaining. It somehow keeps you from being elevated too far above me," he said with a light laugh.

Sarah's lips parted slightly in surprise. "I hardly think a doctor's daughter is considered more worthy in the eyes of society than the son of an earl," she said.

"Ah, but you are far above me in my eyes. And you forget that I am considered an outcast by the Beau Monde. One does not become a man of business without some censure in the world into which I was born."

"Surely, you exaggerate, my lord. Your father has not disowned you," she said flippantly.

Luke emitted an unpleasant sound somewhere between a grunt and a laugh. "Make no mistake, my sweet, the earl and countess tolerate what they see as my eccentricities for practical reasons. They like to live well, as does my little sister."

"I have heard that aristocrats disdain those who choose to earn a living, but I cannot believe one's parents would scorn a son and heir for such a petty reason."

"Believe it, Sarah, my parents take no pride in my accomplishments." His shrug indicated a casualness that Sarah suspected Luke did not feel.

She linked her arm through his and moved closer to him. "I like you exactly as you are," she said.

Luke kissed the top of her head. "Now that, my dear, is what makes life worth living."

Sleet and freezing rain turned the weather nasty for a time. Luke went to his office in the mornings, but he would return to the house early in the afternoon.

Matilda and Mary curtailed their visits to Lady Cheney's and sat sewing and gossiping while Sarah and Luke played piquet or backgammon in the drawing room warmed by a roaring fire.

One afternoon Luke came home from his office and said to Sarah, "The weather has improved into something quite decent. There is a jewel of a park nearby which, though small, is as satisfying as Hyde Park and not as crowded. I thought you might enjoy a ride, and if you dress warmly, we might even get down from the carriage and walk."

"Oh, yes, that sounds delightful," Sarah said, running to get a warm cloak and a woollen bonnet.

Luke had his driver stop at the curb beside a path which circled the park. Sarah linked her arm with Luke's as they set off on their walk in the bright sunshine.

"Do you always work late at night in the library as you were doing last night?" she asked.

Nonplussed, Luke looked down at her. "How do you know that? Has one of the servants been talebearing?"

She shook her head. "I couldn't sleep and went for something to read. You looked so engrossed in your papers, I feared to interrupt and tiptoed back upstairs without disturbing you."

"I want to devote as much time to you as I possibly can," he explained. "There are fewer daylight hours during a given day for sightseeing this time of year, and that coupled with the uncertain weather, our time together would be shrunk to almost nothing if I went to the office for my usual hours. I try to catch up on some of the tasks at night so I can be with you during the day."

Sarah felt warmed by his consideration for her.

Neither of them paid attention to a town coach with a crest on the door which pulled up next to the curb until the window came down and a woman's shrill voice cried out, "Luke!"

Luke turned toward the carriage and muttered an unmistakable obscenity beneath his breath. A footman jumped from the rear of the coach and opened the door for the occupants.

A glum young man of average height, dressed in smart winter attire, stepped down onto the pavement from inside the fine vehicle. Lady Isabella Leighton took her escort's proffered hand and alighted, elegant in a fashionable, fur-lined rose velvet cloak and matching ermine hat.

Isabella sashayed from her companion's side and put her small gloved hand intimately on Luke's coat sleeve. "It has been an age since I have seen you, Lucien," she said, running the hand up and down his arm possessively before she looked pointedly at Sarah, who had removed her arm from Luke's and stood a little apart from them. Isabella recognized Sarah as the woman she and Bernice had seen with Luke at Gunther's.

"Lord Darnay and I are old and dear friends, Miss . . . ?" She raised a perfect brow and glanced at Luke to fill in the name for which she was fishing.

"Buchanan," Luke supplied. He turned to Sarah. "Miss Buchanan, may I present Lady Leighton." All traces of his annoyance were civilly hidden.

Isabella took in Miss Buchanan's cloak and saw that although the cloth was good, it was not the work of a London modiste. Wherever could she have come across this female?

"Have we met before, Miss Buchanan?" she asked, anxious to solve the mystery.

Before Sarah could answer, Luke interjected, "Miss Buchanan is visiting with her aunt."

His phrasing suggested that Sarah's aunt lived in London and that she was visiting her. Somehow Sarah knew Luke's choice of words was not a slip of the tongue. He did not want this aristocratic beauty to know that she was a guest at his town house.

"And who might her aunt be?" Isabella asked.

"Mrs. Drayton," Luke answered. "She is an intimate of Lady Cheney's."

"Oh, yes, the duchess. Of course, I am rarely in the dowager's company. For the most part, we travel in very different circles. That is, probably, the reason why I have not met your aunt," she said to Sarah.

Biting back a clarification which Sarah was certain would greatly displease Luke, she remained silent.

Lady Leighton's escort, who had been scowling the whole time Luke and Isabella spoke to one another, said rather forcefully, "Isabella, we shall be late for tea with Lady Capens."

"Hush, Havercole, Lady Capens can wait," Isabella said, not taking her eyes from Luke's face. "You know Lord Havercole, don't you, Luke?"

Luke acknowledged the heir of one of the leading families of the Ton with a curt nod. "We met very briefly at Thornystone," Luke said, noting that the young wastrel, who had been sent down from Cambridge a number of times, was clearly besotted with Isabella.

Luke had no desire to engage in a prolonged conversation with either the sullen young man, who was several years Lady Leighton's junior, or with her ladyship herself, but the matter was taken from his hands. Isabella linked her arm with Luke's and stepped forward down the path, forcing him to walk along with her. She turned a smile on him, which was meant to seduce.

"I am giving an intimate dinner party on Thursday," she said, her voice low. "I want you to come."

Luke suspected that the intimate party might be a little too intimate with him as the main course. "Sorry, Bella, I am engaged on Thursday." He kept his voice mild, but he felt nothing but contempt for her. She would catch cold at her game. Never again, drunk or sober, would he fall into the lady's trap.

Some distance behind them, Sarah walked side by side with Lord Havercole, overcome with a jealousy she had not known that she could feel. She recalled Luke and Sir Roland discussing Lady Leighton in unflattering terms at Thornystone, but she had not imagined that the woman was so incredibly attractive. She glanced up at the young lord beside her. His eyes were burning into the couple's backs.

"She is a monstrously selfish creature, you know?" he said.

"My lord?" Although she had heard him clearly, her response was caused by his shocking indiscretion.

"Isabella," he clarified. "Selfish. She does exactly what she pleases no matter whom she hurts. But you would think the chit would have more sense than to try to rekindle her affair with Darnay."

Sarah knew from the conversation she had overheard at Thornystone between Luke and Sir Roland that there had been no affair; but she was as smitten as this young lord, and her heart hurt as she viewed Lady Leighton familiarly attached to Luke.

But Luke made short work of the unwanted *tête-à-tête* with Isabella. He delivered an unequivocal rejection of an alternate date for a liaison with her and returned the now petulant lady to Lord Havercole posthaste.

"Come, Havercole," Isabella commanded, as if the young man had been responsible for delaying her. "We are very late for our appointment with Lady Capens."

For some time as the carriage carried Luke and Sarah back toward Berkeley Square, neither spoke. Luke broke the silence when they were in sight of the house.

"That was unfortunate, but don't refine on it, Sarah. Regardless of the scurrilous rumors you might hear, Lady Leighton was never my mistress. She means nothing to me and never has."

"I don't expect you to be chaste, Luke. In the country we are not entirely cut off from the world. I know that men have mistresses, often many of them," she said, feeling her cheeks becoming warm with her own plain speaking.

Luke patted her hand and smiled down at her. "But not nearly as many as you are imagining, my sweet."

She curled closer to him. "That is a relief." His chuckle melded with her timid laugh, and he picked up her gloved hand, holding it to his cheek.

"You did not want Lady Leighton to know that I am stopping with you," Sarah said. It was not a question.

"No, Bella is the sort of woman who smiles at you while she drives the proverbial knife into your back. She can make something sordid from nothing."

Sarah could not have remained in London with Luke for even a day had she not believed with her whole being that he loved her. Yet, with the exception of his cousin and Lady Cheney, whose *raison d'etre* was evident, he had never voluntarily introduced her to any of his friends or family. Perhaps in the eyes of the polite world her lodging with him was, if not precisely sordid, at least suspect. Or did he keep her to himself because she was not quite the thing, too countrified and an embarrassment?

Sarah did not have an opportunity to speculate further, for when she and Luke entered the drawing room of the town house, she was distracted from her previous anxieties by the presence of the young couple who sat together on a love seat talking to Miss Westlock and Sarah's aunt.

"Here are Cousin Lucien and Miss Buchanan, now," Mary Westlock said to the man, whom Sarah recognized as

Sir Roland Kirkwood, and the dark-haired young woman
with bright blue eyes, whom she surmised correctly was
Lady Jane Sutter, Luke's sister.

After the usual greetings, Mary explained to Luke, "Mrs.
Drayton and I went for a stroll right after you and Miss
Buchanan left for your carriage ride. Not a block from the
house we met Cousin Jane and Sir Roland. The two are at
loose ends, for your parents are hosting one of those afternoon card parties for the older set, so I took the liberty of
inviting them here for a cup of tea."

"I see," Luke said, noncommittally. "Lady Jane and Sir
Roland are announcing their betrothal at my mother's Valentine Ball in a few days," he said to Sarah, who had taken
a chair near to her aunt.

Sarah murmured all the appropriate felicitations as she
reached out to accept the cup of tea which Mary handed
her from the tea trolley. Sir Roland rose from the sofa and
stood beside Luke, who had moved to the fireplace and was
holding his palms toward the cheery fire. Neither of the
gentlemen was attending to Jane, who was a relentless chat-
terbox and was swamping the ladies with the most minute
details of the upcoming ball.

"Miss Westlock has informed me that Miss Buchanan is
here to help you in your quest to tempt a doctor to Thorn,
Luke," Roland said in a stilted voice. "Have you been successful yet?"

Sarah, who was sitting nearest to them, heard him.

Roland intercepted the blank expressions that passed between Luke and Miss Buchanan. He noticed the con-
science-stricken look that sprang into the young woman's
brown eyes before she became quite interested in the con-
tents of her teacup.

Sarah could not believe that she and Luke had put the
securing of a doctor for the village completely from their
conscious minds. As soon as Luke's visitors departed, she
must speak to him about attending to the matter.

Reinforced in his suspicion that Luke had launched an

affair with the country beauty, Roland waited for his friend to speak. He was appalled that Luke was keeping his paramour under his roof and allowing her to mingle with decent females.

Unruffled, Luke said to him, "I have it on good authority that the passage of the Apothecaries Act a few years ago has left a scarcity of qualified doctors from which to choose, but I plan to send one of my men to tack up notices in the teaching hospitals tomorrow."

Luke was relieved to see that Sarah had regained her poise with his response. While her cheeks were flushed, she was once again listening to Jane, who had continued her conversation uninterrupted, too immersed in her own discourse to be aware of Sarah's abashment.

Roland drew Luke a tactful distance from the ladies to a window which overlooked the walled garden. With all the contempt and scorn he could muster, he said, "Why didn't you tell me that Miss Buchanan is your *petite amie?*"

"Don't be a cork-brain, Roland. Sarah is no such thing. Do you think me such a bounder that I would insult Cousin Mary by keeping a doxy under my own roof and that I would be so insensible of proprieties as to introduce a lightskirt to my sister who is just out of the schoolroom?" Luke said with some heat. "Roland, give me some credit for good sense."

The derision in Roland's eyes barely slackened. "It is certainly not what I would have expected of you. Nevertheless, I'm waiting for your explanation. But don't do it up brown with Banbury tales of looking for doctors or signing transfer papers with a solicitor. I'm not as gullible as Mary Westlock."

Luke drew a long breath. "I knew from our first meeting that I wanted Sarah and that she felt the same about me. I could not remain in the country with my business here in the City. Inviting her here, well chaperoned by Mrs. Drayton and Mary, seemed the sensible way to further our relationship and get to know one another better. I think, we are both ready to announce our engagement now."

"Then why don't you? Why have you been hiding her?"

Luke smiled faintly. "I haven't been hiding her. We have been all over the City together. You may find this hard to believe, Rollie, but I have held back because I did not want to overshadow your own betrothal to Jane."

"Dash it all, Luke. Do you expect me to swallow that rapper?"

Luke sighed. "Think about it, my friend. An announcement of my engagement to Sarah, a female from outside the Ton, is going to be fodder for the gossip mill. What would everyone at the Valentine Ball be whispering about, do you suppose, if I declared for Sarah before the dance?"

Roland could imagine the endless speculation over such a match or mismatch, if the truth be told. "I suppose you are right. Jane's moment in the sun would be spoiled. I guess instead of ripping up at you, I should thank you." He ran a hand over his sandy hair. "But, Luke, are you certain that you want to marry Miss Buchanan? I don't know anyone more thoroughly sensible and cautious than you. It is not like you to enter into a madcap romance."

"Make no mistake, my friend, my feelings for Sarah are genuine. We have talked and talked, and with each passing day, my first impressions have only strengthened. Sarah is no milksop miss. Yet, I have not even kissed her. That should tell you something of my frame of mind. This is no reckless affair. I intend our union to be permanent."

Lady Jane cut off any further private communication and forced the men back within the women's circle when she called, "What are you two whispering about over there? Come taste these delicious cakes."

Luke recognized the nut cakes, for he had become fond of them; the thought that Sarah had given the recipe to Cook passed through his mind.

Sarah was certain that Luke knew she had baked the cakes. When he smiled at her, she relaxed. She knew that real ladies did not putter in the kitchen, and she had wondered if he would be vexed with her. But her curiosity had been piqued when Miss Westlock had mentioned that Luke had recently installed the latest modern cooking equipment. She had not been able to resist testing the new model oven.

"Roland and I have tickets for *Twelfth Night* at Drury Lane tomorrow night," Lady Jane was saying as Sarah once again became aware of the conversation.

"Lord Darnay has tickets as well," Sarah said, pleased to see that Sir Roland had replenished his plate with two more of her nut cakes.

"Oh!" Jane cried. "If you and Luke are also going to the play, Miss Buchanan, let's make a party to the theater. Rollie, Luke could take us up, and we could all go together."

"If that is your desire, my dear," Sir Roland said with a lack of zeal. "My mother *is* expecting us to join *her*."

"She won't mind," Lady Jane said heedlessly. "We could share your box, Luke, unless you have invited some others."

"No others," Luke acknowledged. He knew Jane would persist until she got her way, and he would appear churlish if he refused her. Roland never seemed to be able to deny Jane anything, so he could not look to his friend for support.

"All right, then," Luke gave in. He had wanted to be alone with Sarah in the privacy of his theater box, but maybe this was better. He could ease Sarah into his family's life and, perhaps, make Jane and Roland his allies. He would need all the support he could get when he presented Sarah as his bride-to-be to his obstinate parents.

Sarah's smile sparkled as she bid *adieu* to the guests. Her very recent fears that Luke might be finding her common and an embarrassment now vanished with his acquiescence to his sister's suggestion.

FIVE

When Luke unlocked the front door and stepped into the vestibule, delicious aromas from the kitchen assailed his senses. Cook had apparently outdone herself, he thought. He was famished, for he had left early in the morning and skipped a midday meal to compose a notice to be posted in the teaching hospitals as he had promised Sarah after Jane and Roland left the previous afternoon.

He still had to dress for the Drury Lane performance, and he was in a foul mood, which was the inevitable result of his harangue with his mother. He did not like to cajole and threaten to get his way, but the countess would never have come through with the invitations to the Valentine Ball for Sarah, Matilda, and Mary without his exercising considerable pressure.

Billings appeared, greeted Luke, and took his hat and cane.

"Something smells delicious," Luke said, putting aside the black mood his difficult parent had caused.

"Yes, sir," Billings said, "Miss Sarah has prepared the dinner in Cook's absence."

Luke frowned; a new bearishness replaced the irascibility brought on by the countess.

"Miss Buchanan? Where is Cook?"

"Her daughter went into childbed early this morning,

and Mrs. Westlock gave her permission to stay the night with her son-in-law and to help out."

"That does not explain why Miss Buchanan has been recruited as a cook," he said. For Sarah to prepare meals for him and his staff was unseemly to say the least. He did not like it.

Before Billings could respond, the door which led to the servants' wing opened, and Sarah walked into the hall, her dress covered with an enormous holland apron. Unruly strands of damp brown hair trailed at her neck and onto her flushed cheeks.

"You are home, my lord," she said. "Did you get the advertisements for a doctor posted today?" It was the first thing that sprang into her mind, for she had been fraught with guilt all day for shirking her duty to her fellow villagers.

Luke gave her a curt nod, his face a thundercloud of disapproval. "Come into the library," he said as he dismissed Billings with a brusque hand signal.

He stepped aside to let Sarah precede him into the room, closed the door with a snap, and leaned against it. Sarah faced him, sweeping strands of hair from her cheek with the back of her hand and eyeing him with a bewildered expression.

"Just what possessed you to cook a meal in my kitchen like a common servant?" he asked at his most wooden.

Sarah raised a proud brow. "You sat in my kitchen in Thorn and watched me prepare food for our journey. I never heard a word of objection to my cooking or talk of my being a common servant."

"Gad, Sarah, surely you can see the difference. You cannot transfer your country ways to town. Life here is regulated according to strict social rules. You have lowered your consequence before my staff and allowed the servants to become entirely too familiar. *Miss Sarah?* Indeed! I would have reprimanded Billings for his insolence, but I suspect the lapse is not his fault."

"You are being snobbish," Sarah accused with an airy toss of her head.

Their equally irate glares met and held, neither giving quarter.

Luke saw the gold sparks of righteous indignation in Sarah's brown eyes. A trace of color rose in her high cheekbones and flushed down to her creamy neck. Her hair was sensual in its dishevelment, and he pictured her in his bed, the rich brown tresses spread onto his white pillowcase. Never had she looked more desirable.

Fascinated, Sarah watched his dark stormy eyes change to a lustful mossy green.

Luke's gaze fixed on her mouth; her cherry lips were lush and ripe and tempting. "You are beautiful," he said, his voice low and husky.

One step and he was beside Sarah, his hands on her shoulders. His craving mouth lowered onto the velvet softness of hers.

"Gad, I'm hopelessly in love with you," he murmured against her lips. He swept her into his arms in a powerful embrace, and Sarah felt her heart pounding wildly as her arms wound around his neck. His warm mouth touched hers, and her lips parted instinctively. Their kiss was breathtakingly long and deep.

How they came to tumble into a large leather man's chair, Sarah could not recall, but she was on his lap, still being kissed and kissing in return, their rift forgotten in passion.

When Luke at last lifted his lips from hers, he said, "I am not being impertinently forward. We will be married, Sarah, I promise you. But you know a little of my family and their toplofty views."

Sarah bit her lip. "They will not be pleased."

"Not at first. But we will win them over. Today, I convinced my mother to send invitations to you, your aunt, and Cousin Mary for the Valentine Ball."

Sarah turned in his arms to see his face. "Oh, my, I have never been to a real ball, only village dances. I do hope I will know how to go on."

Luke smiled a little and moved her gently from his lap and stood up beside her. He leaned down and kissed her cheek. "We will talk more about that at another time. If we do not eat now and dress immediately after, we shall be very late in taking up Jane and Roland and will miss the curtain at Drury Lane."

He walked with her to the door, his hand around her shoulder. "What did you prepare for dinner?" he asked.

"A chicken pie with the flakiest crust you are ever likely to eat," she boasted. "And, a green salad with a special wine vinegar dressing of my own creation. This being the wrong time of the year, I could not find fresh herbs at the greengrocer's, but I did get fairly decent dried ones."

"You went shopping for food?" She listened for rebuke in his voice but heard none.

"Billings guided me to the best poultry shop and greengrocer and carried the shopping basket for me. I was certain that you would appreciate a hot meal after such a long day at your business, rather than the cold fare the cook left for dinner."

"My little domestic," he said, but the mockery was gentle.

"Since the ladies are dining with the duchess, I asked Billings to serve the two of us in the breakfast parlor," Sarah said, leading them toward the more intimate room.

When Luke had seated her, and Billings had served the salad and returned to the kitchen, Sarah said, "Please don't scold Billings and the others for addressing me as Miss Sarah. It seemed more friendly. I'm not accustomed to being called Miss Buchanan."

Luke's shrug was neither acquiescence nor condemna-

tion. Instead, to divert her, he praised the meal. Cooking
and cleaning and maintaining an easy relationship with
servants were natural to Sarah. The girl Jilly, who did for
her and her aunt, sat down to meals with them. He would
have to curb Sarah's familiarity with the help or, at least,
warn her to be discreet when speaking with others about
how things were done in their own home once he and
Sarah were married. He meant to protect her from the
slights and slurs she might encounter in his parents' world
of social maneuvering and indelicate snobbery. But while
there would have to be some inevitable changes in her
behavior, she was perfectly to his taste, and he had no
intention of reforming her into a replica of his mother or
sister.

Later that evening, Sarah and Luke were ascending the
staircase to Luke's box at Drury Lane when he whispered
to her, "Once we are wed, we shall have to find some way
to give the cook many days off. After sampling your supe-
rior culinary talents, I am not certain I can resist your
cooking for me some of the time."

A ripple of mirth rose in Sarah's throat, and her laugh
drifted forward toward Sir Roland and Lady Jane.

The soon-to-be-betrothed couple looked back, but their
notice went unheeded, for Sarah and Luke were treating
each other to the special smiles of lovers.

The small party had barely settled in Luke's box, when
the curtain rose and the play started. Sarah was too intrigued with watching one of Shakespeare's dramas come
alive to pay attention to her surroundings. But many eyes
were on her, wondering about the identity of the attractive
woman whom Lord Darnay attended with such devotion.

Lady Leighton sat beside Lord Havercole, covertly watching Sarah and Luke through her opera glasses. Isabella had
verified that Lady Cheney did have a Mrs. Drayton in her

circle of friends, but the woman was unfashionable and had no position in society. She saw Luke Sutter's behavior as a personal affront, for she was Isabella Leighton, a titled lady born and bred and an indisputable Incomparable. It was inconceivable that he would cast her aside for some nobody so lacking in style. She decided to be generous. At intermission she would seek Luke out and give him one more chance. With this resolution determined, she lifted her fan to shield Lord Havercole from prying eyes and permitted the young man to lean in and touch his lips to hers.

"Are you enjoying the play?" Lady Jane asked Sarah as their party mingled with the crowd in the hall during the intermission.

"Oh, yes, very much so. I have read all of the Bard's works, but have never seen any of them performed," Sarah said.

"I do like you, Miss Buchanan," the outspoken young woman told her. "I'm glad that Luke coerced Mama into inviting you to our Valentine Ball, even if she is being insufferable about it and making Papa miserable."

Sarah was taken aback and had no suitable reply for the frank remark. Luke stepped to her side.

"Bridle your tongue, Jane," he said softly.

Lady Jane clapped a gloved hand over her mouth. "I'm so sorry. I wasn't thinking."

Luke's brows knit, but Sarah saw that his displeasure was no longer directed at his sister. Lady Leighton was bearing down on them with Lord Havercole in her wake.

Isabella brushed past the ladies and struck Sir Roland in the chest playfully with her fan.

"So, Rollie, at last, you are being allowed to squire your infant bride-to-be in public."

"I am eighteen, hardly an infant, my lady," Jane snapped. "I have been out these six months."

"Really, dear? I suppose your protective swain has been shielding you from his wicked friends." She looked up at Roland with innocent blue eyes. "You have been remiss, dear boy. You must bring Lady Jane to one of our stimulating evenings."

"Perhaps, after the Valentine Ball, Bella, when our betrothal will have been formalized," Sir Roland said with a cool smile.

Isabella tittered knowingly. She whispered for his ears only, "Or better yet after the wedding, or should I say, the bedding, when the conversation will be less obscure to little Jane."

With a laugh Isabella moved next to Luke and attached herself to his coat sleeve. Speaking to her escort, she said, "Havercole, be a dear and fetch me a lemonade before the intermission ends." Lord Havercole remained rooted in place, glaring at her and Luke.

"Go, go," she ordered. Left with a choice of either obeying her or initiating a public quarrel, the young blade prudently chose the more sensible course.

"I must speak with you privately, Luke," Isabella said, ignoring Sarah as if she were invisible.

Pointedly, Luke removed her hand from his arm. "Forgive me, Bella, but Miss Buchanan and I need to return to my box immediately. This is her first time to see *Twelfth Night,* and I do not wish her to miss any of the drama. If you hurry, you can catch up with Havercole."

Luke turned his back on his nemesis and missed the venom that blistered the lady's eyes. As he walked back toward their seats with Sarah on his arm, he gnashed his teeth. He had thought that the encounter in the park would be the end of Isabella's flagrant attempts to entice him into her bed. Now he wondered if she would ever tire of stalking him.

"I hate that strumpet," Lady Jane said as she and Sir

Roland walked behind Sarah and Luke. "I don't know why Mama invited her to our ball."

"Lower your voice, my love," Roland cautioned. "People are staring. Lord Leighton is an important man who has the Prince Regent's ear. One cannot say to him, 'Sir, you are welcome, but leave your wife at home,' you know."

Jane was not mollified and was suddenly jealous. "Lady Leighton is part of that fast crowd that you spend so much time with, Roland. What is she to you?"

"Nothing," Sir Roland said. "You need never consort with that set. After we are married, we will have for our friends those people whom we mutually agree upon."

His promise pacified Jane, and she walked with proper decorum back to their seats.

Later when Luke and Sarah were alone in the dark of the carriage driving home after putting down his sister and Sir Roland at the Sutter mansion in Albemarle Street, Luke noticed that Sarah was unusually quiet.

"What is it, darling?" he said.

At first she shook her head in denial, but then said, "I had not realized just how disturbed your mother is by my presence in your life. It is obvious that she does not want me at the Valentine Ball."

"You are right, Sarah," he said honestly. "I had a devil of a time securing an invitation for you. But it is done. I assure you that my mother is too well bred to snub you in her own home. Your initial acceptance, however tenuous, will be a step toward complete acceptance."

"I don't think I should attend, Luke. It will only exacerbate the dissension between you and your parents."

"Sarah, I have no intention of giving you up. Now, we can either strive to bring my parents around, or we can elope. Boats sail frequently to Guernsey from Southampton. One does not need a license to wed there. We could

marry secretly and present the earl and countess with a
fait accompli and chance alienating them forever. Would
you prefer that?''

Sarah glanced through the window into the dark night.
"No, of course not. I want to be married properly in
church with our families present," she said. "I don't want
to elope."

"Good, because I don't want a hole-in-the-wall wedding
either," Luke said.

For several moments Sarah considered his words against
the clip-clop of the horses' hooves on the pavement of the
deserted London street. If she and Luke were to have a
life together, she could not hide from his parents indefi-
nitely. He would be perpetually unhappy in such a state.
It would be cowardly on her part, and she was not a coward.
She straightened her spine.

"All right, Luke," she said. "I will look over my dresses
with Aunt Matilda to see which one can be altered into a
suitable evening gown for the ball."

Luke relaxed with her capitulation, but another concern
rose as she broached the lack of the requisite evening
dress. Any conversion of a country gown that Mrs. Drayton
could execute, however skillfully, would leave Sarah open
to disparaging gibes and contemptuous snickers from the
arrogant aristocratic tabbies. He had to squelch the idea
without wounding her feelings.

"Why don't you and Mrs. Drayton treat yourselves to
new gowns from one of the London modistes for this special occasion? It would be a shame for your aunt to be
spending the few days left to her in the City cooped up in
her room laboring over dresses that can so easily be purchased in one of the shops," Luke said. The coach turned
from the street into the town house drive.

"Remodeling a gown can be an arduous task," Sarah
admitted as the coachman brought the carriage to a stop
in the porte cochere.

"Frocks are not my strong point," Luke said as the groom unlatched the coach door, "but I imagine Lady Cheney can give you the names of some reliable dressmakers."

Luke stepped onto the brick walk and held out a hand to Sarah as she climbed down. He had already devised a plan to present to Lady Cheney which would insure that Sarah would attend the ball dressed in the height of fashion.

The next evening Sarah shared recollections with Matilda and Mary of her afternoon visit with Luke to the Tower of London.

"The Royal Menagerie was disheartening," Sarah said. "An elephant was confined in cramped quarters. I am certain the poor beast would have preferred to be romping and trumpeting with his own kind in the wilds of Africa."

Luke looked up from his newspaper with an amused grin. "I believe that was an Indian elephant," he said.

Sarah made a small noise of exasperation. "Well, then, romping in India."

"I think Indian elephants are used as beasts of burden," Luke chimed in again.

"Luke, I thought you had compassion for the animal?" Sarah protested. "You said as much."

"I do, Sarah. The conditions are abominable. The animals should be moved to a more favorable habitat."

"I think I shall write a letter to the *Times* to that effect," Sarah said, looking at the newspaper in Luke's hands.

He folded the paper and handed it to her with an indulgent grin. "Do that. I have some work to do if you ladies will excuse me," he said and left them to go to his desk in the library.

Mary put the tapestry she had been embroidering into her work basket and got to her feet. "I think I shall seek my bed, for I need to be up early. Cook should be back by noon tomorrow, but I will take care of brewing the coffee in the morning and heating some rolls for breakfast."

When Sarah and her aunt were alone, Matilda said, "I spoke to Lady Cheney today about our gowns for the Valentine Ball. She gave me the direction of a seamstress who is just now catching on. She has assured me that we can get unexceptionable gowns from this Madame Lisse at a greatly reduced price. She apparently has ready-mades that have been turned down by customers for one reason or another which she allows to go cheaply."

"How cheaply?" Sarah asked, putting aside the newspaper Luke had handed her.

"Perhaps ten or twenty pounds."

Sarah slumped in her chair. "Aunt Mattie, ten pounds is more than a year's budget for my clothes."

"I know, dear, but Lady Cheney says that a custom evening gown cannot be had for less than forty pounds, and I would venture to say that most of the women who will be attired in the first stare of fashion at Lady Covington's Valentine Ball will have paid even more for their dresses."

Sarah gasped. "I cannot imagine any of our friends spending so lavishly on clothes."

"No, but the villagers do not attend fancy balls given by members of the Ton. I have heard that some of these people have ten or fifteen thousand a year at their disposal, and a few considerably more."

"Heavens, do you suppose Luke has that kind of money?" Sarah blurted out. She had always thought of him in a rather unspecific way as being well-off.

"The thing about being accepted into a duchess's inner circle is that her wealthy friends tend to gossip a great deal," Matilda said. "Lord Darnay's income is rumored to be in the neighborhood of thirty thousand pounds."

Sarah swallowed hard. "Thirty *thousand*? Luke? Oh, my!" The very thought of such wealth overwhelmed her.

Small wonder that he did not blink an eye when he had agreed to buy her house.

"Of course, people tend to exaggerate," her aunt went on, "and he does support his family in style, but he has more than enough in his own right to be considered rich. You must make Lord Darnay proud before his family, child. I am certain that he means to offer for you."

A smile creased Sarah's face. "How did you guess?"

"No one who is around the two of you can miss how he is always watching you. Whenever you are near to him, he touches your sleeve or brushes your hand. There is the aura of Cupid about the pair of you when you smile at one another. So let us purchase a dress worthy of a future viscountess, even if we have to deplete our entire bank account."

Sarah laughed. "We shan't go that far, but we will spend more than we customarily do, I promise."

The next morning found Sarah and Matilda stepping from the street into the front room of Madame Lisse's Dress Salon a block off St. James's Place. A small, dark woman came from the back of the shop at the clang of the bell above the door. Her black eyes swept over Sarah and Matilda, her lips tight as she took in their country cloaks.

"Yes?" she said in a condescending tone.

Matilda mentioned Lady Cheney's name as the duchess had instructed her to do. "Ah, yes, Mrs. Drayton and Miss Buchanan, here to purchase gowns for Lady Covington's Valentine Ball. I am Madame Lisse." The woman's stiff lips tamed into an agreeable smile, and she got right to work.

"Please remove your cloaks," she requested. When Sarah and Matilda had done her bidding, she had each woman turn slowly while she appraised their figures with a professional eye, then waved them to a padded bench to be seated.

The modiste clapped her hands, bringing an assistant

scurrying through a curtained door from the back room. Speaking in French, Madame Lisse gave the young woman her orders, and her helper disappeared into the nether regions from which she had come while the modiste made small talk about the weather with Sarah and her aunt.

Soon the assistant returned, her arms filled with gowns. She handed each in turn to her employer, who displayed each elegant dress draped over her forearm. Matilda decided almost at once on a green satin suitable for an older woman and went to try the dress on. She received her niece's approval and changed back into her own modest attire. Sarah, however, still lingered over each of the remaining offerings, unable to settle on a single gown, finding some imperfection, however small, in each garment.

Madame Lisse forced a smile. "Let me see if I have anything else in back that might please you, Miss Buchanan," she said and left the room. She had a dress that she was saving for one of her more discerning customers, but she could not allow this young woman to leave without buying. It would reflect badly on her with Lady Cheney.

The moment Sarah saw the dress the modiste brought out, she knew it was the one she must have. She fingered the garnet silk. The sweetheart neckline was cut fashionably low, lower than any gown Sarah owned, while the short sleeves were not puffed in the prevailing style, but were created of fine lace.

The elegant gown fit Sarah's trim figure to perfection. "It's lovely," she said, looking at her reflection in the long mirror, "but I fear, Madame, that it is probably beyond my means."

"Not at all, Miss Buchanan. I know something of your situation from Lady Cheney. I make drastic allowances at times as a form of advertising. You need only mention where you and your aunt purchased your gowns. Nothing tasteless, but just an honest word if the dress is admired, you understand? Lady Covington's Valentine Ball, while not a major event, will draw a select number of the Ton, particularly since Lady Jane Sutter's betrothal to Sir Roland Kirkwood will be announced by her parents that evening."

"But Madame Lisse," Sarah said, "I must know the price."

Madame held up her hand. "The gown is well within your means, my dear Miss Buchanan. Trust me. I will mail the bill to the Berkeley Square address Lady Cheney gave me." She was off to supervise the boxing of both dresses before Sarah could question her further.

Matilda whispered to Sarah, "Perhaps this is the custom in London society. Madame Lisse seems to have some idea of what we can afford. If she is somehow mistaken, the dress is so perfect, Sarah, it will be worth the extra cost. Remember, we are not as strapped as before. There is the money from the sale of the house to fall back on."

Sarah lowered her voice to match her aunt's. "Yes, I had not considered that, although we cannot rely on those funds until a doctor agrees to bring his practice to Thorn. Madame Lisse will probably want payment before then. Yet I cannot think that Lady Cheney has steered us wrong. I suppose, it is just that I have never bought anything before without knowing the price. But, 'When in Rome . . .' as the saying goes."

After the ladies left with their packages, Madame Lisse wrote up the bill for the full amount of the dresses, tucked it into an envelope, and addressed the letter to Lord Darnay in Berkeley Square as she had been instructed to do.

SIX

Preparations for Sarah's debut at the Valentine Ball bustled along smoothly. Mollie took her to the shops frequented by ladies of the Ton, where Sarah purchased suitable dancing slippers and a beaded reticule to go with her ball gown.

The young maid had proved an expert at arranging hair and had devised a stylish coiffure which would add the crowning touch to Sarah's appearance on the important night.

Much to Sarah's surprise, Lady Cheney had hired a dancing master to spend two hours a day with Sarah and Mrs. Drayton.

"The duchess thought we could use some brushing up on the latest dance steps," Matilda said when she passed on the news to her niece. "We are accomplished at only a few country dances, and neither of us knows how to waltz. Why, we have never even seen the dance performed."

But in spite of all the advance preparations that should have bolstered her confidence, Sarah found herself becoming edgy about the ball. When she had first accepted the invitation, her sole concern was not to look too countrified before Luke's parents. But now she saw there were other pitfalls. And when the dancing master presented her with a fan and showed her the nuances of using it effectively, she despaired of ever getting through the evening without making a cake of herself.

Thus, when she nearly collided with Mr. Bertram as she stepped from her bedroom into the hall the day of the dance, she had worry lines on her face.

"Such a fierce expression, Miss Sarah," the valet said, teasing her.

She gave him a wobbly smile. "I confess I am a tad nervous about tonight's ball, Mr. Bertram. There is so much to remember."

Bertram liked Sarah for her unspoiled manner and hoped that his lordship would offer for her. Since she had been at Berkeley Square, Lord Darnay had been happier than he had ever been, and the reason was Miss Sarah. Billings and Cook and the girls had all remarked on it.

Bertram looked at her with kind eyes. "It's natural for you to be a mite unsure of yourself under the circumstances, Miss Sarah. You have never been to a ball before. But his lordship will be at your side. He will look after you, for he's a good man, but don't tell him I said so." He chuckled. "Can't have him thinking I like him. But you have pluck, miss. You shall think of all sorts of brilliant things to say and will win the lot of them over."

Sarah was grateful to him for caring enough to want to invigorate her spirits, but she claimed, "I shall be content just to muddle through. I fear I am one of those people who think of witticisms long after the talk is over."

"Not so, Miss Sarah. I find you are always ready with a clever reply."

Their exchange terminated when Mary Westlock approached, clutching a blue velvet jewelry case in her hand and looking determined.

Bertram nodded to the housekeeper and continued down the hall on his unspecified errand.

"Could we go back into your chamber for just a moment, Miss Buchanan?" Mary requested.

"Of course," Sarah answered. Closing the door, she said, "Please sit down."

Mary shook her head. "I will take but a minute of your time. I would like you to wear these jewels to the ball this evening," she said, her thin voice cracking. With trembling fingers, she lifted the lid of the velvet case.

Sarah gasped when her eyes rested on the exquisite necklace of tiny diamond- and garnet-studded hearts linked together in a gold setting. The magnificent piece could have been designed especially to add the finishing touch to her evening gown.

"Oh, Miss Westlock, I couldn't. The necklace must be very valuable."

Had Sarah taken her eyes from the jewels, she would have seen Mary chewing her lower lip nervously. "The garnets are the exact dark red of your gown and will complement the dress perfectly. I insist you wear the necklace," Mary said, snapping the case closed and shoving it into Sarah's hands.

"Are you certain?" Sarah asked. Luke's cousin stepped to the door as if anxious to make her exit. With her hand on the knob, she said, "Very certain." She opened the door and was gone, her footsteps muted by the thick hall carpet.

Sarah stared for a long time at the flawless gems, puzzled by Miss Westlock's persistence and strange behavior. Unsure whether she should borrow the necklace from so recent an acquaintance, she decided to seek her aunt's counsel.

"Miss Westlock wants me to wear the piece. And, I must admit, I am tempted," she said to Matilda, who sat with a book in her hand in a boudoir chair in her bedroom. "The necklace is so right for my dress, but she seemed nervous about lending the jewels to me and, yet, insistent that I take them."

Matilda put her book aside and lifted the necklace and held it against her own drab brown dress. The diamonds and garnets sparkled with a newness that strongly suggested that the necklace had never been worn. The velvet case was not faded or threadbare, nor was it dingy from handling. Moreover, the white satin lining was pristine. Matilda opened her mouth to point this out to Sarah, thought better of it, and said instead, "Mary would not have offered you the jewels if she did not really want you to have them. The necklace is just the thing to complement your ball gown."

"I can see it is," Sarah said. "If you think it is all right, Auntie . . ." Her brown eyes glowed in wonder. "How terribly generous of Miss Westlock."

"Yes, isn't it," her aunt replied, managing somehow to keep the irony from her voice.

Splendid in black-and-white evening attire, Luke was lounging near the fireplace with a snifter of brandy in his hand when Sarah came into the room. One glance at her and he felt as if the breath had been knocked from him. He set his glass on the mantel and took in her glorious appearance. She looked radiant in the garnet gown with her hair elegantly dressed. She was beautiful, he loved her, and she would soon be his wife, he thought proudly

His eyes went to the chain of little hearts against her alabaster throat. He had commissioned the jeweler to replace the original pink stones with genuine garnets and had paid dearly to have the work completed in one day. It had been worth every penny.

The adoration in Luke's eyes told Sarah that he cared for her deeply. Whatever Madame Lisse's bill turned out to be for the dress, she thought, it would be well worth the price for eliciting so worshipful a gaze from this handsome, vital man whom she loved with all her heart.

* **

At the Albemarle Street mansion, Luke and the ladies were conducted up the marble staircase to the ballroom on the second floor by Phelps, the Sutter family butler.

Matilda and Mary walked directly behind Phelps while Sarah followed the ladies with Luke at her shoulder.

As she approached Lord and Lady Covington, who greeted their guests just outside the ballroom door, Sarah inhaled a deep, calming breath to settle the butterflies in her stomach.

The countess looked haughty even from a distance. In appearance, she seemed to be an older version of Jane while Lord Covington, Sarah was certain, even in his younger years, had never been as good-looking as Luke, although there was a distinct family resemblance between father and son.

The aristocratic couple exchanged a few words with her aunt Matilda and Mary Westlock. The two ladies moved on, and Sarah stepped forward.

Lady Covington smiled patronizingly at Sarah as though she were confronting an inferior being. Luke, at Sarah's shoulder, said very properly, "Miss Sarah Buchanan, I have the honor of presenting my mother, Lady Covington." Determined not to show her unease, Sarah smiled and curtsied as the dancing master had taught her to do.

"Ah, yes, the young woman who is here in London to secure a physician for her small village." She saw Sarah as an insignificant creature who was using her son to elbow her way into society. She would give the interloper short shrift. "How . . . selfless," she said and turned to her son.

The countess offered her cheek for Luke's kiss which he dutifully supplied. But not trusting the battlefield look in his mother's eyes, Luke moved Sarah in front of his father before the countess could say something cutting to him that would reflect badly on Sarah.

Sarah curtsied to the earl. Lord Covington's false smile

did nothing to raise Sarah's spirits. "I trust you are enjoying your sojourn in our City," he said.

The remark was delivered in a cold manner and was not meant to elicit a response. Just as his wife before him, he turned from Sarah and gave his attention to Luke. "It has been a while since you have deigned to be in my company, Lucien."

"I called on the countess the other day, sir," Luke replied, "but you were at your club."

"Yes, I heard about that visit . . . for days, it seems. It would be a nice diversion if you could call on your mother at some time without causing a bumblebroth."

There was more reproof than irony in his parent's tone. Even though Luke had earlier assured Sarah that his parents would not be rude to a guest in their own home, he saw nothing in either his father's or his mother's manner toward Sarah to want him to push his luck by prolonging a conversation with either of them. Luke put a light hand on Sarah's elbow and moved her into the ballroom.

Hundreds of red velvet hearts edged with white lace decorated the silver walls while dozens of red roses spilled from a myriad of Cupid-shaped white vases. Crimson candles stood tall in the glass chimneys of the wall sconces and flamed overhead in the chandeliers.

Making his way around the ballroom with Sarah on his arm, Luke nodded to many acquaintances and stopped now and then to introduce Sarah to select friends before taking her onto the dance floor for a waltz. She floated in Luke's arms and never missed a step, thanks to her practice with the dancing master.

Afterward, she danced with Sir Roland and a number of the men to whom she had been introduced and a few more who pressed Luke for an introduction. Her light feet carried her through the steps of the more intricate dances and flew gracefully in the spirited reels. She found herself having fun. Lady Cheney had warned her to expect puffed-up praise from rakes who might have less than honorable intentions. Yet, while Sarah was aware of the open admiration in more than one stranger's eyes, not a single gentleman who stood up with her crossed over the boundaries of correctness.

Luke kept a close watch on her. He danced a few obligatory dances, but did more observing than participating. He was there whenever Sarah was escorted from the dance floor. As the evening wore on, her sunny smiles and vivacious spirits diminished his fears that she might be subjected to subtle insults or risque innuendos.

Luke had collected Sarah after a Scottish reel when their path toward the refreshment table took them directly to where Lord and Lady Leighton stood. Lord Leighton was a contemporary and bosom friend of Lord Covington. It was incumbent on Luke to stop and exchange a few words with the diplomat. Isabella took the opportunity to pull Sarah aside for a private word.

"I saw a necklace like yours at George Burrell's," she said, naming a prominent Bond Street jeweler, "except the stones were pink. Is your necklace his work?"

Sarah did not know how to respond. It seemed gauche to admit her jewels had been borrowed from Mary Westlock. Her honest nature made it difficult for her to lie outright. Finally she said, "I'm not certain."

Isabella had wanted Lord Havercole to buy the necklace for her since the pink stones had matched her own gown, but he had been unable to make the purchase because his father had drastically cut his allowance after his last catastrophic caper at Cambridge.

"It was a gift, then," Isabella presumed. Some soft bell went off in her head. In that moment two things came together in Isabella's mind. She knew just who had paid for Miss Buchanan's jewels, and she had a strong suspicion where she had seen Sarah before.

"I know you are visiting your aunt, Miss Buchanan, but where is your home?"

Sarah was relieved to have talk of the necklace put behind her and answered readily, "Thorn, Lady Leighton." But as soon as the admission had left her mouth, she wondered if she had acted wisely.

Isabella merely said, "Oh, yes, Lord Darnay just bought some property there," and turned back toward her husband. But the wheels of Isabella's mind were turning. She was right. Miss Buchanan was the woman in the cloak whom Roland had helped into the rig at Thornystone. Luke's mistress's hair had been covered with a hood, and her face partially obscured, the reason her identity had remained elusive. But there was no doubt now as to who she was, for the chit had admitted as much. Sarah moved beside Luke once again, and the two took leave of Lord and Lady Leighton.

Isabella watched Luke lead Sarah to the refreshment table. Malice and vindictiveness began to build up in her heart. Luke had had the gall to foist his paramour on the decent people of the Ton. He must not be allowed to get away with it unpunished. Her duty was to see that he got his comeuppance.

Sarah raised to her lips the champagne flute Luke had handed to her. Lady Leighton stood a short distance from her, her blue eyes fixed on Luke with unadulterated hatred. Sarah shuddered, and an ominous shiver slipped over her skin.

"What is it, my dear?" Luke asked. "You can't be cold; the room is stifling."

Sarah could not bring herself to disturb his contented air by mentioning Isabella. Fortunately for her, the orchestra played a fanfare. "Oh, look, Luke, I think the earl is going to announce the engagement," she said, deflecting his attention from herself.

Lord Covington made the anticipated formal declaration of the betrothal of Lady Jane Sutter to Sir Roland Kirkwood. The guests surged forward to congratulate the happy couple. The orchestra struck up a Viennese tune, and Roland led Jane onto the floor for a romantic waltz. Others were invited by the orchestra leader to join in. Lady Leighton was forgotten, and Sarah happily whirled about the floor in Luke's arms.

Watching them, Isabella Leighton shook with rage at Lucien Sutter's affront. He had had the temerity to reject her for a trollop. The earl and countess would not overlook their son's shameless behavior in bringing that tart into their home. This time Luke would pay for flouting the conventions of his class. She waved off Lord Havercole, who would have led her onto the dance floor, and moved toward where Lord and Lady Covington stood, rejoicing in their daughter's excellent match.

Lord Covington caught his son's eye as the younger man waited with Sarah for a country dance to commence.

Luke responded to the silent summons with an acknowledging nod. He refused to let his thoughts dwell upon the reason for his father's scowl, but he felt the muscles in his stomach knot.

Sarah was speaking to another couple who was also waiting for the music to begin.

"Sarah," Luke said, "would you mind joining your aunt and Lady Cheney there by the window. The earl seems to want a word with me."

"Not at all, Luke," she said. She looked for Lord Covington where she had seen him a short time before, but he was no longer there. Only Luke's mother stood in the vicinity, fanning herself rapidly.

Luke waited until Sarah had reached Mrs. Drayton and sat down beside her aunt before he walked to where his mother waited.

"Your father is in his study," she said in a freezing tone. "You have much to answer for, Lucien."

Luke did not indulge in fruitless speculation, but made his way down the marble stairs and opened the library door. His father ceased his pacing and faced him.

At once the earl commanded, "Remove that woman from this house. Not in an hour or ten minutes, but immediately. I want to see the back of your Miss Buchanan by the time I return to the ballroom."

Unintimidated, Luke crossed his arms. "What is this about?" he asked. He was not moving from this room until he got to the bottom of his father's demand.

"It is about your bringing your harlot into this house." If Lord Covington expected to hear an admission of culpability from his son, he was soon disabused.

"Harlot?" Luke repeated. "Miss Buchanan might not be of the fashionable world, but she is as much a lady as any of your highborn, aristocratic female guests. Wherever did you get the notion that she is a lightskirt?"

Although the two men were better than two arm lengths apart, figuratively they were toe-to-toe.

"When Lady Leighton was at Thornystone recently, she saw that woman leaving your house early in the morning after spending the night with you."

"Ah, now I see," Luke said. His tension ebbed. "Isabella Leighton is a vicious, petty woman, my lord. She put her own warped coloration on what she saw. Miss Buchanan was there that morning to ask for my help in securing a doctor for the village, not to warm my bed."

"It won't wash, Lucien. Defaming the wife of a respected diplomat and close friend to boost the consequence of a loose woman does you no credit."

"Isabella is lying," Luke said firmly.

"And is Sir Roland lying as well?"

Stupefied, Luke looked at his father for a long moment. "Rollie? What the deuce does he have to do with the matter?"

"Roland is the one who revealed to Isabella that the woman is your mistress."

"What kind of madness are you perpetrating? Roland knows better. He would never say such a thing."

Lord Covington's eyes remained hard and resolute. "I have had quite enough of your insults and dissembling. This interview is terminated. Get yourself upstairs and remove your paramour from under my roof. Now."

"I will obey you, my lord, not from any admission of guilt, but because I will not have Miss Buchanan hurt. She means too much to me for me to allow her to suffer the embarrassment of being cut dead by you or my mother. However, this is not over. I will return after I have seen Miss Buchanan, her aunt, and Cousin Mary safely home."

Luke turned on his heel and was nearly through the door when Lord Covington took a step toward his son's receding back and extended a combative chin. "You are damn right this is not over, you insolent pup," he shouted. "You and Roland will answer for having the audacity to introduce Jane to Miss Buchanan, a woman who you were both aware was of sullied virtue."

Luke gathered together the ladies for their immediate departure with the excuse that something unforeseen of a business nature had come up. Most of the older guests had already left, so the two senior women needed no extra prodding. A core of indefatigable young people continued to dance, but Sarah had no desire to remain, for she could see that Luke was distracted by something more serious than business. Her suspicions were heightened when she was prevented from taking leave of Luke's parents by his claim that the earl and countess were involved in a small family crisis and would not want to be disturbed.

Back at the town house, Matilda and Mary, worn out from the unaccustomed late hours, went to their respective rooms immediately.

Luke drew Sarah into his arms without removing his overcoat. "I love you, Sarah," he said, and kissed her.

She returned his kiss in full measure before drawing back and looking up at him. "Your family's crisis has something to do with me, doesn't it?" she said.

He nodded. "Darling, it is all a misunderstanding. I must return to my parents now and clear it up. Tomorrow I have several appointments which cannot be canceled, but we will talk when I come home for dinner. I promise by then everything will be made right. I don't want you to worry." He ran a gloved hand down her cheek. "Now, remove that frown from your pretty face and smile for me."

Sarah tried, but her lips refused to form into more than a faint movement of her mouth. Somehow being told not to worry made her worry all the more.

SEVEN

The last carriage was pulling away from the mansion on Albemarle Street when Luke rang the bell and was admitted by Phelps, who rid him of his hat and coat.

"The family and Sir Roland are in the small parlor, my lord," Phelps said, stepping in that direction.

"I'll show myself in," Luke said and walked past the butler and down the hall to the parlor door, where he could hear voices coming from inside the room. He fingered the knob and without knocking opened the door.

The conversation came to an abrupt halt, and all eyes were on Luke. He moved forward a few steps and remained standing with his hands resting on the back of a wing chair. Looking directly at Sir Roland where he sat beside Jane on a rose brocade settee, he asked, "Is what the earl said true, Rollie?"

"Gad, Luke, I'm sorry," Roland answered, his face crumpling.

"Why, my friend? You knew Sarah's reason for being there." Luke was more puzzled than angry.

Lord Covington leaned forward in a side chair. "Roland thought he was doing you a service, Lucien. He has explained everything. I'm satisfied that Miss Buchanan is as you purport her to be."

His eyes still on Roland, Luke wondered, "What were you thinking, Rollie?"

"Just what your father said. I thought I was doing you a good turn. Isabella saw me hand Miss Buchanan up into her rig that morning and jumped to the conclusion that Sarah had spent the night with me. I figured if Isabella believed that Sarah was actually your new flirt, she would leave you alone. You know Bella's vanity. I expected her to consider it beneath her to vie for your attentions when you were smitten with a country nobody."

"Sarah is not a nobody," Luke said. Although his voice remained soft, his eyes were becoming perilously dark.

Looking miserable, Roland said, "I know that, Luke. I meant it from Isabella's point of view. She has this high opinion of herself. I never thought she would put herself in a position where she would have even the slightest chance of being thrown over for someone she considered her social inferior."

Lady Covington fanned herself negligently where she sat on a Sheraton sofa beside the French doors which opened onto the terrace. "You need not apologize to Lucien, Roland. Miss Buchanan *is* a nobody." She turned to her son. "You wronged me, Lucien, by forcing me to invite that woman to the ball. Now look at the disaster she has caused. I should have put my foot down when I heard that she was installed under your roof. No respectable female would even consider moving in with a bachelor."

Luke sneered. "Mother, even you cannot think I am such a shameless scapegrace that I would romp in bed with Miss Buchanan under Cousin Mary's nose."

"Lucien, I warn you," his father put in. "I won't have that kind of crude speech in front of your mother and sister. Watch your tongue or I'll . . ."

Luke stood up ramrod straight. "What are you going to do, sir, disinherit me? I have more money than I shall ever need and the ability to make as much more as I want. And as far as the damned title is concerned, give it to Jane's firstborn son. I much prefer being plain Luke Sutter."

"Lucien, Lucien," his mother cried. "Are we forever to hang our heads because of your willful acts?"

Not mincing words, Luke replied, "May I remind you, madam, that were it not for my willful acts, your husband would have ended up in debtor's prison and you would not live in this fine house or wear those expensive jewels and dresses."

Lord Covington gasped. It was not in Luke's nature to be deliberately cruel. The uncharacteristically harsh and unchivalrous words stunned the earl. He had quarreled with Luke in the past, but the altercations had been no more than annoying bickerings that could be overlooked. He feared this clash was pushing them into a permanent breech. Luke was not just out of curl; he was bitterly incensed. It was obvious to the earl that he and the countess had underestimated their son's devotion to Sarah Buchanan.

Thinking to make himself a voice of reason, Lord Covington said, "You are not yourself, Lucien, speaking of disinheriting and alienating yourself from your family. I'm certain any rumors concerning you and Miss Buchanan will be eradicated in time and, regardless of your mother's fears, will not reflect badly on us."

"You are too optimistic, my lord," Lady Covington said to her husband. "Isabella Leighton is not one to hold her tongue." She turned to her future son-in-law. "She is your special friend, Roland. Find a way to insure her silence, or we will lose the respect of some important people for subjecting them to Miss Buchanan's presence at the ball."

"I won't have Roland speaking to Lady Leighton, Mama," Jane said, pouting. "Rollie has promised me that she shan't be in our circle of friends once we are married. She is a horrible woman, and I don't want her at our wedding."

"Nonsense," Lady Covington said mildly. "Lady Leighton is excellent Ton."

Luke's face hardened. Without forethought he said, "I am marrying Sarah Buchanan."

His announcement seemed to have caught only his mother unaware. Her surprised look deepened into one of strong displeasure. "No, Lucien," she said. "You have a duty to marry well. The woman is a penniless nobody. She may have looks, but that is all. If she is not already your mistress, offer her the role if you must have her, but don't ruin your life with a legal entanglement."

Luke bristled. If his mother referred to Sarah once more as a nobody, he just might do the unthinkable and strike his female parent. Sarah was more important to him than anything or anyone. He could slough off barbs directed at himself. Slurs at her, however, tore at his heart and soul. He had had enough. Caustically, he issued an ultimatum.

"Reject Sarah Buchanan and you reject me," he said, addressing both his parents. "Your Sutter grandchildren will be lost to you forever. Moreover, I shall send you the names of two or three reliable men of business who can handle your affairs from now on. If you disregard my wishes, I intend to cut all ties with this family."

"But my wedding, Luke," Jane wailed. "I ordered the invitations, the expensive ones with the gilt edges when Mama and I set the date last week. I like Miss Buchanan. Ask Roland. Rollie, haven't I said as much?"

Sir Roland patted her hand. "Shh, my dear, don't overset yourself."

"Rest easy, Jane," her brother assured her. "I will pay for your wedding. I just may not attend." He knew he was being needlessly heartless in baiting Jane, but at the moment, he was not in charity with any of the people in the room.

"Oh, Luke, don't be a brute," Jane said, tears forming in her pleading eyes. "You are to be Roland's groomsman. Rollie, speak to him."

"Not now, Jane. Let it be," Sir Roland said. His spirits

were low. Were it not for his own stupid tactic, no matter how well meant, Luke would not be in the soup.

Lord Covington once again undertook to placate his son. "I think we could all benefit from some sleep," he said. "Lucien, call on me tomorrow. We will work something out," his father promised.

But Luke was intractable. "No, Father. I am marrying Miss Buchanan. That fact is non-negotiable. No more talk. My choice is made and is irreversible."

Luke heard the burst of voices, but paid no attention as, on those last words, he turned and left the room. He waved off Phelps when the butler would have assisted him into his overcoat. He slapped his hat onto his head and stuffed his gloves into his pocket. He was still shrugging into his coat when the cold air hit him full in the face as the butler opened the front door for him and closed it behind him.

He had reached his carriage at the curb when the house door gaped once again, throwing a beam of light into the street, and footfalls tapped down the steps.

"Luke, wait," Roland called to him. Luke removed his hand from the carriage door latch and waited for his friend to reach his side.

"I know it was gormless to play an idiotic trick on Bella. But I never dreamed she would confront your father. I was dumfounded and tried to make things right. Dash it all, Luke, don't shun me for putting my foot wrong this one time."

"Forget it, Rollie. This hasn't much to do with your error. It is about my parents," he said, jerking his head toward the house. "I have asked nothing of them in the past. But I want them to accept Sarah, for her sake and for family peace. Never have I needed a woman in my life before. I need Sarah. And I mean to have her as my wife with or without their approval. If the earl and countess think I am blowing smoke, they have another think coming."

"Give them time, Luke. Lord and Lady Covington will

come around. Deuce take it, if you refuse to stand up with me at my wedding, I will refuse to get married.''

Luke cuffed Roland's arm. "Don't be a gudgeon, I have no intention of missing my sister's wedding.''

Luke swung his long form into his carriage, and the coachman sprang the horses, leaving a much relieved Sir Roland standing alone in the empty street.

Sarah came downstairs late the next morning to find that Luke had already left for his appointments and Aunt Matilda and Miss Westlock had gone to spend the morning with Lady Cheney and her Orphans' Committee, who were knitting warm scarves, mittens, and hats for needy children. She went to the breakfast parlor for a light repast and was drinking her second cup of coffee when Billings brought her a silver tray with a calling card.

Sarah read Lady Covington's name on the card and frowned. "The countess asked for me?''

"Yes, miss, specifically. I have seated her in the drawing room,'' the butler said in his usual correct manner.

Sarah set the card down on the white tablecloth. It had not escaped her notice that Luke had pushed her through the receiving line last night with undue haste. While she was ignorant of the outcome of the family crisis that he had hurried away to resolve after bringing her home, of one thing she was certain: Luke's mother was not here to make idle chitchat.

With some trepidation, Sarah pushed aside the cup of untouched coffee and made for the drawing room. She perched on the edge of the sofa, facing the countess, who sat imperially in one of the less comfortable chairs in the warm room where a fire had been laid earlier that morning.

Not wasting words, Lady Covington said, "It has come to my attention that my son wants to marry you. You must turn him down.''

Sarah squared her shoulders and sat back against the cushions. "And why should I do that, my lady, when we love each other?"

Lady Covington emitted an inelegant snort. "What has love to do with it? Lucien is an aristocrat. He has a duty to select a bride of consequence who reflects positively on him. He is already tainted, for he is seen as little better than a Cit because of his business dealings. But if he marries a titled woman of wealth, he can redeem himself and regain his rightful place in society."

"Frankly, I don't understand how you can put social status before your only son's happiness, particularly when he has done so much for you," Sarah said with a determined tilt to her chin.

"My dear Miss Buchanan, you are being presumptuous. What Lucien has done for his family is none of your business. But any happiness Lucien would have with you would be short-lived. Someone of low birth such as yourself can know nothing of the importance of honor and duty in an aristocratic family. Believe me, Miss Buchanan, when I say that Lucien cannot afford to lower his standards and marry you."

"Apparently, Lord Darnay does not see me as a drawback. I do not think I embarrassed him before his peers at the Valentine Ball."

"You are a brazen bit of baggage," Lady Covington said. "You can make such a statement without shame?"

Sarah raised an offended brow. "I have nothing of which to be ashamed. My conduct was all that it should be."

". . . if one overlooks that a man who is not your husband bought your fashionable dress and gifted you with the elegant necklace everyone admired. I assure you, had your dancing partners been privy to the information, you would have been treated as a courtesan, rather than a lady," the countess said with a derisory sniff.

Sarah shook her head. "Madame Lisse gave me a good

price to model the gown as a form of publicity, and the jewels were leant to me by Miss Westlock," she protested, but a speck of doubt was penetrating her brain.

"Fustian! Madame Lisse dresses the cream of the Ton. Why should she need you, a country rustic, to advertise at my ball? What advantage could she gain from dressing a woman without the slightest connection within high society?"

For what was a matter of seconds, but seemed longer, Sarah and the countess looked at one another. "None," Sarah admitted, at last, astonished at how clear it suddenly all now seemed to her. Was this a new meaning to "Love is blind?" How easily one could delude one's self when love got in the way.

Luke had duped her. He had paid for the dress. The jewels, too, were from him. How could she have believed even for a moment that mousy Mary Westlock could have owned such a treasure?

Lady Covington watched Sarah with gloating satisfaction. "I think you have guessed by now, Miss Buchanan, that Lucien purchased the jewels," she said, echoing Sarah's thoughts. "Cousin Mary is as poor as a church mouse. A spinster, she served as her father's housekeeper until his death three years ago when she was left destitute. She would have gone onto the county's poor rolls had Lucien not intervened and taken her into his home."

Sarah sat still, neither angry, nor even bitter. Instead she was tremendously sad. She was so much in love that her good sense had deserted her. How could she have been so obtuse and ignored the obvious?

"I can see by your countenance that my son has tricked you. But if you choose to fly in the face of convention and insinuate yourself among your betters, like some encroaching mushroom, you must suffer the consequences when you are unmasked," Lady Covington said callously. "But better now than when it is too late. Marry my son and you will never move in first circles. He will come, in time, to resent being saddled with a wife whom he must constantly defend against slights and outright rudeness."

The countess rose from her chair and went to the bell pull to summon Billings to show her out, for she saw with glee that Sarah was numb and unable to move. "Go back to Thorn, Miss Buchanan. Find yourself some man of your own class to marry. Frankly," she scoffed, "I don't think you even have the panache to make Lucien a suitable mistress."

Lady Covington's taunt was a knife cutting into Sarah's heart. She knew she had to leave before Luke came home. She did not want to see him; she could not cope with his excuses, not now.

The butler came back into the room after seeing Lady Covington out. By then, Sarah had regained her outward composure.

"Billings," she said, "please fetch Mrs. Drayton's and my luggage from the storeroom and send Mollie and Chloe to me to assist with the packing. I want to quit London within the next few hours. Also, I need someone to fetch my aunt from Lady Cheney's immediately." Rising from the sofa, Sarah walked to the door and turned back into the room. "Oh, yes, Billings, one more thing. Do you know of a large town near Thorn which is a public coach stop?"

"No, Miss Sarah, but Mr. Bertram would. He travels with Lord Darnay all the time. I will send him to you."

Sarah was throwing clothes onto the bed as she waited for Billings to deliver her trunk when Bertram came through the open door. "Billings says you plan to leave this afternoon, miss," he said, his collected manner belying his distress at her rash decision.

"Yes, I need to know where I can secure public transportation that could get me from London to Thorn," she said.

Bertram looked aghast. "Miss Sarah, such a trip would be tedious, take an impossible number of changes in transport, and require at least an extra day. Wait until Lord Darnay returns this evening, and I am certain he will see you back to Thorn himself."

"I wish to be well away from here before his lordship arrives home," Sarah said. There was a painful ache around her heart. Perhaps in time she could listen to Luke's explanation, but not today. She did not want to hear from his lips how unsuitable she was.

"Then, Miss Sarah, I must insist that you borrow his lordship's traveling carriage. I know that would be his wish."

For once Sarah let her good sense overrule her pride. She did not want to spend a wasted day wandering over the unknown countryside and sleeping in a flea-infested bed in some second-rate inn. "All right," she agreed. Her reply did much to restore Bertram's inner calm.

"I have sent a carriage for Mrs. Drayton. She should be here within the half hour," he said and left. He hurried to the servants' wing, and said to Billings, "Stall Miss Sarah. I will bring Lord Darnay back lickety-split."

But when Luke entered the house, it was already dark, and Sarah and her aunt had been gone five hours. He had been to Chelsea to visit a client and had neglected to inform his office staff of his whereabouts. Luke had been far from his usual haunts in the business district through which Bertram searched diligently before giving up his futile quest. The valet spilled the day's events from Lady Covington's impromptu visit to the hasty departure of Sarah and Mrs. Drayton in his lordship's traveling coach.

Luke remained surprisingly calm. "It's too late to do anything this evening," he said. "Miss Buchanan and Mrs. Drayton will be safe enough under the care of the coachman and groom. Both are reliable fellows. Have my curricle ready tomorrow an hour before dawn. I'll drive myself. It will be quicker."

That evening Luke sipped a brandy seated behind his desk in the library as he sorted through the mail which his office clerk had given Bertram that afternoon to bring home for Luke's perusal. He unfolded a letter from a teaching hospital where days before he had asked one of his clerks to post an advertisement for a doctor. He read the letter and was putting it aside when Billings announced Lord Covington.

The anger was gone from Luke now. There was just a compulsion to get to Sarah and make things right between them.

"Father," he greeted Lord Covington and waved him to a seat. "Brandy?"

"Thank you," Lord Covington said, sitting down in a comfortable leather chair. While his son poured the dark amber spirits into a snifter, he repeated some of the confession his wife had made to him less than an hour ago relating to her confrontation with Sarah.

Luke already knew of his mother's morning call from Bertram and had guessed that she was the stimulus that had goaded Sarah into leaving. Left behind were the necklace of diamond and garnet hearts lying on the vanity in silent indictment and the exquisite silk gown hanging in solitary accusation in the armoire as damning signs that Sarah had discovered his deception.

Lord Covington took a generous swallow of the brandy which Luke had handed him before he had reseated himself at his desk.

"Your mother is convinced that the harm you have done by engaging in trade will never be repaired if you marry beneath you. In her opinion, you need a wife of consequence to reestablish your position in society."

Leaning back in his chair, Luke inhaled the aroma of the brandy, holding the snifter with both hands to warm the bowl.

"And what do you think?" he asked his father without any particular emotion.

"I think you are too old for me to pick your bride. I do

not want you lost to us, Lucien. Someday I want to play with my grandchildren. You have been an excellent steward of the family finances. Oh, don't look so surprised, but try to understand that a man my age finds it difficult to deal with his pride. It is not easy to own up to the world that your son, at a rather early age at that, became your financial savior."

Luke felt an unexpected lump in his throat. He had become accustomed to hearing a litany of his faults from both his parents. This was the first time he had heard even a hint of gratitude from his sire. But he knew enough to let the matter rest.

"I suppose you are still bent on marrying Miss Buchanan," Lord Covington said into the moment's silence.

Luke nodded. "Definitely. She returned to Thorn after the countess's lecture, but I am going to her tomorrow."

"I don't blame her for wanting to put some distance between us," his father said. "Your mother said some very hurtful things to her, but, I promise you that they shall not be repeated. Your Miss Buchanan need never fear a repetition of that disgraceful scene."

Lord Covington left fifteen minutes later. His visit gave Luke hope of establishing a closer relationship with his father. His lordship's last words at the door were, "I pledge to you, Lucien, that I will see that the family pulls together and puts up a united front in accepting Miss Buchanan as one of us."

Sarah had just started across the field beyond her house for a walk when Luke's curricle pulled into the yard in front of the barn. The temperature was mild; the sky a deep blue, dotted with white fluffy clouds, one of those rare perfect days that is especially welcome in winter.

Sarah felt her heart lift at the sight of Luke's tall form jumping from the vehicle's box. Perversely, she had a de-

sire to flee from him, but decided such an action would
be both childish and futile. With his long legs, he would
catch her up in no time at all no matter how fast she ran.
Instead she stood where she was and waited for him to
come to her, knowing she still wanted him and loved him
to distraction.

Bareheaded, his hands in the pockets of his blue super-
fine coat, Luke strolled toward Sarah at a leisurely pace,
never taking his eyes from her enchanting figure wrapped
in a woollen shawl.

He stopped in front of her and reached for a letter in
his pocket. "This came after you left. It appears you have
a prime candidate for the village doctor's position. I have
read the resumé, and he seems eminently qualified."

She took the envelope from his hand, but did not open
it. "Is that why you came?" she said.

"Why else? When do you want to move into the woods-
man's cottage?" He felt like a cad for teasing her when he
saw her lips quiver and her eyes pool with unshed tears.

He placed his hands on her shoulders and said tenderly,
"Before I found you, I never met a woman with whom I
wanted to spend my life. I had all but decided that I would
make Jane's and Roland's son my heir, for I never hoped
to have children of my own. You changed all that."

"Your mother believes I acted like a fallen woman accepting the dress and jewels from you. Why did you do it,
Luke?"

He stepped back and dropped his arms to his sides. "I
know the shallowness of the polite world and how cruel
the ridicule can be toward someone who is less than fashionably turned out at those affairs. I knew you would be
scrutinized. I did not want you to be scorned."

Sarah said, "Even Aunt Matilda suspected about the
necklace . . . and I have the impression Lady Leighton
thinks you seduced me."

Luke rubbed a hand across the back of his neck and

looked at her with forthright eyes. "You are not going to like this," he said and told her candidly about Sir Roland's ruse.

"I suppose I shouldn't have told Lady Leighton that I was from Thorn," Sarah said.

Luke shrugged. "She would have found out from someone else. In any case, it has all been cleared up now," he said. "Without anyone to back her up, once we marry, any gossip-mongering Isabella engages in will be discounted as sour grapes. I know you want to curse Rollie for what he did, and he deserves it. But I hope in time you will find it in your heart to forgive him for his bad judgment."

"I am not concerned with Lady Leighton's machinations or Sir Roland's feelings, Luke," she said in truth. "I want to know how it is with us."

"I should have told you the truth about the dress," he admitted. "Madame Lisse's couture does not come cheap. You would not have been able to afford even her most modestly priced gown. Would you have allowed me to buy you a dress?"

She shook her head.

"No, I thought as much. As for the Valentine necklace, I wanted it to be a betrothal gift, but I did not feel it would be fair to take away from Jane's and Roland's celebration by making our plans to marry known before the ball. Our declaration would have minimized their big moment. I already had a hint of how you would feel about accepting money from me when you rejected the payment for the house until a doctor was definitely secured. I knew you would have scorned the dress on principle and the necklace without a formal announcement. And, if the truth be known, I wanted to see you turned out in style. You floored them, my love."

Sarah moved to him and rubbed her cheek against the fine wool of his coat and slid her hands up his sleeves. She had long ago admitted to herself that one of her old gowns would have been woefully inadequate in that august company. "I did look quite splendid," she said with a small laugh.

"Quite the kick of fashion," he agreed, grinning down at her. He put his arms around her and pulled her close.

"Did you pay for the dancing master, too?" she asked.

Luke shook his head. "No, actually, that was Lady Cheney's idea, and she insisted on footing the bill."

"There is still your parents' disapproval," she murmured into the front of his coat.

"I am not a man who would allow himself to be coerced into marrying a woman I did not love. My father has already come around, and he will see that my mother does, too. But I would be doing you a disservice if I painted too rosy a picture. The countess will not openly oppose you, but that may be the best we can hope from that quarter. There is hypocrisy and artificiality in polite society, but there are also many good people like Lady Cheney and Rollie and some others you met at the ball who will stand our friends."

Sarah knew she would have to make adjustments, but with Luke at her side that would be all right. A feeling of total love and trust filled her.

Luke turned her around. "Sarah, look at that cloud," he said, pointing into the distant sky. "I'll be darned if it isn't in the shape of Cupid. See the chubby legs?" He traced the outline in the air with his extended finger. "And there's the bow and arrow."

Sarah stared at the formation he indicated and tilted her head. "My goodness, you are right," she said.

"Now, if that isn't an auspicious sign that we belong to one another, I don't know what is," Luke said with a roguish grin.

He turned her back into his arms and brought his lips down on hers in a warm kiss. When he lifted his mouth, Sarah peeked over his shoulder at the cloud which the wind had already reformed into an indistinguishable mass. Cupid had flown off to shoot his arrows into some other unsuspecting lovers' hearts, she thought whimsically, but had left her and Luke with a love so right and so strong that she was very sure that it would last until the end of their days.

LOOK FOR THESE REGENCY ROMANCES